TREASON   1

TREASON

T. STYLES

By T. STYLES

By T. STYLES

TRANNY 911: DIXIE'S RISE
FIRST COMES LOVE, THEN COMES MURDER
LUXURY TAX
THE LYING KING
CRAZY KIND OF LOVE
SILENCE OF THE NINE
SILENCE OF THE NINE II: LET THERE BE BLOOD
SILENCE OF THE NINE III
PRISON THRONE
GOON
HOETIC JUSTICE
AND THEY CALL ME GOD
THE UNGRATEFUL BASTARDS
LIPSTICK DOM
A SCHOOL OF DOLLS
SKEEZERS
SKEEZERS 2
YOU KISSED ME NOW I OWN YOU
NEFARIOUS
REDBONE 3: THE RISE OF THE FOLD
THE FOLD
CLOWN NIGGAS
THE ONE YOU SHOULDN'T TRUST
COLD AS ICE
THE WHORE THE WIND BLEW MY WAY
SHE BRINGS THE WORST KIND
THE HOUSE THAT CRACK BUILT
THE HOUSE THAT CRACK BUILT 2: RUSSO & AMINA
THE HOUSE THAT CRACK BUILT 3: REGGIE & TAMIKA
THE HOUSE THAT CRACK BUILT 4: REGGIE & AMINA
LEVEL UP
VILLAINS: IT'S SAVAGE SEASON
GAY FOR MY BAE
WAR
WAR 2
WAR 3
WAR 4
WAR 5
WAR 6
WAR 7
MADJESTY VS. JAYDEN
YOU LEFT ME NO CHOICE
TRUCE: A WAR SAGA (WAR 8)
TRUCE 2: THE WAR OF THE LOU'S (WAR 9)
AN ACE AND WALID VERY, VERY BAD CHRISTMAS (WAR 10)
TRUCE 3: SINS OF THE FATHERS (WAR 11)
TRUCE 4: THE FINALE (WAR 12)
ASK THE STREETS FOR MERCY

TREASON

WWW.THECARTELPUBLICATIONS.COM

By T. STYLES

TREASON

By

T. STYLES

Library of Congress Control Number: 2021906891

ISBN 10: 194837336X

ISBN 13: 978-1948373364

Cover Design: Book Slut Girl

First Edition

Printed in the United States of America

By T. STYLES

What Up Fam,

As always, I do hope and pray that this letter finds you well. We have a lot going on around us these days, so please, please make sure your energy is positive as much as you can. I always find that doing something that I love brightens my mood and can shift my energy. Self-care is key!

Now (clasping hands together in excitement) jumping right into this here! *TREASON* is a story I didn't know I wanted or needed, but it is, and soooooo much more. This unique tale that T. Styles has masterfully created will leave you breathless! You'll be craving for more, I guarantee it ;)

With that being said, keeping in line with tradition, we want to give respect to a vet or new trailblazer paving the way. In this novel, we would like to recognize:

Will Smith

Willard Carroll Smith Jr. is a rapper, an American actor, producer and most recently an author. His first novel entitled, *WILL*, drops November 2021 and promises to be a glance into the life of one of the most groundbreaking entertainers of our lives. I absolutely cannot wait for this one! Make sure you check it out too.

Aight...I've taken up too much of your time, get ready to be emersed into a whole new world from the beautiful mind of T. Styles!

Catch you in the next one!

God Bless!

Charisse "C. Wash" Washington
Vice President
The Cartel Publications
www.thecartelpublications.com
www.facebook.com/publishercwash
Instagram: publishercwash
www.twitter.com/cartelbooks
www.facebook.com/cartelpublications
www.theelitewritersacademy.com
Follow us on Instagram: Cartelpublications
#CartelPublications
#UrbanFiction
#PrayForCece
#WillSmith

#TREASON

By T. STYLES

"I had the sun but longed for darkness.
And when darkness came, I longed for the sun.
But we don't always get what we want.
Am I doomed?"

- Cage Stryker

PRESENT DAY

The forecaster called for a thunderstorm, but it was giving hurricane season. As rain and wind beat the top, sides and back of the rented vehicle, two parts of three sisters were propped in the back seat.

Dressed in all black, the color suited them perfectly. In their early twenties, they had the faces of 40-year-old women who played on the harder side of life. Money hungry, superficial, and selfish, they were going to the hospital after being called by the doctor for one reason and one reason only.

To see if the *wicked old bitch* was dead.

They had been out all night, tricking an unsuspecting older perp out of his cash, and as a result they smelled of dried spit and sex. Women of no regard, their lips were swollen and their down belows were raw and bloodied.

The perp may have come up off six G's, but he made sure they paid for each dollar, even inviting the meanest perverted men the two had ever encountered to join the party.

Thinking about the future, Jeannette looked over at her sister who was placing lipstick on a mouth which hadn't been cleaned in days. "You think this is it?"

Chloe tossed the whore red lipstick in her fake Louis Vuitton bag and adjusted the collar of her sister's jacket. "It better be. 'Cause I'm not fin' to waste no more of my time on her old ass. If she don't die soon, I'ma put a pillow over her head."

"And I'll guard the door."

They both giggled while the driver stared at them with disgust in the rearview mirror. If he knew what the streets knew about the sisters, he had better adjust his gaze to the road, or he could find himself tucked neatly under a newly paved driveway.

"Where is Violet?" Jeanette asked, looking at her phone.

"Who knows?" She shrugged. "But if I know her, she probably never left her side."

"Sucking up and shit."

They were on point, because already in the hospital Violet sat at her grandmother's side, reading her favorite stories. Prettier than both of her sisters put together, the only way people knew they were related was from their birth certificates.

When she finished the last chapter, her Abuela touched her hand and smiled.

Violet enjoyed many things in life.

Like the smell of her Abuela's lavender hand lotion. Lemon stewing on the stove in the summer. A lukewarm bath after a jog on her favorite trail.

But there was nothing on earth that meant more to her than her grandmother's love and touch.

"I'm tired, my Violet." She said with little to no energy. "Why don't you leave and come back tomorrow? So, I can take a nap." Her grey hair sat on top of her head in a bun that had been brushed softly every day by Violet.

Unwilling to go, she set the book down on the table and wiped her long dark brown hair over her opposite shoulder. "I'm not leaving while you're awake. Because...because." Suddenly she began to cry heavily.

Wanting to make her feel better, Abuela squeezed her hand lightly. "Death is the end of life. Not love. You have to let me go."

"But I don't wanna miss a moment."

"Why worry about a moment when we've had a lifetime, Violet?" She smiled. "So, what's a few hours of rest? Go home. Take care of yourself."

When there was a soft knock at the door, it opened, and Dr. Perry entered. He was the top in his field and was the reason Violet had her transferred from the other hospital which had far too many neglectful tendencies to care for someone she gave a fuck about.

Touching her Abuela on her hand again, she followed the doctor out of the room.

"Your sisters are here," he sighed. They were already getting on his nerves. "Are you ready for the meeting?"

She crossed her arms over her body, as if her Abuela was hugging her tight. "You can tell them whatever you need them to know. I'm going to stay with my grandmother until she falls back to sleep. And then I'll join you."

"Violet, I'm concerned."

"Why?"

"Because I think you aren't willing to come to the understanding that she's—."

"Don't say it," she said, pointing in his face with a trembling finger. "I like you but...but..." She was suddenly struck with grief which threatened to bring her to her knees.

"Violet, are you okay?" He asked, placing a gentle hand on her shoulder.

Ripped to shreds over the idea of losing her grandmother, she dipped back into the room, slamming the door behind herself.

PART ONE

By T. STYLES

PROLOGUE

MANY, MANY YEARS AGO

"It's 'cause of Matthew 2:16."

Roaches were everywhere and the air smelled of raw sewage and bananas.

The electricity hadn't been paid in months. And so, the scented candles, different in size and structure provided the bathroom with a soft glow and sweet funk.

Needing more light, Wendy walked barefoot to the small window and opened it wide. This allowed a cool breeze along with the moonlight to shine inside. With the wind threatening to blow out the candles flame, the filthy brown chiffon curtains danced as dust particles floated in the air like glitter.

Satisfied, Wendy sat on her knees in front of a tub of running water. Next to her, on the floor a baby cooed softly atop a pink blanket.

Wiping her natural dirty brown hair out of her face, she looked down at the child and lifted his foot.

It wasn't a loving touch.

This was an examination of sorts.

What was this damn thing?

She looked at his leg, arm, hand, and his face. Unsatisfied, she released his limb. "You look fine to me," she said glaring. "But you aren't, are you?"

Silence.

"Otherwise, why would you be here?" She whispered. "When she knows I can't stand kids."

By T. STYLES

The child smiled and rocked in a happy baby yoga pose, as he fell under her hateful gaze.

When the tub was full, she turned the water off and sighed. What was to be done, could've taken place hours ago, but she was bored. And boredom to those who chose wickedness instead of kindness, was recess.

Raising the child up, she held him over the tub. "I'm doing you a favor. Because ain't nothing like being born unwanted. I know..." She sighed, as a glimpse of humanity threatened to expose itself on her light-skinned, red freckled face.

KNOCK. KNOCK. KNOCK.

When there was a bang at her front door, her head whipped around as she looked in the direction of the sound.

"No, no, no! It's too soon!"

Focusing back on the child, she dropped the baby in the water and ran toward the exit.

Liquid splashed everywhere as it covered the child.

Walking slowly toward it, she took her time opening the door.

She knew who it was and ignoring them would not be an option. And just as she suspected, on the other side was Magnus and Lala Stryker.

This was bad news for the funky bitch.

Lala stood behind him, and her face was red with anxiety. It was obvious that she had been crying. Her freckles were the only indicators that Wendy was her sister, as Wendy was truly one of the ugliest women inside and out that you'd ever meet.

Magnus, on the other hand, stood over 6'4 inches with muscles popping in all the right places. Nothing about him said meek, weak, or timid.

And right now, he looked as if he had chosen violence.

"Where is my son?" He said plainly, as his chest rose and fell heavily.

Although his voice level was medium, his tone was authoritative and murderous.

Wendy gazed at her sister, who wiped her long black hair out of her face and looked away.

"I don't know what you—."

He stepped closer. So close she could feel his body heat.

Wendy trembled under his gaze.

"I won't ask you again." He said. "Where is my fucking son?"

Wendy swallowed the lump in her throat. "He's inside. The bathroom."

Feeling something was off, he exploded ahead, knocking Wendy to the right with his presence and body.

Within seconds, he screamed out in agony. It was a painful wail that rocked the soul.

Irritated with her sister, Wendy stomped closer and crossed her arms over her chest. Feet spread out like frog toes on the wooden floor. "Why did you tell him he was here? Now—."

"He could sense it," Lala cried, wiping the tears away harshly.

"I don't think you understand what you just did." She whispered. "He will forever hate me behind this shit. When all I was doing was what you asked."

"Did you do it?" Lala sniffled. "Did you…did you…" She couldn't bring herself to finish the question.

Wendy could've answered but said fuck her sister. "I guess we'll see."

It seemed like forever, but five minutes later Magnus exited the bathroom, with the baby in his arms. The infant may have been wet, but he was cooing as if nothing happened. It was at that time that Wendy remembered that babies are often natural born swimmers.

Walking slowly toward the door, there was a look of hate in Magnus' eyes.

And yet, the baby was alive so for now all was well.

Or was it?

Magnus's shirt was drenched. "You had her do this?" He asked Lala. "To your own child?"

Silence.

"ANSWER ME!"

"It's cause of Matthew 2:16." She sniffled. "And I thought you didn't want him." Her gaze fell downward. "And I…I wanted things to be okay."

"The drugs, Lala. You have to…you gotta take your…med…"

He took a deep breath, as both sisters braced for his next move.

"Years will pass, and I will never look at you the same. Ever." He said to his wife before looking back at Wendy and then Lala again.

Wanting both of them out of his air space, he rushed out, with the infant cooing playfully in his arms.

"I was trying to save his life," Lala whispered, before walking away.

By T. STYLES

CHAPTER ONE
SEVENTEEN YEARS LATER
"I Want To Be A Savage."

In less than a week, seventeen-year-old Cage Stryker would become a full-grown ass man.

As beautiful as a Kehinde Wiley painting, he sat propped in an audience so crowded, he was squished between two strangers who smelled of burgers and sweat.

One of them, a lazy man, begged him to hold his bag because his arms hurt. Truthfully, he was hot and uncomfortable and couldn't be bothered to hold his own shit. The other violator didn't make shit better. She leaned against him as she took up more room than what was necessary, just to be up under the fine young boy.

But Cage didn't care.

The only thing on his mind was the traditional father and son hunting event that occurred on the eighteenth birthday for a boy child. And although Magnus hadn't confirmed the event, Magnus was a man of convention so Cage was sure he would honor the code.

Because lately, over the past couple of years to be exact, his relationship was strained with his father, and he desperately needed that to change. Because there was nothing on earth that Cage adored more than him.

As he looked at Magnus, who was on the stage giving a sermon, the soft yellow overhead lighting managed to highlight the shimmer of Cage's chocolate skin, causing it to glow as if he were bronzed.

Although this wasn't a traditional church, every Sunday he and his four siblings went religiously to witness Magnus deliver powerful words to a crowd who needed his strength to maneuver in life.

His overall message didn't include a bible but was simple.

Either you control your world, or it will consume you.

And nobody needed to hear the message more than his own son.

Cage was a pushover, the type of kid who erred on the side of reducing as much conflict as possible. And still, if he had to pick out one trouble, it would be his concern that on his eighteenth birthday, he would be thrown out of the house.

He didn't even care if he got a gift, besides, despite their wealth, Magnus didn't allow them to wear designer clothing anyway.

Nah...for Cage, Archer, Bloom, Tatum, and Flow, it was always simple jeans, unpatterned shirts, and inexpensive shoes. Which caused problems for Cage since he was in high school.

When asked why they couldn't get more popular clothing, Magnus said, *"If you don't know who you are in your own skin, you'll die early in cloth."*

"...sex, money and betrayal, is the only thing most of you know." Magnus preached, his voice booming behind his podium. "And because of it, you don't demand more from yourself and the people you allow in your life. And this will be your undoing. No one will be able to—"

Suddenly three men entered, and their presence put the entire room on pause.

They wore grey sweatpants and no t-shirts which showcased their chiseled physiques. Tall in stature, their dreads rolled down their backs like snakes as they stood in the rear of the audience with authority.

Cage was in awe because in that moment, he saw what looked like fear in his father's eyes for the first time in life.

Who were they?

Fuck it...their names didn't matter.

Their presence spoke volumes.

Turning his head slightly, Magnus looked at security and nodded in their direction.

On point, the guards rushed in defense mode. But even as security walked upon the threesome, they didn't move until they made it clear that they couldn't be touched.

"We won't let you divide us for long!" The tallest yelled. He was tatted from the neck to the waist. And he, and the others, looked like rock stars.

Flow, Archer, Tatum, and Bloom were also in awe at their power.

"Leave!" Magnus yelled loudly, reclaiming his church. "I won't tell you again!"

Having provided more questions than answers, slowly they walked out.

When they were gone, Cage looked at his father whose gaze was now on his mother's worried eyes.

"It'll be fine," Cage saw his mouth say.

Would it though?

TREASON 25

The couple weren't the only ones wondering what had just taken place. Because whispers were heavy with everyone desiring to know who the mysterious men were.

Taking a deep, long breath, Magnus exhaled as if recharging and focused back on the crowd. "I want to call my oldest son to the stage right now," Magnus grinned. "To close us out for the evening."

Thunderous claps rang throughout the auditorium, reminding everyone who was in control.

"Get on up here, son."

In an attempt to disappear between burger butt and sweaty cheeks, Cage sunk deeper into the chair, hoping their bodies would shield him, as everyone peered his way.

"Cage, it's okay," Magnus smiled. "Get up here."

Looking downward, slowly his head rose.

Walking unenthusiastically to the podium, he stood next to his father. Magnus' heavy hand weighed on his shoulder, making him feel smaller. But Cage didn't care, because with Magnus he knew he was safe.

"My son's birthday is coming soon!"

The crowd applauded.

Magnus slowly raised his hand and without saying a word, the crowd fell in a hush.

The act was so small, but it placed his father's power in full view for the newcomers who were unsure of his command.

When he dropped his hand, looking down at Cage he asked, "Son, what is your wish for your birthday?"

Cage looked up at him with hopeful eyes.

Was this a trap?

After all, Cage made it known on many occasions that the only thing he wanted was the father son hunting trip which Magnus had yet to confirm.

"Really, dad?" Cage whispered, where only he could hear him.

Magnus covered the mic, lowered his head, and whispered in his ear. "Tell them no matter what you get, you only want peace."

But he didn't though.

He wanted the hunting trip.

Eager to please his father, Cage nodded and looked out in the audience. He was preparing to honor his request. At that exact time, he saw a pretty girl with dark vanilla skin and long black hair. She was wearing a mini skirt too slutty for an eighteen-year-old.

And yet with a snap of her chipped red nail polish, she yanked his soul.

He heard of love at first sight and thought it was corny, but after seeing her he would never doubt the concept again.

But it was the cell phone in her hand that threw him for a loop. On the black screen, in white block words it read:

SAVAGE SEASON

She looked mischievous, and although he had never been around a girl outside of school and his baby sister, he found himself drawn to her presence.

That moment, it was as if they were all alone.

And when she crossed her legs, briefly revealing her pink undies, Cage stiffened in a way he never had in public.

"Son, what's wrong?" Magnus whispered in his ear. "Tell the people what I said."

Mesmerized by the bad girl he said, "I want to be a savage."

Everyone gasped.

The bad girl dropped her phone in her purse and closed her legs.

Playing the tapes back in his mind, when Cage heard himself utter the words, it was too late. The sign and her presence threw him for a loop that he wasn't prepared to jump through.

"I was just playing," he told the crowd who laughed heartily. He could feel Magnus' eyes on him and did his best to clean up his mess. "Truly, I don't want anything but peace."

"Awwwwww." The females in the audience cooed.

Magnus, still embarrassed, nudged him slightly to the side and grabbed the mic. "Did I tell you he was a comedian too?"

Half chuckles followed by boisterous laughter filled the hall.

But when he looked at his parents, it became obvious that not everyone was laughing.

The Stryker family rode seven deep in a white BMW truck. Every now and again Magnus would look at Cage from the rearview mirror and he would find him staring.

Still embarrassed by the ordeal, Cage sat in the middle row, on the outside seat. He was sitting next to Bloom, his thirteen-year-old sister who maintained a hate for her body so deep, she often took to marking up her skin.

On the left of her was the youngest of the clan, eleven-year-old Flow, who possessed some traits that most of the members of the family preferred to pretend didn't exist.

In the back was fifteen-Year-old Tatum, a social media influencer, with an online following of close to a million. This caused him to sometimes come across as arrogant which rubbed people the wrong way.

Next to him was Archer, fourteen, who was considered ugly by most. With acne so bad covering his skin which bubbled in papules; he repulsed most girls which made him bitter and play the bully to those he assumed would reject him.

The only thing the four of them had in common, was that they loved their big brother Cage.

"Dad, who were those men from earlier?" Flow asked.

"Don't worry about all that," he responded.

"Can you open this for me?" Bloom nudged Cage while handing him a bottle of diet soda.

He took it and twisted off the cap. "What you drinking this for? Thought you wanted to gain weight."

"I do. But I don't wanna get ugly either because—."

"What I tell you about talking like that?" He whispered, touching her leg.

Silence.

"What I tell you?" Cage said firmer.

He may have moved around weak in real life, but when it came to them, he found the strength to be what they needed. Because they saw him as Superman, and he wanted to live up to that persona, despite feeling nowhere near as strong.

She looked down. "You said ain't nothing wrong with me."

"Then why do you keep talking like that?"

"If you say I'm so pretty, how come you don't like girls the same size as me? Like the girls you look at on the internet. Or that girl you were smiling at today in church?" She looked down at herself. "She don't look nothing like me."

She watched him too closely.

Just like the others, she watched everything he did and that made him uncomfortable.

He was about to respond when Cage saw his father staring in his direction. Unable to meet his gaze, he looked toward the window.

It was time to smooth things over.

Taking a deep breath, Cage jokingly said, "dad, did I tell you I have Tourette's? And that I yell out things I don't mean in public?"

Crickets.

Since his bad joke didn't land, he tried to sink deeper into his seat.

"Not everything is funny, Cage," Lala said.

"Exactly." Magnus added, "I mean what was wrong with you?"

He looked at him and then his mother who looked away. Whenever things got heated between him and his father, Lala always avoided his gaze and Cage never knew why.

But how was this his fault?

By T. STYLES

Had the girl not been there, he never would've lost his mind. It was time to tell him what happened. Sure, it could resort in the girl being banned but her antics fucked up his birthday.

Plus it wasn't like he would see her again.

"I got confused, Dad. I'm...I'm sorry."

He couldn't snitch.

"We aren't going to the hunt." Magnus responded.

Cage exhaled.

Due to losing his mind temporarily, he had destroyed the one thing he wanted. The one thing he heard from other boys was that once he returned, he would be a man.

So, learning that this would not be the case, fucked with him in weird ways.

"Dad, I'm sorry. I...I got kinda messed up and—."

"There's nothing we can do about it at this point." Magnus sighed. "So let it be."

"But we're supposed to go for my birthday. I mean, do you hate me that much?"

Cage's siblings gasped.

He never asked a question so deep from his father and certainly not in front of them.

"Why would you ask me something like that?"

"Magnus, leave it alone," Lala said softly, touching her husband's leg.

"If I hated you, I wouldn't have given you a beautiful home. I wouldn't have made sure that you have everything you needed," Looking back in the rearview mirror he said, "So you tell me, Cage, does that sound like hate to you?"

Cage sighed and remained silent.

TREASON   31

"Son, one of these days you are going to remember our conversations. And if you are talking to your son when it happens, I pray he never questions your loyalty."

"I understand."

He didn't.

But he wanted the spotlight off him.

"I saw you looking at that little girl today in the audience. I saw how your body reacted too."

Okay, now Cage wanted to push the door open and roll out into the street.

"You must control your urges. You must control your flesh."

Having been caught up, Cage leaned his head against the window.

Damn he felt miserable.

He didn't have friends and he didn't have hope.

When Magnus turned onto a small road leading to a row of million-dollar homes where they lived, their truck was almost sideswiped by a caravan of moving vehicles going in the same direction. The final vehicle in the lineup included a brand-new Christmas white Benz with a bow on the roof that was sitting on top of a flatbed next to a silver Range Rover.

Driving one of the moving vehicles was a white man with brown dreads and he was staring attentively in their direction.

"Looks like we have neighbors," Lala whispered before looking at Magnus worriedly.

"Yeah," he nodded. "Looks like we do. It was just a matter of time. And we might have to act now."

What did that mean?

As the married couple spoke quietly amongst themselves, Cage sat in the backseat wishing hard.

He wished for something major to happen in his life.

He wished for adventures his mind couldn't fathom.

In a sense, he wished for trouble.

CHAPTER TWO

"Say My Name Again."

A full moon sat above the million-dollar estate where Cage was helping his mother unpack groceries and a fresh order of beef from the butcher. As he removed the items from paper bags, he felt her eyes on him.

Judging.

The older they got, the more they grew further apart. "Mom, did you want me to whoop up on you on the video game later? You know you whack when it comes to—."

"You play too much. That's your problem and it needs to stop."

He looked down. "Yeah, you're right."

"And pull your pants up, Cage." She wiped her long luscious dark brown hair out of her face. "You'll be a man soon and you should appear more presentable."

He nodded and adjusted his gear.

"Mom, I...I mean...do you think you can talk to dad? About the hunt? I was hoping we could still go so—."

"He said no already!" She yelled, slamming a flat palm on the table. "Leave it at that! I don't like you participating in violent things anyway."

They never listened to him.

Apart from his siblings nobody cared what he said, and it was making him resentful.

By T. STYLES

Suddenly, he swiped the groceries off the counter with his forearm. A few pieces of fruit rolled under the table, and the slab of meat hit the floor.

He was immediately sorry.

But the damage was done.

With widened eyes after seeing what he did, he rushed toward her, but she shoved him away.

"Just...just stop." She tossed a palm his way.

"You're growing hateful, Cage. You try to hide it with jokes, but I see beneath that sweet interior. It's in your nature."

He had no idea what she was referring to, and it made him ashamed. Because in his eyes he didn't want anything other than their approval. But in his mind his worst fear was coming upon him.

And it was that he would be thrown out, the moment he turned eighteen. Besides, if his parents didn't fuck with him why would they have him around?

Before he could say anything else, Tatum yelled, "Who been in my fucking room?! Stay out!" He continued to spew obscenities.

"Aye, Tatum!" Lala hollered. "Watch your mouth!"

But he didn't though.

Instead, his young ass continued to go the fuck off. "I don't care about that shit! Y'all better stay out my room!"

"Tatum, please stop!" Exhaling deeply, she looked at her oldest. "This house is driving me crazy."

In that moment Cage noticed she was kinder to his younger brother than she ever was to him.

After all, he just displayed rage too.

Where was his scolding?

"What are you looking at?"

TREASON   35

Silence.

"Go get my purse. I left it in the car."

With his head hung low, he walked out the house. The moonlight was beautiful and commanded his entire attention. With the weight of the world on his shoulders, Cage was a sweet soul doing his best to maneuver in a place he felt didn't want him.

Trudging to his mother's car, he stopped suddenly.

Because at that moment, he was witnessing a girl, hanging inside of their truck. She was bent over, and her dress was hiked up so that he could see a peak of her black underwear.

Concerned, he approached her and yelled, "Aye, what you doing in our car?"

Slowly she eased out. And under the stars he was shocked to see it was the girl from church.

She was holding his mother's purse.

Not a day had gone by when he didn't think about her and wonder what made her react so wild in the audience. Up until that moment he swore he would never see her again.

He was wrong.

Damn, shawty was a ten.

Her naturally long hair cascaded down her back, and her body curved in all the right places.

She would be his girl in this lifetime.

He knew it.

"I remember you." Cage whispered. She was about to take off when he said, "Don't run. P...please."

She paused and faced him, while being sure to keep her distance.

"What's your name?" He stepped closer.

By T. STYLES

She stepped back. "Why? So you can call the police?"

"I wouldn't do that." He moved closer. "Besides, you seem cool. Even though you robbing me and shit."

She hung the straps of the Louis Vuitton over her shoulder as if it were her own. "You funny and nice, Cage Stryker. I like funny and nice boys."

"How you know my name?"

"Everybody knows your name."

He walked closer. Now he could smell the cocoa butter on her skin. "Say my name again."

She didn't move.

Licking her lips, she smiled and said, "Cage Stryker."

He grinned because her voice was so perfect it felt like she was singing.

Unlatching the purse off her shoulder he dug inside. She watched him suspiciously until he removed his mother's wallet.

"How much you need?" He asked.

"Need to what?"

"To stay in my life?"

She grinned. "Everything you got. And more. Can you afford that, Cage Stryker?"

A young nigga was on his dick, but he planned to try.

Feeling reckless, he gave her every bill in his mother's purse, which totaled up to 350 dollars.

She held it between her fingertips. "You really giving me all this?"

Silence.

"One day I'ma pay you back."

"No need."

Just then a tall dark-skinned seventeen-year-old teenager approached. He had tiny old scars on his face that were slightly raised in a keloid fashion.

Cage thought things were about to get heated, but the moment grew awkward when he smiled at Cage.

As if he were in awe.

"I told you he lived here," he said walking up to Cage and Angelina.

"Who are you?" Cage asked.

"The name's Onion and this is my girl, Angelina." He said with a grin on his face.

Cage was gut punched.

If she belonged to him, how could she be his?

"I'm not your girl," she said, nudging him.

Relief.

"Not like a girlfriend. Like my homie."

More relief.

She rolled her eyes and focused back on Cage.

"What you doing at my house?" Cage asked them both.

"Is it true that your birthday's soon?" She asked him.

Silence.

"You should answer," Onion grinned like he knew something Cage didn't. "So, she can tell you her idea. She always has the best ideas."

Cage nodded. "Yeah. Why you asking?"

"Is it true you wanna be a savage?"

Cage looked down and back at her. "You know, you really shouldn't do stuff like you did in the audience. I got in trouble. It's not—."

"You gotta answer her for this to work," Onion said playfully.

Cage wasn't certain, but he had a feeling that Onion's mind may have been younger than his age, and it made him look at him differently.

With kinder eyes.

"I was just talking," Cage said.

Angelina looked disappointed. "That's too bad."

"Why?"

"Because I'm here to change your life."

"How you gonna do that?"

"I guess it don't matter because you want to stay in your perfect world. When everything about me is a wrecking ball."

"What that mean?"

"I destroy old things, so new things can be born."

I'm ready for you to fuck up my life. Cage thought.

They turned to walk away.

"Wait!" Cage yelled.

They both paused and faced him.

"It's true. I wanna be a savage."

She grinned. "We'll be back soon."

"I hope so." Cage waved.

"You got it."

"I'm dead serious," Cage continued playfully. "Maybe we can play tag or something."

"You'll never be able to catch me."

"I guess we'll see."

Loving his personality, she winked, looped her arm around Onion's and skipped away.

When Cage turned around, he was shocked to see a beautiful woman standing before him. She was wearing a black pantsuit and no shirt, and so her cleavage exposed her Double D breasts.

But it was her skin that stunned.

It literally resembled the color of melted caramel and due to her designer perfume, she smelled good enough to lick.

She was giving model behavior and stood at 5'7 with straight fire red hair that ran down her back. Despite the strong color, it was obvious that she came from extreme wealth. The diamonds on her neck and rings on her fingers were worth 500 grand alone.

"Nice purse." She said. "Is it yours?"

He glared. "Nah."

"You live in this house?" She asked.

Cage nodded, unable to look the beautiful woman in the eyes.

"The name's Joanne, but my friends call me JoJo." She extended her fingertips. "What's your name?"

"Cage?" He accepted and found himself not wanting to let go. "Was that your daughter or something?"

"Nope. I don't have any kids."

He looked at her in awe.

"Well, I'm new around here, Cage. We just moved in up the block. Come see me when you get a chance." She kissed him on the cheek. "You have an open invitation."

He nodded again.

"You going to let go of my hand?" She asked.

"Oh...I was trying to hand wrestle." He released her. "I win."

She giggled. "I like you, Cage. And I'll be waiting."

In one night, Cage went from the most unpopular to the most popular boy on earth.

With the luck he was having, he was feeling on top of the world.

CHAPTER THREE
"They Let Me See Their Kitten."

It was a cool night as he jogged in his neighborhood just to see JoJo again. Essentially, he was hoping to take her up on her offer, whatever that meant.

Since he met her the night before, she was all he could think about. And prior to that moment he thought Angelina was the most beautiful girl in the world.

But why bother with a girl when he could have a woman?

Plus, he didn't know if Angelina and Onion were really a couple.

DING. DING. DING.

Sweating and panting, he pulled out his phone and checked his messages. Under the night sky, he sighed when he read his mother's texts.

Where are you?
You're supposed to be in this house.
This is unlike you Cage.
Come home.

Shaking his head, he dropped the phone in his sweats and continued his run. Within minutes, he ended up in front of the new neighbor's house.

From where he was, he had the perfect view of her backyard.

Peeking from across the street, he stopped when he saw JoJo shimmering under the patio lights. She was sitting next to her pool and wearing a white Louis Vuitton bikini set. Propped in a red sling chair her shoulders were being massaged by a tall dark skin man from behind.

His skin was also flawless, and they were giving model vibes.

At that moment Cage couldn't move.

He was drawn to them both as he continued to stare from a distance.

He was just about to inch closer, when suddenly JoJo looked at him and licked her lips.

They glossed up as if sprayed with water.

To his surprise instead of being angry that he was snooping, she smiled.

With her sight firmly on his, she removed her right breast, gripped it from below and ran her pink tongue across the nipple. It hardened and glistened under her tongue stroke.

Cage's eyes widened.

Was she doing all this to get his attention?

Because it fucking worked.

He was stuck.

Since Cage was a virgin, he didn't know how to handle the sensation coursing through his body and so he turned around to run.

First, he started slowly and then ran faster.

At this speed, he almost ran past his house and into the next state.

"You big freak! Now everybody gonna know you gross!" He said to himself.

He wanted to get rid of the shame of what he saw even though he didn't want the memory out of his mind.

Before he knew it, he was standing by his own yard when suddenly he heard loud voices. A high wooden fence surrounded the property and he walked toward it slowly.

Looking through the slat, he saw his father yelling at his mother. Whenever Magnus tried to walk around her, she would step in his path, and he would yell at her again.

Cage couldn't hear what was being said, due to them being an acre away from the fence but he could tell things were getting heated.

Feeling like he was violating their privacy, he walked away.

Once in the house, he decided to check on his siblings first. Back in the day his parents didn't fight much. But lately they were at it all the time and he couldn't help but think it was because of him.

The least he could do was go into big brother mode and console them.

After searching the estate, he found the young ones in Tatum's room looking out the window.

Concerned, Cage walked inside and closed it when he saw they were also looking at their parents.

"Where were you?" Tatum asked.

"Going to see a man about a dog. They gave me two poodles instead."

"Really?" Bloom asked with wide eyes. "Where are they?"

"He lying!" Tatum interrupted. "And he gotta stop because mom and dad were arguing because of you, you know."

His eyebrows rose. "Really?"

"I'm worried you gonna have to move soon," Bloom said. "Please be nice to them and don't break the rules."

He grabbed her hand and sat on the edge of Tatum's bed. Waving his brothers over he took a deep breath.

Standing in front of Cage, the four of them inhaled deeply.

"I don't know what they fighting about, but I'ma smooth stuff over so I don't gotta go nowhere."

Flow was sold, holding onto his brother's every word.

"You promise?" Bloom asked.

"Yeah, because I gotta be here to take care of y'all," he nudged her cheek softly. Looking at Tatum who used anger to hide the fear that he was scared his big brother would be put out he said, "Plus if I don't, Tatum gonna take care of you. Ain't you big man?"

Tatum smiled proudly.

"Everything will be fine. I promise. Let me go see what's up. I be back."

Exiting the room, he was shocked to see Lala on the other side of the door.

Was she listening?

She grabbed his hand and led him to the front door. Next, she locked it from the inside, and ushered him toward the basement. Upstairs Cage could now hear his father yelling at the top of his lungs.

He sounded drunk.

"Lala, we aren't done!" Magnus continued. "Do you hear me? We aren't done!"

"Where did you go tonight?" She yelled, stepping closer to Cage.

He walked toward the couch and flopped down. Looking up at his beautiful mother, he was confused at why Magnus was getting louder.

"What were you guys arguing about?" He whispered. "I saw you both. On the lawn."

"Is this your way of skipping the subject?"

"Can you please tell me what's wrong?"

"The neighborhood is changing. And we may have to move."

"If you do, am I going with you?"

"Cage, where were you tonight?"

Why did she ignore the question?

"I went down the street."

"Down the street where?"

Silence.

"Cage, where did you go?"

"The neighbors. They let me see their kitten."

She was sick of his ass at this point.

She sat next to him. "Listen to me, what's happening between me, and your father is not an issue. I can handle it. But you need to stay away from that house because he has a problem with them moving in the neighborhood and I do too. Okay?"

He looked down. "You know them?"

"Cage, promise me."

The way she looked at him made him feel her seriousness. Because Lala never looked directly in his eyes. "I promise you."

"You know breaking a promise to your parents is the greatest disrespect, right?"

"I won't go back again. I promise."

She kissed his cheek, grabbed the remote and turned on the television. "Now what was all that shit you were talking about with the video game?"

Cage smiled brightly. "Oh, so you do want to get whipped?"

"We'll see about that," he continued, as the two played into the night.

With the house down the street on both of their minds.

Nothing but your run of the mill public high school complete with an underpaid staff, who were forced to teach students whose outfits cost more than what they made in a month.

Magnus pulled up in front of the school and parked. "I'll see you later." He said with an attitude.

Trying to connect to his father he said, "Dad, I'm sorry about disrespecting curfew yesterday. I wanted to work out so I can make the football team and--"

"Cage, this is your last year. You aren't good enough to play sports. I keep telling you that. So why waste your time?"

"I was thinking if I worked really hard I could--"

"Focus on being a man of honor. And getting a job. Nothing more."

"You're right, dad," he sighed. "I'll see you later."

Magnus examined him a bit longer and then popped the lock.

Cage nodded and gave a half smile.

After closing the door, he walked up the stairs leading into the school building and was greeted by the usual assholes. A jealous group of young niggas led by their goofy ass leader, Ziggy.

When they made sure Magnus was gone, Ziggy grabbed his arm.

"Get off me," Cage yelled, yanking away.

Ziggy flipped off his hood and said, "Oh, so you feeling yourself all of a sudden huh?"

"Why? Because you keep trying to touch me?" He paused. "Because I caught you several times staring at me in the locker room?" He gripped his dick. "I ain't even know you go that way."

Ziggy's eyes widened two sizes bigger. "What you just say to me?"

"I mean you ain't my type but when you wanna suck my dick?" Always in joke mode, he leaned in for a fake kiss and Ziggy shoved him back.

"I should break your--."

"You ready to go?" Onion asked, stepping up.

Angelina stood at his side.

Perfect timing.

Cage looked at him. "Yeah, let's go do that thing we were going to do."

"So you running with this nigga now?" Ziggy asked Onion.

"If he is, it ain't none of your business," Angelina said.

Ziggy looked at her and tapped the crease of his arm.

She looked away.

Cage wondered what secret Ziggy had on her.

Focusing back on Cage he said, "I'll catch you later." Ziggy smirked.

Cage winked. "You got it."

When he was out of sight, Cage said to Angelina and Onion, "What y'all doing here?"

"So, we ain't allowed to get no education?" Onion laughed.

Cage held back a smile. "Serious," he said looking between them. "What's up because this getting weird now."

Angelina whipped out her school ID. "I told you we go here." She flashed it in his face.

"How come I ain't never seen y'all before?"

"I just started last week," Onion said. "And this one is never in class." He pointed at her with his thumb.

Cage was about to walk away when Angelina grabbed his hand, "I got plans for your birthday. So, I gotta give you the details. Come with us."

A few minutes later they were in an excluded section in the back of the school. As they smoked, Cage looked them up and down, admiring their clothing. One day he would be able to wear anything he wanted too.

"So, the way I see things, you look bored with life," Angelina said.

"Not really bored but—."

"I know bored when I see it. Because whenever my stepfather was bored, he used to come in my room."

Cage frowned and Onion looked away.

"Come into your room and do what?" Cage asked.

Onion shook his head no, for him to stop with his line of questioning.

She smiled and shook her head. "So, look, I think you need to do three things before you turn eighteen. First, break your parents' rules. Second have sex with a complete stranger." She batted her eyes. "And I'm available if need be."

"I thought you said you didn't fuck your friends?" Onion interrupted.

Cage didn't know their dynamic, but if she was going to be his girl, he was going to have to get to the bottom of it soon.

"I'm just playing, Shhhh." She focused back on Cage. "See you're too nice. You can't go into the world as a grown man who's too nice because people will take advantage of you."

"She's right," Onion said. "The man who took care of me was too nice. Then when he got married, his best friend took his wife."

Cage frowned. "That ain't gonna be me."

"You never know," Onion continued.

Angelina frowned and focused back on Cage. "I'm going to lead you into disfunction." She said, closing her hands together in front of him. "And you're going to love every minute of it too. Trust me."

The sun gave Cage a headache as he stared out the window.

He thought about what Angelina and Onion said about cutting up before he turned eighteen. Over the years he tried his best to be the model son, but his parents didn't appear to appreciate his efforts.

By T. STYLES

When the teacher, Gordon Tole, saw him daydreaming, he closed the blinds.

Cage didn't mind.

He always felt off balance in the daytime anyway.

"Why you close the window, Teach? I was looking out of it," a student yelled.

"Since you flunked five times in a row, you need to be focusing on your test."

The classroom erupted in laughter before settling into silence.

Slowly, Gordon approached Cage. People would take him for a model before they did a teacher.

"What's wrong?" The scowl on Gordon's face was concrete. In fact, behind his back he was referred to as Mean Face Gordon.

"Nothing's wrong." Cage moved uneasily, not liking the attention he was drawing from the other students.

"We're taking a test. Why aren't you focused instead of looking out the window?"

Cage slid the test paper in his direction. "I finished last week," he said sarcastically.

Gordon looked down at the sheet and smiled. "Good work. Hopefully your score will match your mouth. So, what's on your mind?"

Cage opened and closed his mouth. It was evident that something was on his heart that he was trying to get off.

"Let's take a walk," Gordon said.

Getting out of his seat, he bopped out the door with Gordon with all the students watching in confusion. Every one of them knew he liked Cage but what they didn't understand was why.

Moving deeper down the dark hallway, until they reached the area that stored the school supplies and was virtually void of people, Cage said, "Is it normal for your father to want you gone at eighteen?"

Gordon leaned against the wall. "What's happening?"

"I feel like my father doesn't like me. Nothing about me. And I don't get it. Before this year we were close but now..."

"Did something change recently?"

"No. And I can't explain it. All I know is he yells and fusses a lot at night."

"How often?"

"At least once a month. And when he does he gets my sister and brothers worried."

Gordon shifted a little. "I don't think your father would hurt your mother."

"I never said he would."

"Listen, son, it's difficult sometimes when you're growing up. You often feel like you gotta protect everyone, even your mother."

He frowned. "I just want my family to stay together and be happy. I'm not ready to go just 'cause I'm eighteen."

"Magnus is smart. He's a man of honor so he won't release you until you're ready. For now, remember the lessons he's teaching you. Because when you become a man, you'll meet people who give no respect to what it means to have a code. And you'll wish you had him to rely on in those dark days."

When school let out, Cage walked slowly toward the front door. Glancing out the window, just as he expected the group with Ziggy in the lead was waiting on him.

Welp, he couldn't hide forever.

Slowly he descended the steps.

His heart pounded against the wall of his chest, and he felt his breath quickening because he was out of his league. When it came to fighting Cage was fearful.

It was all in his eyes.

He preferred to use his mind.

But it didn't mean he wouldn't fight to the death.

He thought about swinging a few blows but was sure he would be bloodied and beaten within every inch of his life.

Afterall, this had happened many times before.

And whenever it did, he would lie to his parents about his bruises. Claiming he had played too rough in the gym and lost his balance.

The thing was, Cage didn't play.

He did get his ass beat though.

So, no one at his house ever believed him.

As Cage moved closer, Ziggy stomped up to him outside and cracked his knuckles. "This later, right? What you wanna do since you had so much mouth earlier in—."

"Cage!"

When he heard someone call his name, he was shocked to see the white man with brown dreads staring at him from a white Benz on the curb. The last time he saw him and the vehicle, Cage and his family were leaving Magnus' church and he was driving a moving truck.

Was he JoJo's friend?

Instead of answering, Cage stared at him.

"You're Cage right?" He said.

Cage nodded.

"You need a ride?"

Technically he didn't.

His father would be coming at any moment, but he was facing getting jumped now.

Maybe if he accepted the ride, he could avoid the madness.

Looking back at Ziggy and the gang, he said, "I hate to beat your ass in front of your friends, so I'ma let you live for now. But we'll always have tomorrow."

Ziggy clenched his fist and said, "Nigga, I should--."

"I wouldn't do that if I were you!" The man from the Benz yelled. "He has some really powerful friends now."

I do?

"In fact, I would steer clear of him for the rest of your life!" He continued. "Unless you wanna die."

Cage winked at Ziggy again, jogged down the steps and slipped into the Benz before it pulled out of sight.

An hour later instead of being at home, Cage was standing in front of the neighbor's house. Although they lived literally down the street from one another, he was shocked at how different their homes were in daylight.

Their grass was so green it looked fake, and they had motion detecting lighting everywhere. There was also a garden on the left and right of the estate, with roses that were so red and vibrant they were prize worthy.

"You coming in?" The man asked, holding the door open.

Cage looked at him and thought about the promise he made to his mother. For some reason he felt if he accepted, everything in his life would change.

It can't be that serious. Maybe I'll go in for a little while.

He bopped inside and the dreaded man disappeared within the home, leaving him in the foyer alone.

This house was showing the fuck off.

Cage was stunned at the decor.

Their home put his to shame. There were crystal chandeliers even in the hallways and the entire mansion was laid out with plush beautiful white carpeting and intricate gold design.

He made mental notes that when he was rich, he would have a home just as lavish.

Five minutes later the dreaded man entered the living room holding sandwiches. "Figured you were hungry. After having been at school all day."

Cage shook his head. "Nah, I'm good."

He dropped the plate on the table, causing a sandwich to flap open on the floor.

"You okay?" Cage asked, looking at the food before staring back at him.

The man smiled. "My name is Flan. And I'm the housekeeper."

He glared. "Housekeeper?"

"I always get that reaction. But yes, the housekeeper. I do everything the Ledgers need."

He shrugged. "Why did you want me to come here?"

"Why did you agree?"

"I didn't agree. You drove, parked and I followed you inside."

He smiled. "The lady of the house met you the other day. Do you remember her?"

Cage sat back and then forward. There wasn't a moment that passed where he didn't give her some of his attention.

"Nah, who you talking about?"

"JoJo."

He placed a finger under his chin and looked upward. "Ohhhh yeah. I remember her."

"She said your birthday's coming up."

"Why should she care?"

"I don't know. I'm just the housekeeper, remember?"

"Where are they?"

"They keep late hours."

Cage glanced around. "Drug dealers?"

He smiled. "Anyway, they wanted me to invite you over for dinner, the night of your birthday. You can bring your friends if you'd like. That way you can feel safe."

"I ain't got no friends."

"That sounds like a lonely life."

Silence.

"Do you accept the invitation, Cage?"

"What about her husband?"

"He'll be here too." He leaned closer. "Cage, You'll find they have many dinner parties. Parties that bring the best people." He grew serious. "You aren't putting them out. So, after learning, through his wife, that a neighbor had an upcoming birthday, Mr. and Mrs. Ledger decided it would be a special occasion. They're just being gracious."

"So, I guess they want me to bring my parents too."

"Do you want to bring your parents?"

Silence.

"Do you accept their invitation?"

Cage thought about his mother again and rose slowly. "I have to go." He walked toward the door.

"You know..."

Cage turned around and looked at him. "You know what?"

"Whenever they offer you something, you really should be nicer. It's dangerous not to accept invitations. Especially from the Ledgers."

Grabbing the knob, Cage shook his head and walked out.

Was that a threat?

The invitation played on repeat in his mind as he remembered seeing Mrs. Ledger lick her own titty. Part of him wanted to honor his mother and not make things worse, and the other part wanted to know more about the strange couple.

He was halfway down the street when he ran into Angelina and Onion. They were sitting on the curb on the side of his house smoking weed.

"It's time for part one of your savage birthday week," Angelina announced loudly.

Cage was so scared he felt faint. "What you talking about? What are you even doing here?"

"You going to the party tonight at school?"

"Are y'all crazy? You could've gotten me in trouble sitting on the side of my house smoking and shit."

Angelina smiled. "I thought you wanted to have fun. Because this is a part of it."

He crossed his arms over his chest. "I'm starting to think y'all stalking me."

Angelina looked at Onion and then back at Cage. "So how you know Tino?" She stood up and dusted her butt off.

"Who's Tino?"

"The man who owns the house you just walked out of." Onion rose too.

"Wait so you know him?"

"Everybody knows him."

Cage grew suspicious.

"Stop the fucking games!" Cage yelled for the first time. The voice was so authoritative it almost didn't sound like him. "What's going on?"

"I earn money sometimes dancing," Angelina admitted. "I mean...before I met them it was a little money. But after meeting them shit changed. I went to their house one night, did my set but when I woke up, I was bruised. And they acted like they didn't know what happened."

Speaking of bruises, while she was talking, Cage noticed her bare arms.

Grabbing her wrist softly, he said, "Wait, y'all use drugs?"

"Not me," Onion said, throwing his hands up in the air.

Angelina snatched away. "I only use when it hurts."

"When what hurts?"

She walked away.

Onion approached him as she stormed quickly up the street. "Look, she ain't perfect. But I promise you, when you get to know her, she'll be the most important person in your life."

When Onion looked up, he saw Bloom looking at them from her bedroom window. He winked at her and she grinned.

"Don't turn around just yet but your little sis got eyes on us."

"She won't say nothing to my parents but it's time to go." Cage looked over at Angelina who was now sitting on the curb crying. "My parents be home soon." He paused. "But what did she mean when she said she only uses when it hurts?"

"She'll tell you when she can trust you. Until then you gotta wait."

Feeling bad he hurt one of the few people on earth who cared to plan his birthday, he walked over to her and extended his hand. "So you a crying savage or...?"

She giggled. "Never said I was a savage. I'm too weak for that."

"And you think I'm stronger?"

She took his hand. "I know you are, Cage Stryker. And soon you will too."

She stood up, looped her arm through his and Onion's. "You wearing that?" She asked Cage, looking at his clothing.

"I ain't got no gear. Plus, if I go home now my folks gonna make me stay inside. So, I gotta rock this."

"No, you don't. Go with me to my job and then we can hit the mall."

"What job?" Cage frowned looking at them both.

"You'll see."

As they walked away, Onion waved at Bloom once more.

She smiled.

CHAPTER FOUR

"Why They Call You Onion?"

The stars were high when Angelina strutted into the fence surrounding a small house with Cage and Onion following.

Walking to the side door, she looked at them both. "You see this window right here?" She pointed downward with her chipped red fingernail.

Cage nodded.

"I'ma open it up when I get inside. If you see me let down my hair, come get me. It means I'm in trouble, okay?"

"Hold up, what's going on again?" Cage asked, looking at the two.

"You gonna watch my back or not?" Cage shifted a little and she grabbed his hand. "Please don't leave."

He didn't even know them niggas.

"We got you," Onion said.

She looked at Cage. It was important that he stayed.

"I'll be here when you get out."

"Okay, when I open the window don't be judgmental. I'ma take a little bit to cut the edge. But I'll be fine." She stood on her tiptoes and kissed them on the lips before rushing down the steps and entering the door.

When she was gone, Onion and Cage dropped onto their bellies on the cool damp grass and waited for her to come into view. The window was covered at first until suddenly the curtains opened just enough for them to peek inside.

She looked sad but wanting to lighten the mood, she walked to the window and gazed up at them. Placing a finger under each one of her cheeks, she pushed upward, forcing a smile on her pretty face.

When they gave it back, she walked away.

Sitting on a chair with a black torn leather seat, she looked like a little girl waiting on the worst.

Within minutes a sloppy older white man entered and dropped his red and black pajama pants. Angelina rose from the chair and crawled on her knees.

Snaking her hand into his boxers, she removed his limp penis and placed it in her mouth. Stroking it while licking the balls too, within seconds he hardened up.

What the fuck is this? Cage thought to himself. He didn't know what he expected but it definitely wasn't a live blowjob show.

Cage was disappointed and embarrassed.

"She's a virgin you know?" Onion said off the commentary tip.

Cage looked at her and back at him. "If she doing this, she ain't no virgin. She's—."

"Everybody gotta have a way of thinking to prevent going crazy. Ain't nobody ever go between her legs, so she still clean that way."

"This is too much."

"Some women do what they gotta to survive. Others do things like this, for the ones they love."

Cage didn't understand.

"Don't judge her." Onion continued. "Please."

They both looked at her give a blowjob with precision and Cage fought the urge to harden up. He felt guilty and angry for her at the same time.

Cage had never seen anything this sexual in his life.

Apparently, the John hadn't either.

The man she was giving a blowjob was in such ecstasy, that he cried. Literally. Tears rolled down his cheeks.

For some reason, shame continued to wash over Cage. He felt bad for Angelina. And he felt bad for himself because he still liked her. Once she was his, she would never have to move like this again.

Looking away he said, "Why they call you Onion?"

Onion focused on the window. "I don't talk about those things."

"Why?"

"Look through the window, Cage. We gotta make sure she's safe, remember?"

Five minutes later when she was done, the man handed her money and a small baggie before disappearing from the room, leaving her alone. Standing up, she reached for her purse and removed a heroin kit. It included everything she needed to cook and get high.

As they waited on her to come out, Cage watched a needle go through her arm.

It was at that moment that he was certain he was dealing with people that were deep in the streets.

So why did he feel at home?

An hour later they were in the mall.

For the blowjob Angelina commanded six hundred dollars. It was a cheap amount in her opinion to get head from a young Filipina and black girl, but it was her fee all the same.

As they went from store to store, she spent most of the money on Cage.

When he walked out of the dressing room, wearing the clothes that Angelina just bought for him, both she and Onion hyped him up.

"Aw, shit," Onion said, holding his fist over his mouth. "This nigga ready for savage week for sure."

Cage tried to stop blushing, but it was literally the first time anybody ever bought him something he wanted.

The gift hit him so hard, that for a second, he paused as he was overcome with gratitude and suspicion.

"Why you doing this for me?" Cage asked seriously.

"Because I like you. Plus you gave me $350 from your mama's purse. I said I would pay it back. Can't that be enough?"

The moment the threesome stepped onto the dance floor at the school party; all eyes were on them. Angelina and Onion were known for looking the part but Cage not so much.

But tonight, things were different.

As he peeped the attention being given to him, Cage tried his best to play it off like he didn't care. Like he dressed that way all the time.

But he did and it was obvious that he was proud of himself in that moment.

"This just the beginning," Onion said to Cage with a hand on his shoulder. "I see big things for you."

"Nah, for me this is as good as it will get."

"Not true," Onion said seriously. "I promise."

"Yep, we doing it all week too." Angelina added. "I'm going to get us something to drink. I be right back."

Onion walked up to him. "So, she likes you."

Cage nodded to the music. "That's cool."

"Do you like her back?"

Cage shifted a little. Liked her was an understatement but he wasn't prepared to let on how much.

"I mean if I had a few bucks I would buy her a couple of poodles and shit."

He frowned. "Everything is not a joke. For real."

"Listen, I don't know her," he said seriously. "I don't know you. Let's just enjoy savage week and I'll let you know then."

Cage saw him drop his head sadly. "You aight?"

Onion sighed. "Look at me, man. I'm the ugly nigga girls be talking about when they describe the dude in their nightmares. And the only female whoever wanted to spend time with me, put me in the friend category the moment she saw my face. And she didn't do that with you. So if you have a chance to be with her, don't fuck it up. Because I would for sure take my shot."

Cage thought about what he said.

In his opinion, despite the marks on his face, Onion had a style that he thought females could get with and a face that money could correct. In his mind he had to wait for age and his paper to catch up.

"You ain't ugly," Cage said. "Just not fine as me."

Onion looked at him and suddenly they both broke out into laughter.

"Just give shit some time," Cage said seriously. "You gonna be good."

"Maybe you right."

Cage looked at Angelina across the room.

She was a star and the boys gravitated toward her. Outside of her beauty her laugh was contagious, and her personality was electric which made her a hot commodity.

After a short while, Angelina returned. "The line too long." She rolled her eyes. "All that for some dry ass punch? They doing the most."

"I'll go," Onion said, wanting to please his friend.

"Cool," Angelina said.

As she danced in front of Cage, he looked away. He saw what Onion liked about her because her personality was huge.

Her face was perfect.

And when he was around her, he felt on top of the world.

Cage wasn't the only one taking notes. Angelina was checking him out hard.

"Having fun yet?"

Cage shrugged. "Yeah, thank you."

While Onion hung over the drink table, leaving the two of them alone, Cage took the opportunity to get serious. But there was something else on his mind besides her beauty. She was dancing happily on the floor, and he could tell she was high.

"You know what, I think you better than what you gotta do for money."

She frowned and stopped. "Why would you bring that up?"

"Um, not saying it's a problem. Just didn't know you got down like that, that's all. You too pretty to—."

"So, you're wearing the clothes I bought for your birthday and pointing fingers at me at the same time?"

He could tell she was embarrassed, and it wasn't his intent. "I'ma be honest, it's not my thing. All I'm saying is between the drugs and whoring yourself around you can do better."

"I don't know what happened in your life that makes you feel like you can judge everybody, but I really hope that changes. Because if it doesn't, you're gonna miss out on some really cool people. And one of them will be me."

"I was just—."

Suddenly, everything seemed to pause when Cage looked over at the door and saw his father enter. Maybe it was the fact that he was 6'4. Or maybe it was the glare on his face. Whatever it was, all eyes were on Magnus at that moment and Cage was stunned.

No longer was he a fake ass savage.

Suddenly, under Magnus' gaze he was a scared little boy.

Cage wasn't even sure how he knew about the party. Because he never mentioned it to his parents knowing they would say no. And yet there he was staring at the man he loved and feared while trying to prevent an embarrassing scene from taking place.

Thinking on his feet, quickly he walked in his direction to diffuse the situation.

But Magnus was faster. And before he knew it, he was upon him.

"What are you doing here?" Magnus roared, causing everybody on the dance floor to look their way. "I thought you were jogging."

"Dad, I'm..."

"What? I can't hear you! Why are you whispering now?"

"Dad, I—."

"And where did you get them clothes? Huh?" He pulled at the shirt Angelina bought him and tore it off his body, like paper from a stick of gum.

Cage was so ashamed he almost dropped to his knees.

"What you doing? Trying to seduce these young girls?"

He was confused. "What? No, I--"

"Take off them shoes."

"Dad, please don't. I—."

"NOW!"

Looking back once at Angelina and Onion who were staring in his direction, Cage removed the shoes.

"Is everything okay?" Onion asked, stepping to the two with Angelina at his side.

It was at that time that Cage decided never to question his motives again. Because the boy was either dimwitted or fearless.

Either way he was someone he wanted on his team.

"I'm fine, go away," Cage said in a low voice.

Onion looked up at the massive man and then Cage before trudging off.

"Why are you even here, dad?"

"That's not the question or the answer. You don't go anywhere without my approval. What is wrong with you, Cage? Ever since your antics at church you've been different."

"Let's go, dad." He tried to walk past him.

"I asked you a question!" Magnus said louder, grabbing his arm.

Cage heard him.

But knew the battle was lost and wanted to save what was left of his dignity.

"Apparently everything, dad. Now you got even more reasons not to love me." Barefoot and embarrassed, he walked around him and toward the door.

CHAPTER FIVE

"Son, Please Stay Away From Them. I'm Begging You."

As Cage jogged under the purple starlit sky, he thought about how he was embarrassed beyond belief by his father at school.

At that moment, he experienced so many emotions when he was caught at the dance. Juggling between shame and annoyance, he also felt anger at Magnus.

You must understand, this was a man that he loved.

So, to feel this way, brought many questions. The questions had him wanting to work harder to build their bond, and he had plans to do just that.

Despite being welcomed to the house by the Ledgers, he decided to jog in the opposite direction.

He was already in trouble due to going to the high school party. With his birthday approaching, the last thing he needed was to be on punishment because he went into the Ledger's house again.

After finishing his workout, he was about to turn around, when suddenly a beautiful white Benz pulled alongside him. When he lowered his height to see who was inside, he was shocked to see JoJo.

"Can we talk for a minute?"

He looked to the left and right to be sure there were no eyes upon him, although he was a half a mile away from his house.

When he noticed the coast was clear, he slipped inside. She was wearing a red top that cut so deep, her breast fullness was on display as well as the top of her belly button.

He couldn't keep his eyes off her if he tried.

"I heard about what happened at school." She placed a warm hand on his thigh and rubbed erotically.

He frowned. "Who told you?"

"It doesn't matter."

"Actually, it does."

She grinned. "It's like this...you aren't respected where you are. You aren't even taken seriously."

"I would appreciate it if you got to the point."

"When you turn eighteen, I hope you think about what you want out of life. Because you need to give consideration to it right now."

Cage scratched his head. "Why you so interested in me? I'm a nobody. I have nothing."

"That's not true."

"What do you want with me?" He asked firmer.

"We have a job we need you to do for us. Although you aren't in possession of the skills, we believe with training, you'll rise to the occasion."

"A job? Why would you offer me a job?"

"That's not the point. Because at the end of the day, you're living in a house worth a lot of money, yet you dress like a bum, and no one respects you. Is that what you desire for yourself?"

Cage looked out the window and back at her. "Angelina, and Onion. Do you know them?"

"You mean the weird duo I see you hanging with?"

"Yes." He shifted a little. "Did you send them to me?"

"You don't trust them?"

"I do but they seem too good to be true."

"You're smarter than a lot of people give you credit for. But the answer is no. Angelina is a neighborhood drug addict who wants a life that she isn't suited for."

"How do you know her?"

"She came to a few parties we had back in the day. A pretty girl with a bad habit. She claimed someone hurt her at the last party. And now she circles the neighborhood hoping we would see her and invite her back into our world. She's a nasty girl. Not someone I'm interested in having around me."

"Please don't talk that way."

"What way?"

"Don't talk about her like that."

"Somebody has a crush I see."

"That's not it. I just—."

"What do you want out of life, Cage? You haven't answered the question. And I can assure you that whatever you desire, we can provide."

"We?"

"Yes. You'll meet Tino soon. He's—."

KNOCK. KNOCK. KNOCK.

When Cage turned his head, he was shocked to see his mother looking through the window. She was pissed. And he was certain that her expression was dipped in pure rage.

Pulling the car door open, only after JoJo unlocked it, Lala snatched her son from the seat.

"What are you doing with her, Cage? I thought I told you not to be around those people."

JoJo leaned down, "Hello, Mrs. Stryker." She grinned.

"I want you to stay away from my son, bitch." She said pointing at her. "Or else."

"Or else what?" JoJo glared. "I mean, do you really want to go there?"

"Leave us alone!"

Instead of responding, Lala slammed the door shut, and JoJo pulled off.

"Cage, I don't know what's happening with you." She said, alternating her stare from the ground to his face. But—."

"Why aren't you able to look at me? What is it about me that makes you feel so ashamed?"

"If I'm being honest, sometimes you scare me."

"Why?"

She positioned herself to stand in front of him while staring directly in his eyes. Taking a deep breath she said, "If you deal with those people your life will be ruined. Nothing good will ever come to you. Is that what you want?"

"Who are they, ma? Tell me!"

"Son, please, stay away. I'm begging you."

CHAPTER SIX

"What's One More Battle?"

C age woke up the next morning with a headache as the sun shined through his window.

Mornings were always hard for the growing boy.

Between Magnus embarrassing him at school, and his mother pulling him out of the car while he talked to JoJo, he was certain that everyone around him knew things he didn't.

And he hated them and himself for it.

If people continued to lie to his face, he was certain their relationship would reach the point of no return.

Standing in front of the mirror, he looked at his thick kinky hair, his chocolate skin, and his light brown eyes. For the most part he appreciated the muscular physique he earned due to working out. But he felt his nightly routine of running had far deeper meanings.

Jogging gave him an opportunity to see what the night had to offer.

To see the truth from those who tried to hide.

To play with the darkness.

After slipping on a white t-shirt and grey sweatpants, he heard a knock on the window. Rushing toward it, he smiled when he saw Onion and Angelina on the other side.

Opening the window, he was about to lock the door when he saw his brother Flow in his doorway.

"What you doing in here?" He whispered. "Get out."

"But I don't wanna leave. I wanna see what—."

"Now!"

Embarrassed, he said, "If I can't stay, then I'ma tell dad you let people in the window." He said pointing at Angelina and Onion. "Because you aren't allowed to—"

"You know what...just stay right here." Cage yanked him inside, locked his door and focused back on his friends.

"Snitching will get you hemmed up, lil nigga," Onion said pointing at him.

"And you ugly as fuck," Flow responded.

Cage pinched him silent.

"So, what happened?" Onion continued. "With your father? He looked like he wanted to snap your neck at that party."

"You finally fought dad?" Flow yelled.

"Shut up!" Cage said louder than he ever spoke to him in the past.

Focusing on his friends he said, "You know what happened. My father came in and ruined everything."

"So, you grounded?" Onion asked.

"Did this dude just say grounded?" Angelina laughed.

"You know what I mean." He said to her before looking back at Cage. "Are you punished?"

"I don't know." Cage shrugged. "The other night I was jogging, and my mother pulled up on me when I was talking to JoJo. It's like I can't stay out of trouble."

Angelina and Onion looked shocked.

"Wait, you mean Tino's wife?" Onion asked.

"I don't think you should be messing with her," Angelina said.

"You're just jealous," Onion noted. "If he likes her, I say go all the way."

"Do you like her?" Angelina asked in a concerned tone.

"Nah... it's not like that."

Now it was Onion who was disappointed.

Onion moved closer to Cage so Flow couldn't hear. "But what about the dinner invitation you told us about at the mall? We still going tonight?"

"Can't believe you asked him about that." Angelina whispered. "Didn't you just hear what he said? His father and mother are mad."

"I get all that, but the whole point was to play savage. And you told me Tino's dinner parties be epic." He looked at Cage. "So, if the Ledgers do something just for you, you know it's gonna be official."

"What party are you talking about?" Flow asked, standing next to where they sat. He moved so quietly no one knew he was standing right there. "Because if you punished, you better not go nowhere."

Cage grabbed his arm and tossed him against the wall.

He hiccupped.

"Stay right here and don't say nothing else. If you say one more word, I'm gonna cave your chest in."

Flow frowned. "You're different."

Maybe he was.

In that moment he did feel rage.

Was this why his mother feared him so?

Cage backed up and took a deep breath before walking back over to his friends. Being nice had gotten him nowhere. So it was time to turn shit up.

"I think I'll figure out a way to go to the dinner party." Cage said.

"For real?" Onion asked excitedly.

"Yeah, in the meantime, I have to play along with my parents."

"Whatever you need, we there." Angelina stood up and walked toward the window. Looking at Onion she said, "You ready?"

He nodded and they both crawled out.

When Cage turned around, he saw Flow was sniffing the seat where Angelina recently sat.

Glaring at him Cage asked, "What the fuck are you doing?"

"Nothing. I...I—."

"Did you really just sniff her seat?"

"Nah." He ran to open the door and Cage snatched him.

"You little s—."

Suddenly, his statement was stopped when Magnus walked into the room. Both boys froze, as he always brought with him an alpha presence.

Looking at Cage he said, "We have to talk."

"S...sure. About what?"

"About the other night and how you disrespected me." He looked at his youngest. "Go to your room."

Flow ran out before he was caught in the mix.

Cage focused. "First I wanna say I'm sorry about lying to you. To be honest, I didn't think you would care if I went. Nobody seems to want me around here anyway. It's my--"

"You've been out of pocket lately, Cage. With the disrespect. And I need you to know I'm not having it anymore."

For some reason, at that moment Cage was having trouble agreeing.

And so, he walked away and turned back around to face him.

"I disrespected you?" He pointed at himself. "You came to my school without letting me know and embarrassed me in front of my friends. Then you threw away the clothes they bought me. Why?"

"I told you I don't want you wearing that kind of shit."

"What kind of shit? Designer clothing? Why does it bother you so much that I be seen?"

"Because you must know who you are first, Cage. And superficial shit will make it harder."

Cage hated him.

Magnus stepped closer. "Contrary to what you believe, you are still a child and I make the rules. And if you continue to break them, things will get worse for you, not me. Now get dressed for school." He walked to the door and turned back around.

Cage looked at him, and in that moment, he was certain he was about to say something to let him know that he cared.

To at least acknowledge the day.

"And Cage, stop letting people come into this house from the window. If they aren't worthy enough to enter through the front door you don't need them."

Cage felt like the air was pushed out of his chest.

After all, it was his birthday, and he hadn't said a word.

It wasn't until that moment that he felt that he didn't give a fuck about him. If Magnus just pretended to care, just a little, maybe Cage would not have considered his next move.

But he didn't.

And Cage resented him for that.

The moment he left; Cage slammed the door.

In rage mode, he stormed around his room wondering what to break first.

And then something happened.

He reasoned there were other ways to get at him. If he thought he was the villain, it was time to act like one. And so, he decided to go out the window instead of using the front door.

To his surprise, when he got outside, his friends were there.

Waiting.

"Why y'all ain't go to school?" Cage asked.

"After hearing your father going off, we ain't feel like going." Onion said. "Not without you."

"You heard my father from the window?"

"How could we not?" Angelina said.

"You ditching or what?" Onion continued.

Cage looked at Angelina, grabbed her closely and gave her a Hollywood kiss on the lips. "Fuck it! I'm ready to live recklessly."

Angelina excitedly said, "Let's go!"

Twenty-five minutes later, they were at Angelina's spot.

And if anyone compared her place to Cage's, it would be like night and day. Although adults were present in her home, they didn't care if she went to school. They didn't care if she got an education, or if she lived up to her responsibilities in life.

As long as she didn't expect them to take care of her, and that meant feeding her too, they were good.

After walking in her room, with Cage and Onion following, she locked the door.

"Who you live with?" Cage asked, remembering the six dark strangers that sat in the living room on their way into her apartment. "They not gonna start tripping, are they?"

"I live with my cousins and uncles. Don't worry though. They never come in my room without paying first." There was a sadness with her response that made Cage want to pry.

Paying first?

"They don't care if you have boys in your room?" Cage persisted.

"Nah, they don't care about shit she do," Onion said playfully.

Angelina pulled her feet closer to her body. And when they saw the pain in her eyes, Onion sat down and rubbed her back.

"You know I was just fucking around, right?"

"Yeah...I know," Angelina sniffled, trying to play tough. "I ain't that soft." She wiped her eyes and then placed her feet flat on the floor. "But let me go to the bathroom right quick. To get myself together." She stood up and rushed toward the door.

"Angelina..." Onion said.

She stopped and turned around. "Here." He walked toward her and handed her a baggie of heroin.

Eyes wide with excitement, she grabbed it, stood on her tiptoes, and kissed him on the cheek. "Thank you, daddy."

When she walked out, Cage said, "What was that?"

"You know what it was."

"What's wrong with you? Why would you give her drugs?"

"You see how vulnerable she is right now? You see all them niggas in the front room who share her blood? Just like the old man, they pay her but only after she helps them release a load. And I'd rather have her get it from me, than somebody who will use her more than they already have."

Cage dragged his hand down his face. "I don't know. I think it's still fucked up."

"Until she's yours, and you make it official, let me worry about her."

Cage frowned. "I care about her too, man. And I just...I don't know...I just want her off that shit."

"She'll be fine," Onion continued. "Trust me. I have a plan."

Hours passed, and before they knew it Cage and Onion were drunk, and Angelina was out cold on her bed. Since the sun had gone down, which always placed Cage in a better mood, he was ready to get into trouble.

"So, what we gonna do next?" Onion whispered sitting across from the bed, where Angelina was sleeping. "Because I hate to keep bringing it up, but

I have a feeling that if we go to their house, things will change for the better, man."

Cage thought about his comments.

As excited as he was to break his father's rules, he had a bad feeling.

But at the same time, he wanted change.

"If my father pops up over there, he will go off. And—."

"You in trouble anyway, remember? You ditched school. Might as well make a night of it."

"I don't know..."

"Come on, Cage. It's your birthday. The man didn't care. Your mother either. Let's have a good time. You only live once."

Maybe there was some truth to it all.

But this was a decision not to take lightly.

Cage looked at him and said, "We going!"

Onion gave him dap mixed with a one-sided hug. "Let's do this shit! 'Bout time you seeing things my way."

"Hold up," Cage looked down at his basic clothes. "What am I gonna wear?"

Onion focused at Angelina's bedroom door. "She got three cousins who live here. Two of them about your size. And them niggas don't even wash clothes. They just buy new shit and throw the rest away, so they won't remember what's missing."

"Man, I'm not trying to wear her people's shit."

"You already at war." Onion shrugged. "What's one more battle?"

CHAPTER SEVEN
"I Smell Fruit."

Cage and Onion walked up to the Ledger's front door. The half-moon in the sky was bright enough to hold its own despite not being full. As they contemplated what would happen when someone opened the door, they looked at one another.

"This feels weird." Onion said. "But I like it."

Cage nodded in agreement. "Maybe we should turn around. They could be busy and—."

"You said you called JoJo and she said to get over here."

"She did."

"Then knock," Onion said firmly. "Please."

Before Cage could respond, it opened, and Flan appeared on the other side.

"I'm happy you came," he said to Cage. "Happy Birthday." He was dry but still pulled the door wider.

Cage smiled. "Thank...thank you." Cage looked back at Onion and then him. "So, are they really doing something for me?"

"Yes." He nodded.

"Why though?"

"Would you like to come inside to get all your answers?"

Cage thought the question was odd, considering they both showed up dressed and wearing Angelina's cousin's cologne and clothing.

But he decided to humor the man anyway.

"Yeah. I wanna come inside."

Flan smiled and waved them in.

The moment they stepped inside, Cage felt at ease. They were playing soft rap, his favorite at a comfortable level. And the smells of the food were stimulating to his nose and had him wanting a taste.

When he glanced over to the catered buffet table there were a bunch of beautiful women in revealing clothing and not one was eating. If he wasn't seduced by the sounds and sights, he would've partaken of the cuisine.

As he followed Flan and moved deeper into the house the women waved at him and he waved back.

Were they paid escorts? He thought.

He didn't care.

Walking through the house, past the food and beautiful women, Cage got overly excited as he turned around to look at Onion. And that moment it was like they hit the lottery.

Everything felt as if it was moving in slow motion. Like a music video and they were the stars.

Cage had expected a dinner party and was rewarded with an experience instead.

"This way, gentlemen." Flan said. "Your hosts are waiting."

He walked them deeper into the house, past more women who gave them big attention. Cage was used to being ignored so getting this type of focus felt different.

When they went to the deepest part of the house, Flan opened a lounge-like room.

Inside were Tino and JoJo Ledger.

Bosses.

Sitting behind a desk built for two, they looked like money and power.

Because they *were* money and power.

It felt different seeing them clothed, since the last time he saw them both together, he was massaging her shoulders and she was licking her own titty.

When Tino saw them, he rose and walked over to the teenagers. He was wearing a black suit and smiled at Cage in a way that made him feel like he could trust him.

After shaking his hand, within seconds his beautiful wife walked up to the young men and gave them each a kiss on the side of the cheek.

She then whispered in Onion's ear and Cage wondered what was said.

"Welcome to my home," Mr. Ledger grinned. "My name is Tino, and I have been waiting to meet you."

Cage nodded.

"And you've already met me," JoJo winked at Cage.

Indeed he had.

While Onion nodded so much; Cage had to nudge him still. Onion had him looking like a clown due to association.

"Tonight, both of your lives will change forever." Tino continued. "Are you ready?"

"I know I am," Onion responded, rubbing his hands together briskly. Dude had to slow down or he would start a fire. "I been waiting a long time for this moment."

What did Onion know that Cage didn't?

"What about you, Cage." JoJo touched his shoulder.

He nodded and pressed his lips together. "Me too."

Tino looked at Cage with piercing eyes. His skin looked unreal under the Lights. And if Cage didn't know better, he would say he was wearing makeup.

But what kind of makeup could make a man look that flawless?

Mr. Ledger put his arm around Cage and walked him to another part of the house.

The further they went, the more silent things appeared.

What happened to the music?

And the people talking?

It was as if that part of the house was soundproof.

When Cage looked back, he noticed Onion was being escorted in another direction by JoJo.

"Where is my friend going?" Cage asked.

"Don't worry." Tino said calmly. "Everything will be okay." He shoved them deeper.

Before long they happened upon a gold door. A door with intricate patterns that was alluring. Just like the living room, it was as if every piece of furniture, artwork, and even the carpet was created and placed inside for his liking.

But how could that be possible?

They didn't know his taste.

Mr. Ledger opened the door where a massive mattress was inside the huge room. Although it kept the same design of a bed, it was nothing like it. The structure stretched from one side of the wall to the next and was flooded with gold sheets and matching pillowcases.

Cage squinted. "What's all this about?" He asked Tino.

Before Tino responded, twenty-four of the women he saw in the living room earlier, shoved him lightly

86   By T. STYLES

but further into the room. The moment they touched him, he felt turned on.

Before Cage could say, hold up, he was pushed down, expecting to have his first sexual encounter. And based on the way they looked him in the eyes, he felt he was about to have the time of his life.

As he plopped on the edge of the bed, the first woman got on her knees and kissed him on the mouth.

It was a wet kiss.

A kiss, that would usually be considered too wet if he were outside those doors.

But once again, everything in that house appeared to be created for him because she tasted like honey. Not the man made jarred sugary substance but honey straight from the comb.

Before he knew it, he was kissing another woman and her kiss was just as juicy and wet as the first.

Feeling as if he were floating, the woman between his legs rose and pushed him back gently on the bed. Lying face up, one after the other, kissed him as if they needed to do so to survive.

Within ten minutes, he kissed twenty-four, and all kisses were luscious.

So juicy that if he put their liquid into a container, it would fill jugs.

Suddenly Cage's body became extra sensitized. Every inch of him was stimulated and although his mouth touched the mouths of many strangers, he didn't care.

He wanted this feeling to go on forever.

Just when he thought things couldn't get more sexual, Tino's wife entered and strolled in his direction.

Where was Onion?

Standing in front of him, the others scattered out of her way as if she was royalty.

Maybe she was.

When she raised her dress, he got warm when he noticed she wasn't wearing any panties, evident by the soft curly mound of hair between her legs.

Is this really about to happen?

Pulling his dick out of his pants, she stroked it to a thickness. Within seconds, under her touch, he could tell this woman was a professional, and yet that word didn't seem good enough.

Releasing him before he reached an orgasm in her palm, she eased him into her heated wet body instead. Just like the kisses from the women before him, he noticed immediately that her pussy was soaking wet.

Not the kind of wet that allowed for a regular glide. But the kind of wetness, so juicy, it dampened his body and the bed beneath him.

Her fuck game should be outlawed as she rose and fell on his dick like an expert.

Every time he was about to cum, she paused.

How did she know?

The sensation of her pussy strokes made him dizzy and he contemplated telling her to stop just to regain control of his body.

But why do that when this was without a doubt, the best time he ever had?

And although he never had sex before that moment, in his mind he didn't imagine it would be so good.

As her pussy continued to suck and pull, slowly she fell into him.

88   **By T. STYLES**

In her hand was a red pill.

She placed it on his tongue.

He swallowed.

Suddenly their lips met. And just like the others, her kiss was extra wet except this time the elixir coming from her mouth made him feel drunk.

As if he downed a bottle of the best cognac by himself.

He was feeling different and was certain that under her tutelage, he was becoming a man.

Just when he thought things couldn't get weirder, Tino walked into the room, followed by twenty-four men.

Cage didn't know what he wanted but he wasn't into the gay shit. That was certain. Luckily for him, Mr. Ledger grabbed a woman and fucked her rhythmically at his side.

Leaning over, he kissed JoJo, who was still riding Cage's dick.

What was happening?

The other men, who entered the room, fucked the free women in every position known to man.

Doggy style.

69.

Scissors.

And the like.

The moans sounded like a symphony, and Cage's body vibrated like a tapped cymbal. Women's voices grew higher in octaves as they were overcome with ecstasy. He knew they were about to cum, and judging by their facial expressions, it was obvious the men were preparing to explode too.

Was this really happening?

Suddenly, JoJo eased on her back and guided Cage back into her body.

Deeper.

Wetter.

Slower.

One by one, the women who were filled up with nut crawled toward Cage and opened their legs next to his face.

"Drink," JoJo told him.

At first he wanted to resist, but the pill had him heeding her demand. So he lowered his head and flipped his tongue and drank from all twenty four women's bodies, including the one Tino filled.

When he was done, JoJo kissed him passionately and maneuvered her pussy in a way that set Cage on fire.

But the night was far from over.

Beauty after beauty kissed him again and suddenly everything was in a blur and before long he couldn't keep time.

He thought he would be exhausted, but instead the feeling was the most powerful sensation he ever experienced.

And when he was done, he drifted into a deep, dark sleep.

When Cage opened his eyes, the next night he knew he fucked up.

But where had the entire day gone?

He didn't remember anything after JoJo gave him the pill.

It was a good thing too because things took a turn on the orgie side.

Luckily for him, he was at Onion's house and not under the watchful gaze of his parents. But that didn't mean things would be better because he was certain that once his father learned that not only had he skipped school and stayed out all night, but that he skipped school the next day too, there would be hell to pay.

He was about to roll out of Onion's bed but noticed his body felt heavier for some reason. He was always a fit teenager, but tonight he felt thicker and more solid.

Even his dick felt meatier.

He figured a body change is what happened when you had sex with as many women as he did for the first time.

"Cage, what did you do?" He said to himself with a smile on his face.

Thinking about the night before, when he turned his head, he was surprised to see Angelina in the bed next to him.

Confused, he popped up. "Hold up, I know I didn't have sex with—."

"Calm down. We didn't do anything."

He dropped back into bed relieved. Not because he didn't want her. But whenever they did have sex, it was important that he remembered every detail.

"Where's Onion?" He asked the beauty.

TREASON 91

She shrugged and wiped her hair out of her face. "I don't know. He was sleeping all morning and then when he woke up in a hurry after getting a call, he claimed he had to get out of the house."

He saw an inquisitive look on her face.

"What?" He asked.

"Well?"

He shook his head. "Don't ask me a bunch of questions about what happened last night, Angelina."

She rolled her eyes. "The only thing I want to know is why y'all left me?"

He heard her talking but couldn't get over how sweet she smelled. In the past she wore cocoa butter on her skin, but this fragrance didn't appear manmade.

Her scent mirrored that of a juicy piece of exotic fruit.

Was it a peach?

"You smell like fruit."

"That's different but thank you."

"And we left because you were knocked out. Next time don't get drunk and high and maybe you can roll."

She looked down. "How much longer are you gonna throw what I do in my face? I'm trying to get clean, Cage. Onion's helping me. But being judgmental ain't helping shit."

"You're right. I'll never do that again." He laid on his side. "You getting clean? For real?"

"Yeah. I don't want this for the rest of my life."

He felt like he just received the best news. "That's good to hear, Angelina. I'm proud of you."

"For real?"

"Yeah, man."

She wiped at the air. "Oh, I almost forgot." She hopped out of bed and grabbed a black jewelry box from Onion's drawer. "Here."

"What's this?"

"Open it."

When he popped the lid, he was shocked to see a silver chain inside.

"Whoa."

"Do you like it?"

"I love it."

She grinned. "Let me put it on."

Moving closer, she clasped the chain around his neck and they both laid face to face. He could smell the pheromones of her pussy and that scent again, which was more powerful than the most exotic perfume.

Fruit.

He ran his fingers over the jewelry. "I never had anybody do what you did for me in a little bit of time. But why all the gifts?"

She looked down. "So you can stay."

He frowned. "Listen, you don't have to buy what you already own. Because I'm never leaving you."

"Do you promise? Because people always leave me."

"I'm not going anywhere, Angelina. I swear."

"You feel like a savage yet?" She giggled looking at the chain.

"Something like it." He looked down at it. "What you do for this?"

She sighed. "Don't mess it up, Cage."

He nodded. "You right. And I'll say this...I don't know how, and I don't know when, but one day you will be my wife."

"Cage, don't play games."

"I'm dead serious. It will be me and you against everything. You'll see."

"Do you want to make me smile now?"

He thought about the question and spoke from the heart. "I do, Angelina. I swear to God."

"Start by telling me what happened at the party? Because the people who dropped y'all off said it was the best time of your lives." She asked excitedly.

He glared. "People that dropped us off?"

"Yeah, you don't remember that shit?"

He didn't.

"So, tell me what happened."

"Did you ask Onion?"

She giggled. "You know he don't tell me shit."

Why does she smell so fucking good? He thought as she continued to talk.

"My lips are sealed, bae."

She giggled and her odor grew more intoxicating each time she moved closer.

Suddenly, while staring into his eyes she got quiet. "If I were to kiss you, Cage, would you kiss me back?"

"Why would you do that?"

"That's not what I asked."

"Don't ask me questions that—."

Suddenly she kissed him without permission, and he shoved her lightly but not hard enough to reject her seriously.

By T. STYLES

Instead, he found himself wanting her but in a way that felt violent and dark. The more she kissed him, the more he became aroused.

He was about to give into his urges, until there was a knock on the front door that was loud and authoritative.

Cage knew it was his father immediately.

Angelina did too.

She jumped off the bed and stared at him. The fear took over her body. "That's Magnus ain't it?"

"I think so," Cage sighed.

"You want me to tell him you're not here?"

He eased out of bed. "Nah, I'll deal with it."

After getting completely dressed, slowly, he walked out of the bedroom and toward the living room.

His steps felt heavy and unsure.

In his mind, his clothes didn't fit the same anymore.

That didn't stop him from feeling like he was going to his hanging.

Cage was about to open the door when she grabbed the sides of his face and kissed him passionately.

He wanted to bite her, it felt so good.

"Why you do that, girl?" He asked.

"In case it's awhile before I see you again."

"I'm gonna buy you two poodles one day."

She giggled softly. "What is it with you and poodles? You're--."

He kissed her silently, and with the knob in his hand, took a deep breath and pulled.

The moment Cage opened the door and Magnus saw his face, he stumbled backwards. Within seconds he doubled over in pain and clutched his stomach.

What was going on?

Concerned for his father, Cage ran up to him. "Dad, are you okay?"

Magnus pushed him back so hard, he hit the ground.

Seeing her friend fall, Angelina was furious. "Why you push him like that?" Angelina yelled. "He's your son!"

Magnus focused on her and suddenly remembered her from church. "They always use women." He turned to walk away. "Get in the car, Cage!"

He got up slowly.

"Now!"

Cage was in his bed asleep, when suddenly he rolled over.

Popping up, his breathing felt heavy and rushed.

He didn't know if it was the same night Magnus got him from Onion's crib, or if it was a different moment.

The only thing was certain was that it was nighttime.

When he heard knocking at the door, he eased out of bed.

By T. STYLES

Again, his body felt different.

Dragging a hand down his face, he took a deep breath and opened the door. And when he did, he was looking at Flow, Bloom, Tatum, and Archer.

Each of them looked as if they were bringing the worst news ever to his doorstep. They breathed deeply as they stood in front of him.

"Is it true now?" Flow asked in a low voice.

"What you talking about?"

"Is it true you moving out?"

"What...what you mean? I ain't going nowhere." Cage chuckled once.

"Well, we heard you were leaving," Bloom said, wiping a tear away. "From dad. Please say it's not true."

His heart thumped. Did he really go too far by breaking the rules? "Like I said, I'm not going anywhere."

Rushing up to him, Bloom wrapped her arms around his body and inhaled. "Please don't go, Cage. Don't leave us. If you do, I had a nightmare that everything would change."

After releasing him they walked away.

CHAPTER EIGHT

"There Are Things That Go On In This World That We Protected You From."

Cage looked for his parents everywhere in the house.

It seemed as if ever since he went to that party with the Ledgers, they avoided him like the plague, and he wondered why. They didn't wake him for school. They didn't bring him any meals.

It was like they abandoned him.

After doing a search throughout the house, he decided to go to his mother's favorite place.

The basement.

Just as he thought, she was there.

Walking inside he said, "Mom, why haven't you come to see me? Are you mad at me too?"

She was sitting on the sofa drinking a glass of red wine. With her legs crossed, her foot shook rapidly, and she looked rattled. "What do you mean, Cage?"

He stepped closer. "Are you avoiding me or something?"

"Should I avoid you?" She took a sip, placed the glass down and grabbed her cigarettes.

"No. I'm your son."

She tapped the carton, and one came shooting out. Lighting it, she pulled deeply. "Is that right? You call yourself my son? After all, you disrespected your father and me by leaving this house multiple times." She pulled again and smoke flirted with the air.

"Cage, you have no idea how much you destroyed things in this family."

"Just by hanging out and breaking curfew? I'm a teenager. And it's the first time I've done something like this."

She looked at him and shook her head. "She told you to say that didn't she? The woman in the car."

He didn't remember.

Maybe she had.

"Ma, why don't you tell me what's really going on."

She glared. "You promised not to go to that house, and you lied."

Cage looked away knowing that what she said was correct. In that very basement he promised her to never go to the Ledgers' and that's exactly what he did.

"What is it that makes you hate them so much, ma?"

"It's not about them. It's about you breaking your promise. And lying to me. You may not understand now, but you'll understand soon." She looked in the corner and yelled. "You be quiet. I've listened to you enough."

Cage frowned.

Who was she talking to?

"I'm glad I didn't drown him like you said. He just needs a little love."

He recalled her talking to herself before. But this was the first time her words were loud and clear.

He stepped closer. "Ma, are you okay?"

"There are things that go on in the world that we protected you from. And now it's out of our hands."

"Good. Because you can't protect me forever."

"You know, I always knew some things would change. But we wanted you to know who you were first. So that you would be strong enough." She smashed out her cigarette and grabbed her wine glass. "We'll never get that chance now."

Later that night, Cage was in his room thinking about what his mother said. And although he knew she gave birth to him, being in her presence caused him to have the similar sensation he had when he was around Angelina.

He smelled that same fragrance that was erotic to him.

It was the kind of odor that lit up his mind, body, and soul.

Fruit.

Still thinking about Lala, when he heard soft knocks on his window, he rushed toward it, looked behind himself and opened it wide.

On the other side were his friends, Onion and Angelina.

Just like the last time he saw her, Angelina brought with her the erotic fragrance that was hard to resist.

"The window was already open," Cage said, needing company.

"So, I guess you and Onion not going to school no more?" She crossed her arms over her chest. "Y'all just gonna leave me by myself?"

"You ain't go either?" Cage asked him.

"Overslept," Onion shrugged.

Once they were fully inside, Cage closed the window and Onion handed him a tall drink in a white Styrofoam cup.

"What's this?"

"Something to make you feel good." He sat on the windowsill.

Without asking about the ingredients, he drank every drop.

"Damn, son," Onion said. "How you know I ain't want none? I was just giving you a sip."

"What was that?" Cage asked, holding the cup. "That shit was torch!"

The drink tasted like juice from an exotic piece of fruit. A piece of fruit so mouthwatering, it quenched his thirst and caused his body to vibrate.

Like the smell that seemed to be everywhere.

"Damn, nigga." Onion joked. "It's just a little drink I made with liquor and some chaser."

Cage wasn't sure if it was true or not, but what he did know was that he wanted to taste the drink again, as much as possible.

"So, what's happening next?" Onion asked. "With your people?" He pointed to the door.

"I don't know, man," Cage put the cup on his dresser and Onion picked it up. "I got a feeling that maybe my siblings are right."

"Right about what?" Angelina asked.

He sighed and dragged a hand down his face. "They told me it's a possibility that he's gonna throw me out." He flopped on the edge of the bed.

Angelina's eyes widened. "You can't leave. If you leave, what will happen to us?"

"The man just said his parents may throw him out, and that's all you can say?"

She felt dumb. "I'm sorry I didn't mean it that way. It's just that we've been together for so long, I don't want us to separate now."

"It hasn't even been two weeks," Cage said.

"Still." She looked down. "Feels like forever to me."

She was in love and he knew it.

He was feeling her too.

Young love was intense.

"I don't know what'll happen." Cage said. "Or if I'll move or not. But at this point it's out of my hands."

She got on her knees, and positioned herself between his legs.

Fruit.

"Come with us, Cage." She begged. "If they're going to throw you out, why even be here? It's not like they give a fuck about you anyway. I can hide you in my house. I'll make enough money to take care of us."

"But I don't want you to do that. I mean, if I have to leave, maybe I can get a job. JoJo said I could work for her."

"Whatever you gotta do, don't let him take you away. We need you. I need you."

Crickets chirped under the night sky as Cage lay in bed. His mind raced and he felt isolated in his own home. Over the past few days, he longed for companionship and the connection with his father, but it seemed impossible.

When there was another knock at his window, he sighed.

"I told you it was open," he whispered as he slid out the bed.

He was shocked to see who was on the other side.

With extreme ease, JoJo pushed inside and sat on the windowsill. The half-moon shined on her back, causing her silhouette to be outlined.

No fruit this time.

Just the smell of rain.

"How are you?" She asked, crossing her legs.

Cage nodded, unsure of what she wanted. But if sex was on her mind, he was down for whatever, especially after remembering how amazing she made him feel nights earlier.

"Cage, are you going to answer me or just stare at me like I'm a piece of meat?" She grinned.

"I'm cool, I guess." He crossed his arms. "But why you here?"

"I need to tell you something you may not believe. But I want you to know it's true."

He nodded.

"I saw your father."

TREASON   103

"What you talking about?"

"The night you left the party, your parents were in your backyard and things took a turn for the worse. That's why we took you to your friend's house."

He shrugged. "Okay, what happened?"

"I hate to be harsh, but I saw him beating her."

The rage Cage felt in that moment was hard to describe.

He knew Magnus had a temper which caused his mother to take cover in the basement every now and again.

And still, he never imagined she was being abused.

He stepped closer. "Are you lying to me?" He glared.

The boy had become a man, and she stared at him with different eyes. It looked good on him.

"I wouldn't lie about something like this."

"I don't believe you."

"After everything we've been through?"

"Just because you fucked me, and I tasted your pussy, doesn't mean I believe everything you say."

She grinned. "You're different, Cage. I like that." She paused and crossed her legs to the other side. "Do you feel it?"

Silence.

"Did he tell you he's going to send you away, Cage?"

Silence.

"Well it's true."

"How you know?"

"Why ask questions that don't change your situation? At the end of the day, he's having you

104   By T. STYLES

moved, and it has nothing to do with breaking the rules. And everything to do with the man you're becoming. I mean look at yourself."

She walked him to the mirror.

Standing in front of it, she ran a hand down his chest. Across his arms and through his hair which had gotten looser although it still kept a soft curl.

"Don't you feel different?" She whispered in his ear. "Don't you think differently?"

He did.

"Not that I believe you, but why would he want me gone? I'm his son."

She walked back to the window and sat down. "He wants you gone because you're growing up. And with growing up, you're able to see through the bullshit better. And let's be clear....no household can suffer two men under the same roof."

"This is crazy," he said, rubbing his head.

"And I'm going to tell you this too. If you leave, he will destroy your mother and your siblings. He's not stable, and I know you know that already."

For some reason Cage was hooked onto her every word. And it made him want to hunt his father down and break his neck in the heat of the night.

"So, what can I do? To protect them?"

As if on cue, she reached behind herself and removed an object covered in a red velvet cloth. When she unfolded it, he saw it was a weapon.

A .45 to be exact.

"On August 13th shoot him dead."

Cage's eyes widened. "Are you asking me to kill my father?"

"I'm asking you to save your mother and your siblings."

"I can't do that."

She frowned. "So, you're putting your father over your family?"

"I'm not saying that either."

"Then what are you saying? Because at the end of the day, either you will be a man, or you will be nothing. Your choice."

Cage backed up slowly.

Even though she wasn't talking, her words played on repeat, in his mind.

Loud and clear.

"Who are you?"

"That doesn't matter anymore, Cage. The only thing that matters is that you take his life. If not, one day you will be gone, and your mother and siblings will be dead too. Is that what you want?"

Onion and Angelina sat on the edge of Cage's bed looking at him as if he lost his mind.

"Are you going to do it?" Angelina whispered. "Because you can't."

"I don't know what's going on right now, to be honest." He said leaning up against his wall.

"Hold up, did your father tell you that you had to move?" Onion asked. "Because she could be lying."

"He hasn't said anything to me yet."

"Well, if he hasn't said anything, you can't kill him, Cage." Angelina persisted. "You do know that right? If you do, you could be killing an innocent man."

"All I know is JoJo said he been beating my mother. And I told y'all he gets violent sometimes. I saw him through the slats in the backyard."

"You can't do what she's saying," Angelina whispered. "I'm sorry."

"But it's not your decision," Cage said.

She looked at Onion who in her opinion wasn't fighting for her point hard enough. "Tell him."

Onion stepped up. "Maybe you should talk to your father. See where he's coming from first."

"Don't let this woman gas you up, Cage." Angelina said firmer. "Already I don't like her. I mean who tells a kid to kill his father. She's—."

"He's eighteen," Onion interrupted. "That makes him a man. And you don't know her. She's not just some young dumb bitch. If she told him to be concerned, maybe he should."

"What happened in that fucking house?" She squinted, looking at them both.

"Why do you keep asking me that?" Onion yelled.

"Keep your voice down," Cage warned.

"My bad."

Angelina rolled her eyes at Onion and looked at Cage. "Listen to me, if you do what she wants, you will destroy your mother and siblings' lives anyway. You will destroy yourself too. There's no coming back from killing your parents."

Silence.

"You think your mother will still let you stay if you murder your father?" She continued after being met with silence. "And her husband? Don't make that move, Cage. Please."

Cage looked at Onion. "What do you think?"

"I say do whatever you need to do to protect your family," he said plainly. "And if you want, I'll help you get rid of the body."

August 13th

The next evening, again, Cage woke up in the middle of the night.

It seemed like no matter how hard he tried; he couldn't catch the light of day. But the bigger problem was that once again his mother and father failed to wake him up for school. It was like they abandoned him and his education. And for a young man who hated class, he would give anything to go back now.

When he walked to his bedroom door, to find something to satiate his hunger, he was shocked to see it was locked from the outside. Frowning he tugged, pulled, and jerked the door, many times.

In the end, it was no use.

It wouldn't budge.

Confused, he took to banging on the door with full force. After three minutes of rocking the entire house, he heard a noise on the other side.

It was a set of jingling keys.

They locked him in his room like he was in prison.

When the door opened, his father towered over him while glaring down. "Are you gonna break the door?"

"What's going on, dad? Why y'all not getting me up for school?"

"I have something to talk to you about."

"Before you say anything, can I say something to you?" He took a deep breath. The nervousness of what his father was about to say fucked with him hard. So he wanted to jump in front of it first.

"Now is not a—."

"Please, dad."

Magnus folded his arms over his chest. "Go 'head."

"Can you at least sit down?"

Magnus plopped on the edge of his bed.

"I'm sorry about everything I did. I don't know what came over me."

"It doesn't matter, Cage."

"Listen, dad, please."

He sighed. "I'm sorry for everything I did. And...and, if you let me stay, if you give me another chance, I promise I won't fuck up again."

"We are beyond that now."

"What does that mean?"

"I can't have you in this house, Cage. And I can't be subject to your disrespect every time you feel like you don't want to listen."

"That's what I'm telling you, I'm willing to change."

"And I said it's too late."

TREASON   109

He glared. "How can you say that to your own son?"

Silence.

"Dad, please." He put his hand over his chest. "Talk to me."

"Cage, it's no way possible for you and me to live in this home together."

JoJo was right.

"Ever again, son. I tried to fight against this, but you went behind my back and so this is the result."

Cage walked up to him.

When he did, he couldn't help but notice that Magnus turned up his nose.

"I can't believe it," Cage said, trying to hold back his emotions.

"You can't believe what?"

"I can see the hate you have for me in your eyes."

Magnus looked down, not bothering to deny his statement. Cage was embarrassed about what he was going to do next, but he needed to do all he could to stay with his family.

Getting on his knees he said, "I don't want to go. I don't want to leave. I don't want to be someplace where I have to start all over." He swallowed the lump in his throat. "I have friends now, dad. I'm willing to do better in school. There has to be something I can do to get you to change your mind. You're my father."

"Cage, I —."

"Daddy, let me—."

"Listen, son, you don't know the plans I have for you. And you won't understand now, but you will later in life."

"I know those plans include me leaving this house."

By T. STYLES

"Cage..."

"Am I wrong?"

"Where I'm sending you will be a great place to live. You're going to be around people who can help you. People like yourself."

"People like myself?"

He sighed. "Yes."

Cage looked at him with hate, as what JoJo said played on repeat in his mind. *He's going to ship you away because he's going to hurt your mother.* Again, it was like it had been before. Where, even though she wasn't in the room or speaking he could still hear her voice clearly.

"Do you want me to leave because you want to hurt my mother? Is that what this is about?"

"What?"

"I know you beat up on ma."

Magnus leaned back as if remembering.

"Is it true?"

"Son, we were in the backyard. The night you were gone to the party. And it may have looked as if we were fighting, but we weren't."

"Then what was happening?"

"Sometimes your mother isn't well. And she does things that--."

"So it's her fault now?"

Magnus breathed deeply, realizing there was no getting through to him. "It doesn't matter. Just know that I made the right decision. A decision that will allow me to still take care of your mother and siblings. At the same time, keep you safe. Because I—."

Before Magnus could finish talking, Cage reached under the bed and removed a weapon.

The same one JoJo gave him.

He aimed and cocked.

Slowly Magnus turned his head and looked out of the window.

The moon was full, and the stars were bright.

"Son, don't do this! I'm begging you!"

Cage wiped a tear that crept down his cheek as the other hand shakily maintained control of the weapon. "I can't. Because where *you're* going will allow *me* to take care of my mother and siblings." He said, using his own words against him.

"Son, this is not the way."

"Why? Because you're scared?"

"No, because if you do, you will never be able to forgive yourself. And you will live in a constant state of shame. And I don't want that for you."

Cage raised the gun. "I'll take my chances."

"When you were a baby, there came a time where I saved your life. Let me save you again. Please."

"It's too late."

Magnus was preparing to rush him. "Cage, before you do that, I have to tell you about who you really—.""

Gunfire lit up his room.

Dropping the weapon, Cage fell and scooted away from his father. Seeing the betrayal and pain on Magnus' face hit him in the pit of the gut.

He hadn't expected it to go off so easily.

He made the worst mistake of his life.

He was certain.

Within minutes, footsteps could be heard in the house, and he knew his mother and siblings were probably on the way.

Standing up, he locked the door and looked down at his father again.

Why did it hurt so badly?

Cage was overwhelmed with regret.

And while some mistakes could be fixed, there were very few that could be forgotten.

Backing up against the wall, while watching his father's blood pour from his body, he shed tears.

This was not what he wanted. And yet there was no turning back.

Concerned for her son and husband, Lala pounded on the door with such force, Cage feared she would break it down, only to see his shame.

"What's going on in there?" She cried jiggling the knob. "Open the door!"

Moving to the window, he jumped out and ran into the night.

Wendy loved smoking cigarettes with every door and window closed in her living room. When asked why, she firmly believed that the smoke that remained in the air would have to travel through her lungs twice which provided her with a bigger high.

The problem was that the grungy small house smelled dank due to this habit. And because the air condition was always on, even in the winter, black mold and mildew accumulated in corners of the walls, as well as the carpets.

When there was a knock at the door, irritated, she rose from her sunken brown sofa and opened it wide.

Wearing no bra, her bark titties swung like pendulums.

To her surprise, she was shocked to see her nephew Cage, on the other side.

It had been many years since she'd seen him.

As a matter of fact, the last time she laid eyes on the boy she was kicked out of his house, after Magnus came home only to find her inside talking to Lala in the kitchen.

But a little before then, when he was an infant, she was going to take his life.

Was he coming to kill her?

"My God you're handsome." She closed her robe slowly, in case he liked what he saw. "The most beautiful man I have ever seen this close in my life."

Facts.

"Can I come inside?" He asked with his hands, tucked in his pockets.

She stepped back, and he entered.

Taking the seat in the closest space to the door, he found himself in a recliner that was so tattered, the yellow foam beneath shone through.

"It smells good in here," he said. "Like fruit."

She laughed. "That's different. My place has been called many things. Fragrant is not one of them."

Grabbing her cigarettes, despite having smoked not even five minutes ago, she tapped the bottom and one popped out.

Just like his mother.

By T. STYLES

"What are you doing here?" She asked. "Cause it's not like your rich ass family fucks with me."

He sunk into the recliner. "I made a mistake."

She smiled. "Okay. Now I'm very interested."

"Before I say anything, can you tell me about my mother and father?"

She eyed him suspiciously. "What about them?"

He cleared his throat. "Over the past year they've been treating me differently. I always had a weird relationship with my mother. But—."

"What do you mean weird?"

He glared. "It's just that when I looked into her eyes it was like she was hiding something from me." He sighed. "But my relationship with my father was solid." He was filled up with emotion again after witnessing him die. "Even that changed recently. And when I asked them what's wrong, nobody seemed to want to tell me the truth."

"Your father is a pretentious asshole, and your mother is an uppity bitch. Besides that, I don't know what else you want me to say." She shrugged.

He could've dropped kicked her, he was so mad.

"Are you willing to help me or not?" He stood up.

"Okay, I'll play along. Sit down."

He did.

"There was an incident when you were a baby. I'm not sure what got into your mother. As a matter of fact, I chose not to ask questions. But one night she handed me $500, and you swaddled in a blanket. And for reasons that are still unknown to me to this day, she told me to kill you. Saying that I couldn't let Magnus know that you were gone by my hands, or it would destroy her precious family."

He glared. "You're lying."

TREASON 115

"I have no reason to lie. I don't even like or know you. And still, I'm the only living relative, outside of your little family, that you got. So, if you ask me that means I deserve a little respect."

He disagreed.

Based on what she just said, he thought she was the lowest of scum and now he realized why she was not allowed in their lives.

"Your mother did pay me to kill you. And quoted Matthew 2:16. And she also told me to keep it a secret. Despite you being a baby, I was going to do it."

"Why?"

"Because she was my sister. And family was first." She sighed. "But instead of letting it go down as planned, she told Magnus within an hour of dropping you off."

He leaned forward.

"In the middle of the night, he rushed over to pick you up."

Cage was shaken upon hearing that his mother wanted him killed only for his father to save his life.

It was hard to believe. And at the same time would explain the guilt she appeared to have in her eyes whenever she looked at him.

But why kill a baby? He thought.

"When your mother....that bitch, told Magnus you were in my house. He destroyed my world within a year. I was unable to get employment. My friends who I'd known for years stopped hanging around me. Even now I'm known as the neighborhood pariah." She took several pulls. "It hurt me at first but after a while you find peace in being left alone. And for some reason, no matter what, the grimiest of niggas still fuck with you. And that's all you really need because they keep their ears to the street."

Cage wanted out her house.

He knew now that he'd come to the wrong place.

"Let me ask you something, boy. Do you have any money on you?"

He didn't.

And even if he did, he wouldn't give it to that bitch.

"Because information ain't free," she continued. "You know that right?"

The distaste that he had for her was great.

"Nah, I'm broke." He tapped his pockets.

"Then you better find your way out the door." She pointed at it with a soiled nail.

Cage nodded, rose, and walked toward the exit. It was dumb even coming to her house, but he needed answers. And felt drawn to the one woman he knew was a family outcast.

But his purpose with her was served. And so, without bothering to bid her a goodbye, he walked out the door.

When she smoked the rest of her cigarette, she got up and slinked to the phone. Calling a number she kept to memory, despite never using it once over the years, the moment she heard hysterical crying, she knew two things.

Number one, that her sister's boy had lived up to Lala's worst fears. And number two, that she would never be the same.

In a callous manner she said, "Cage, just left my house. He knows. Everything."

With that, she hung up and smiled.

By T. STYLES

CHAPTER NINE

"All We Have Is This Moment."

G oing to see his aunt was dumb as fuck.
She was washed up and he was certain he would have nothing to do with her in the future.

And as Cage bopped down the dark street, he realized his father was right. He did regret taking his life. His heart was heavy after having committed the worst crime.

Devastated beyond belief, the moon provided light for his path, but he still felt consumed by darkness.

Even though he remembered what he'd done, it took him several minutes before realizing he didn't know where else to go.

He couldn't return home because he was certain his mother called the police.

He couldn't go to Angelina, or Onion's, because his mother knew their addresses and he reasoned the cops would be involved at any moment.

So, he went to the one person on earth, he felt would understand his plight.

The second he walked up to Tino Ledger's house, the door opened and Tino appeared on the other side. With a sense of knowing, he glided out to greet him and placed a hand on his shoulder.

"What's wrong?"

Why the fuck was he playing games? Cage knew he knew why he was there.

With his head hung low he said, "I killed my father."

The moment Cage uttered the words, an emptiness hit the pit of his stomach. It was one thing to commit murder, but a whole different thing to live with it for the rest of your life.

"Say no more," he said, in a voice booming with authority. "Follow me."

Tino walked into the house, with Cage behind him and made a few phone calls. Cage didn't know what was going on, but he felt things would be better for now.

Whatever that meant.

Standing in the middle of the floor, like a guilted toddler who smeared chocolate on the carpet instead of blood, he waited impatiently for the word.

Still on the phone, Tino looked up at Cage and whispered, "You'll be fine. Trust me."

For some reason that appeased him for the moment.

But why?

When JoJo sauntered into the room, Tino ended the call, walked over to her, and whispered in her ear. As he observed the couple, he could tell that he adored his wife, which is why he didn't understand why he allowed her to make love to him.

At least the pussy was good.

As he continued to watch them closer, it was also obvious that they possessed a connection and understanding far greater than what his mother had for Magnus.

Was he witnessing real love?

Touching the small of her back he continued to whisper in her ear. Slowly a smile crept on her face, and she grinned at Cage before mouthing the words, "I'm proud of you."

At that moment, he felt automatic hate for the woman.

Within five minutes, a black van appeared out front. "They're here, sir," Flan said walking into the house.

Cage tensed up.

What was happening?

"Don't worry about anything," Tino assured him, touching his shoulder. Anxious, seconds earlier, he felt calm again. "I'm here for you."

As if he were a good friend, or distant relative, Tino walked Cage to the vehicle and made sure he was tucked safely inside. With a heavy hand on his shoulder, like Magnus used to do, he said, "These are my friends, and they're going to take you to a place where you'll be safe. All your needs will be met. Welcome home."

Welcome home?

"I killed my father," he said softly and to no one in particular. He wanted the world to know, in the hopes that someone would punish him.

"It doesn't matter."

"That makes me a bad person. So why are you doing this for me?"

"That doesn't matter either. All that matters is that you move onto the next part of your life. Because things are about to be different."

"I'm confused."

"You made a mistake, Cage. People make mistakes all the time. That doesn't mean your life should be over. Now go. I'll be in contact soon."

He tapped the top of the roof and the door closed.

The moment the tires moved down the road, and over the pavement, Cage broke down.

He cried about his actions.

He cried about how his mother would feel having to raise kids as a single parent.

He cried about the pain he was sure his siblings would feel while missing their father.

Of course, they would hate him, he thought to himself.

He hated himself too.

But when he was strong enough, maybe he could ask for forgiveness.

Even if it wouldn't be received.

When the doors to the van opened and Cage was in front of a modest house in Catonsville Maryland, he was surprised to see Onion and Angelina in the doorway.

Not only because up until that moment he felt alone but also seeing them automatically brought him a sense of relief.

When Cage eased out of the vehicle, Onion and Angelina rushed up to him. Onion gave Cage some dap, and pulled him in a one-armed hug, and Angelina gripped him in a way that said she was ready to risk it all to be in his life.

It didn't help that Angelina's aromatic smell was heavier than ever, and when they disconnected, Onion handed Cage a cup with a lid and straw.

Thirsty and hungry, Cage accepted like always. "I did it. And it's fucking me up."

"I know, man," Onion said. "Tino told me. But if you did it, I know you had your reasons. Try not to worry about it right now." He looked at the cup. "Drink up."

Cage took deep sips as the drink gave him immediate comfort. "How can you say don't worry about it? I killed my—."

"First off I'm on your side, not Magnus'. And if JoJo said she saw him beating your mother, then I say you did what you had to—."

"I don't trust that chick," Angelina said with her arms crossed over her chest.

"That's not the point," Onion glared. He focused back on him. "All I know is this, you did what you thought you had to do. And at the end of the day there's nothing else that can be done. You can't go back home. You can't go to the police either because they'll never understand. So, what you gonna do but move on? At least your people are safe now."

He was right and Cage knew it.

"So, what am I gonna do? Stay on the run for the rest of my life?"

"We can't think about the rest of your life right now," Onion said looking dead into his eyes. "All we have is this moment. All we have is the present."

Cage noticed that he didn't seem as dimwitted as he had in the past. It was like he was a new man.

Did fucking JoJo change his life too?

"And all we got is each other," Angelina added.

Onion pointed to the cup. "Now drink and feel better."

Without wasting time, Cage devoured every drop of the fruity, juicy, drink. When he was done, not only did he feel stronger, but in that moment, he felt better about life. He felt better about his circumstances. And he reasoned that possibly the choice he made to take his father's life was the right one.

When Cage walked inside the house, he was shocked to see it was fully furnished. A flat screen TV was placed in every social room and soft rap music played in the background. Dark brown leather sofas were propped inside, and it resembled a bachelor's pad.

He felt at home.

Onion led him down a hallway toward the back. "This your room," he said, opening the door.

"What about those other rooms?"

"Me and Angelina are staying in those."

Cage nodded. He didn't want to let them know but he was grateful they were on his team. "Thank you. For being here."

When Cage walked into his bedroom, he noticed that the curtains were blacked out, and that everything was neat and in place. On the bed were shopping bags filled with designer jeans, shirts, tennis shoes and even a silver chain dipped in diamonds.

"Who this stuff belong to?" He asked his friends, holding the jewelry in his palm.

"Everything in here is yours, man." Onion grinned. "Everything in this fucking house for that matter."

"Who gave this to me?"

"You know who gave it to you. Why you even asking at this point?"

By T. STYLES

Cage scratched his head and sat on the edge of the bed. Tino's generosity was rubbing him the wrong way.

"Is this nigga gay?"

Onion laughed. "I doubt that seriously."

"Well what's up with all of this then? I mean, doesn't this shit seem weird to y'all?" He looked at Onion and Angelina.

She looked away.

"Again, you're thinking about things that you don't have to worry about. Tino agreed to help us. Take what he's giving while it lasts."

"Us?"

"I know you don't think we're going to let you go through this shit alone." Onion said. "In my mind if you committed murder, we committed murder too."

"He's right. I don't agree with what you did, but I'm in now too." Angelina said.

"So don't ask no more questions," Onion continued. "Just go with the flow. This is our new world." He placed a hand on his shoulder. "The night is still young. You trying to hit the streets or what?"

Cage didn't feel like fucking going out.

Even as he spoke to them, his father's face was in his head. What he'd done was haunting. And he wanted to get it off his mind, all while knowing it wasn't possible.

Maybe he should leave.

"Where we going?"

"One of Tino's spots. He wants you to meet a few people."

Two hours later, after getting dressed, they were in one of Tino's secret nightclubs.

Affinity.

This place wasn't open to the public and only Tino's guests dared come through the black and gold doors.

The moment the threesome stepped over the threshold; everyone in the club looked his way. He figured it was about the clothing, but the way they gazed at him hit different.

This stare wasn't about his gear.

What was happening?

Physically Cage could feel his body changing and even his muscles were more defined.

He was different in all ways.

When the strobe light kissed him, his complexion shimmered more, and he didn't have a flaw on his skin.

Even the nigga Onion was looking different.

Onion waved two dudes over in their direction. They were wearing all black and gold chains hung from their necks that resembled the white gold jewelry Tino gave Cage earlier.

"This is Pyro," Onion said, pointing to a tall 25-year-old man with a close haircut that connected to his beard.

Pyro shook his hand, and he could tell he was someone powerful.

"And this is Dewey."

Dewey shook Cage's hand with the same confidence. He also wore a smile that Cage was certain held a darker side.

"Welcome to Affinity. Whatever you need, let us know." Dewey handed him a phone. "We put our numbers in this. Get rid of that other cell you got and use this from now on. That other joint too hot."

Cage accepted the cell.

"Thanks."

They nodded and walked away.

"What was that about?" Cage asked Onion. "I need answers."

"They're drug dealers. And they work for Tino."

Finally, he heard something he believed.

"So, all this is about Tino wanting me to sell drugs?"

"Tino will tell you what he wants from you when the time is right," Onion said, as if he'd already been through new employee training.

"But I want to—."

"Let it go, Cage. Trust me. You'll get the answers to everything you need soon. When you're ready."

"This place is packed," Angelina said, whipping her hair over her shoulder. While also trying to skip the subject. "But I'm going to go home. I'm tired."

"You sure you can't stay longer?" Cage asked, looking down at her pretty face. "I need you tonight."

Onion whispered in his ear. "She's having withdrawals."

He released her hand.

"I'll get you a car," Onion said.

Before she left, she looked at Cage once more, and then walked out.

TREASON   127

He was sick of her using her body in that way, but what could he do?

She wasn't his girl yet.

When Onion made sure she was in the car and safe, he returned to Cage.

"I'm telling you; this is just what I needed," Onion said, rubbing his hands together. "I'm gonna finally find somebody for me." He grabbed the money in his pocket and ordered some drinks.

As Cage looked at him, he noticed the scars on his face were not as pronounced.

Many fruity drinks and minutes later, a few ladies walked up to them, and they both fought to get Cage's attention. But he didn't want direct company. He wanted Angelina and so he nudged a few girls Onion's way instead.

"Never mind," one of them said. "That nigga ugly as fuck."

Embarrassed, Onion walked to the bar while all three women engulfed Cage. When he was done letting each of them down to their faces, he met his friend at the bar.

"You good, man?" He asked, putting a hand on Onion's back.

Onion grabbed a glass of wine and gave Cage one too. "Here's to your new life."

Cage held his glass high.

"You deserve it all and more, Cage."

Magnus flashed in his mind.

Cage lowered his glass being unworthy of a toast.

"Fuck that shit, why you not over there with the ladies?" Cage questioned.

"Because they don't want me. They want you. And I can't blame 'em." He shrugged. "I mean look at me.

Ain't no need in faking. I'm gonna always be the ugly nigga at the bar playing wingman to a king like you. And that's alright, because you know what?"

Silence.

"I love to see you shine. And the only girl I want, doesn't want me back."

Cage sighed deeply as a few things went through his head. The first being the fact that he killed his father. So why did he deserve happiness? Why did he deserve Angelina's love? Maybe by giving her to a man he knew would take care of her, he could punish himself at the same time.

"You and Angelina will be together," Cage pronounced. "I promise."

"Wait...she...she said that?" He was so excited Cage swore he saw a tear forming.

"It'll happen, Onion."

"But how can you be sure?"

"Because I know." He paused. "Trust me."

When more women filled the club, the first thing he noticed was that the fruity aroma was so strong, he felt high just being in the room. It was so overwhelming, it caused his muscles to percolate, his knees to buckle and his dick to stiffen.

Suddenly a group of men covered the door, as strangers tried to push in from outside.

"Fuck is going on over there?" Cage asked.

Onion looked. "I don't know. Guess they smell that sweet shit from the street."

Cage frowned. "Hold up. You smell it too?"

Before he could answer, Dewey and Pyro, walked to the door and had the men ushered away.

"What was that about?" Cage asked.

Onion looked in the direction they walked and back at him. With a smile on his face he said, "Where there's women, you'll find fiends. But Tino's goons will handle it every time."

Cage nodded.

"You look thirsty. I'll be back," Onion said before disappearing through the crowd. When he returned, he was holding two cups with lids and straws. "Drink up."

Without another word, he devoured every drop.

And once again, he felt on top of the world.

Suddenly the music with the drink caused Cage to get higher. In the mood, he walked toward the cutie who had been eyeing him from the moment she entered.

She looked at him as if he were important.

As if he were somebody.

He pulled her closely to his body. Her ass was plump but squishy and he placed his face in the crease of her neck to inhale her sweetness.

"You don't have to hold back," She said. "I want you too."

"I want to, too," he said, as his dick stiffened.

"Trust me. It won't hurt me." She said.

Every now and again Cage would allow his mind to return to the murder. And in those instances, Onion would quickly remind him that nothing else mattered before handing him a cup of drunk juice.

He could never go back to the old days.

So, he decided, for the moment anyway, to embrace the dark side.

Cage was in the bathroom about to shower, when Angelina walked up behind him. As the water beat down on his dark chocolate body, her pussy moistened just thinking about what she was going to do to him.

Wrapping her arms around his waist she asked, "Can I join you?"

That second, Cage knew if he didn't cut her deeply, she would never run into Onion's arms. And he needed her to be safe, because if he didn't let her go, he never would.

"Damn, you pressed." He said in an annoying tone. "Fuck!"

She giggled. "You always playing."

He pried her fingers off him. "Playing? I'm dead serious! I mean fuck is you on me so hard for? Let me breathe!"

She looked up at him and took two steps back. "Cage, what's wrong?"

"What's wrong is that you're thirsty. What's wrong is that I can't get five minutes without you being up under my neck. Back the fuck off me, addict!"

As he smashed her heart, tears rolled down her cheek. "Are you serious? You promised you would never bring that up again. Why are you--"

"Great, so now you crying and shit too?"

It broke his heart to rip into her so badly, because seeing her in pain was not on the agenda. But he

TREASON   131

didn't deserve her, and his friend did. Because to hear Cage tell it, Onion was the better man.

"Let me put it this way, I'm not attracted to you. I'm not interested in you and I don't want you in my life as anything other than a friend. And if you can't get with that, step the fuck off, bitch!"

Looking at him as if he ripped out her heart, she backed up and ran away crying.

Not even an hour later, while he was sitting on the back porch under the stars, Onion came outside.

Sitting next to him, Onion took a deep breath and handed him a cup. "Thank you."

Cage nodded.

"I gave her to you, but you better never hurt her," he warned.

"Why'd you do it? I know you love her."

"Because I could tell you cared about her from the moment I met y'all. And I fuck with you like a brother. If I can't have her, I want you to."

Onion looked up at the sky and breathed deeply. "I'll--."

"But I will kill you if you hurt her, Onion." He looked into his eyes.

"I wouldn't have it any other way." He shook his hand. "Still, you can trust me."

CHAPTER TEN

"Did You Do It, Cage?"

After breaking Angelina's heart, Cage realized he needed to do something, anything to get out the house.

So he decided to make paper.

When Cage walked into the exclusive Italian diner, the first person he spotted was Tino sitting at a table in the middle of the floor drinking wine.

Cool as ice, Tino waved him over.

Cage strolled inside and stood by the table. "You called?"

"Sit."

Immediately he did.

"How have you been? Have you been enjoying the house, the women and your new life?"

He nodded. "Kinda."

He laughed once. "You have everything you need, and the answer is kinda?"

Cage readjusted in his seat. "What do you want from me? I know it's something. Maybe drug related. And I need you to tell me now or I'm walking out this bitch."

Tino smiled.

Grabbing a glass of red wine, he leaned back and crossed his legs. "I operate underground gambling rings out of my clubs. Affinity, the club you went to the other night, is one of them. And I want you to run it. To bring in people your age."

"Why me? I don't know anything."

"You're young and without skill. That means I can teach you everything I know."

"And you trust me after everything I did?"

"I need your eyes. I need your looks. So, the answer is yes."

"I have to think about it."

Tino glared. "I offer you the opportunity of a lifetime and you say you have to think about it?"

"Yes. I gotta check on my people first."

Tino nodded. "You have two days."

It had been many nights since Cage killed his father and during the late hours when Onion and Angelina were doing their thing, Cage's mind went back to his family. Ever since he successfully made them a couple things were different.

Two bedrooms became one and he often heard them moaning in the middle of the night. What Cage also noticed was that Onion was looking different. The scars were barely visible on his face and he possessed swag that he didn't have before.

Whoever handled his skincare routine was amazing.

When he caught them fucking in the kitchen one night, he almost lost his mind as jealousy overtook his body.

He started to break his neck and tell him she belonged to him.

But how could he?

He handed her over to him with everything but a bow.

On the other hand, he was happy for Onion.

He never felt about a girl the way Onion did about Angelina until...well...he met Angelina.

Walking to the window, and looking up at the night sky, he decided to check on his family. Using the vehicle Tino gave him, a black Honda with even blacker windows and less than 5000 miles, he drove to the one place he thought his family would be, their home.

When he pulled past the house and parked down the block, to prevent being spotted, he noticed all the lights were out, and it appeared that no one lived inside.

Had they moved?

For a second his mind tried to remember how much time had passed since he killed his father. Although he knew the day he took Magnus' life, he didn't know what day it was now.

He completely lost time and space.

In detective mode, he went to 7-Eleven to get some answers. It took him a minute to search around the front of the store for what he was looking for.

When he spotted the newspapers, he picked one up. Splattered on the front was something pertaining to politics but in the top left-hand corner, he saw what he needed.

"What the fuck?" It had been six weeks since he murdered his father but to him, it felt like a few days.

Getting back in his car, he sat in the parking lot for thirty minutes.

Why did it feel so easy to move on with his life?

Between the strange drinks Onion gave him and the nights at Tino's clubs, he didn't have a grasp of reality.

Where was his mother?

Where were his siblings?

He had to know.

After some time, he went back to the one woman's house he couldn't stand.

Wendy's stank ho ass.

He figured despite hating her guts, she would at least know what went down and where his family was located.

As he continued to drive down the road toward her house, he noticed the grounds weren't lavish and kept like the neighborhood he had grown up in. Because beer bottles, potato chip bags, trash, and other garbage was scattered along the streets.

He was definitely in his aunt's part of town.

Once in her area, he parked down the street from her crib, just to see if he saw anyone he cared about leaving her front door. Although people pretended not to see him, he could feel their eyes upon him as he sat in his car, within the darkness.

To his shock, within five minutes he saw his brother Archer sneaking out the house. The moon was full and provided just enough light, to spot his every move.

"Where you going?" He said to himself.

Following him from behind with the lights out, he was surprised when Archer hopped the fence and walked toward the back door of another house.

Confused on what was happening, Cage exited his car and crept in the same direction. From where he stood, by the fence, he could see Archer, with a gun in his hand.

"Fuck are you about to do?" He said to himself.

Cage tried to enter the fence but for some reason he was stuck. Taking a second to observe his surroundings, from the open window, he could see several men counting what looked like money on a kitchen table.

Within seconds, Archer kicked in the back door, only to be met with a barrage of bullets.

"Archer!" Cage yelled, as he saw bullets pummel his body. Within seconds, he lay face up on the ground as his blood soaked the earth.

Cage went weak at the knees.

Alarmed, Cage made another attempt to jump over the fence when he was snatched from behind by two people.

"Get off me!" He yelled. "Fuck off me!"

Within seconds he was thrown in the back of a van, where Onion greeted him.

With him in the trap, the vehicle pulled away from the scene.

"What the fuck you doing?" Cage yelled. "I just saw my brother get killed! Take me back!" He moved to approach the driver, but Onion pulled him down with extreme force.

"I know what you saw but you're about to get caught. Are you stupid? Or are you trying to go to jail?"

"Who was there?"

"What?"

"When I pulled up, I saw people hanging around in the darkness. Like they were checking out my aunt's house! Talk to me!"

Onion took a deep breath. "All I can say is you are important to Tino. For whatever reason. And because of it there will always be people watching you and everybody you care about."

"Is that a threat?"

"I love you like a brother, Cage."

"I don't give a—."

"Have you forgotten that you wanted for murder? Do you really want to take the chance at going at them and getting caught? What about your sister and other brothers?"

"I watched them just—."

"What good are you going to be to them if you in jail? Think, man!"

"I don't understand what just happened," he said, dragging his hand down his face. "My brother ain't no killer. Why would he go through the back door like that?"

"There will be plenty of time for answers. Now let's just get back on our side of town."

It had been many nights since Cage witnessed his brother be gunned down.

He wanted revenge.

And to be honest, he felt a kind of way that Onion prevented him from killing the people responsible. Instead, every time Cage brought up his rage, Onion would find a way to convince him that there was nothing he could do.

And when he spoke to him enough, after a while Cage would believe him.

Nights later, when Onion and Angelina went on a date, Cage decided to head back to his aunt's. It wasn't enough for him to sit around and wait. He needed to find out what caused Archer to bust up into someone's house, only to get killed.

To his surprise, his little sister Bloom was sitting on the steps.

"Cage..." The moment she saw him, slowly she rose. Her eyes widened as she ran to the gate, opened it, and invited him inside.

They hugged for what seemed like forever. It was obvious that despite everything that happened, that she still cared deeply about her brother. Because at that moment she was home in his arms.

And he was family.

Releasing her he said, "Bloom, what's going on? Where is everybody? Why'd y'all leave our house?"

She wiped the tears that had run down her face and said, "Why didn't you come to dad's funeral? Or Archer's?"

Cage looked down.

To be honest, he didn't know why.

He had every intention of showing up, even if it was to watch from afar. But for the life of him he couldn't seem to awaken in the daytime.

"I'm sorry I couldn't make it, Bloom. And I know you don't believe me, but I had all intentions of being there." He looked at the door and back at her. "Is Wendy home? Where's mom?"

"Wendy's gone to play her numbers and buy cigarettes." She shook her head. "I hate her so much."

"Me too, baby girl. How are you?"

She shook her head, looked back at the house and back at him. "I hate it here. Aunt Wendy doesn't like us, Cage. She says we eat up her food and breathe up her air. And she's tired of it even though she gets a check for us. That's why Archer tried to rob them guys up the street."

"Why he even think of something like that?"

"Me, Archer, Flow and Tatum woke up one night, I think because we all missed dad and were hungry."

Cage's stomach flipped.

"And Archer said he was going to get us some money. So we could get something to eat."

"But where is ma? I'm confused."

"Mom is not good. She started seeing things and talking crazy. At first, we thought she was just talking to herself a little like she did in the house when she was sad. When daddy said she needed to take her medicine. But when she grabbed somebody's baby in the grocery store and walked out, we knew something was off."

"A baby?"

"She kept calling him you."

Cage looked down.

"This doesn't make sense. We had money. Y'all don't have to be here."

"Yeah, but daddy didn't have as much saved up as we thought. When mom was well, she said he spent most of his money buying properties around the states. And nobody knows why."

"Since he's dead, ma can sell his property."

"She says she don't feel like dealing with paperwork right now. Says her heart is still broken."

"Where is she?"

"In Strawberry Meadows Mental Institution."

Cage felt sick. He had single handedly destroyed his entire family.

"Did you do it, Cage?"

"Do what?"

"Did you kill dad?"

CHAPTER ELEVEN

"Can You Handle The Truth?"

He came at night because he felt like he was being watched.

When Cage walked into the mental institution to see his mother, under a fake name, he was shocked to see her sitting in the back alone.

She aged about twenty years, with so much grey hair on her head he had to ask someone to point her out.

Yep. It was his mother.

When asked why she looked so old the nurse started to tell him to go away, until she saw his face. "When your heart is broken your looks are the first things to go."

"Well, what's wrong with her?"

"She has schizophrenia. All her life. And apparently after her husband was murdered, she stopped medicating and the voices got louder."

"Schizophrenia?"

"You didn't know?"

Silence.

"So, what happens now? When will she get out?"

"To be honest, I'm not sure."

After speaking to the nurse, what struck him was that despite being in such a grim place, he still smelled the scent that had been seducing him for so long.

Fruit.

Sweet fruit.

What was it?

Slowly he walked up to his mother. With each step he contemplated turning around and going the other way. But he needed to know how he could help her, even though he was the cause of her pain.

"What are you doing here?" She asked looking past him, as if he weren't there.

"I wanted to see you."

She pulled her grey robe together. "Wanted to see if it was true? Wanted to see if I'm dead? So, you can tell that bitch Wendy who took my kids?"

"Nah, ma, I—."

"She told me you went over her house. To talk about me. What's to stop me from telling the police you're here?"

His jaw twitched. "So, so they are looking for me?"

Silence.

He decided to kick it honestly. "Ma, I'm sorry about what I did. I...I didn't think about—"

"Sit down, Cage. You're causing a scene."

He plopped in a red plastic chair.

Now she focused on his face. "You're a beautiful, beautiful thing. You were always beautiful but now...now you look just like your father. The women will definitely be seduced." As she said the words, she didn't seem proud.

"Ma, I wanted to say—."

"Cage, there is nothing you can do or say that will change things."

"Ma..."

"You ruined my life!" Spit flew from her tongue like venom. "When all we ever tried to do was protect you!"

"Mrs. Ledger, keep it down." The nurse said firmly. "If you can't handle company in the middle of the night, we're going to have to restrict your visits to the daytime."

She stared at the woman until she walked away. "If they did that, my son wouldn't be able to come, now, would you?"

He didn't know what she meant.

Cage took a deep breath as he desperately tried to reach her. "I thought he was going to hurt you," he whispered, placing a hand over his heart. "That's why I killed him."

"Hurt me? What are you talking about?"

"I heard he was beating you. And since I saw you arguing that night, I believed he was—."

"I didn't need you to protect me. I needed you to trust me and your father. And now...now..." She broke down crying.

"What, ma? If you're mad at me, you might as well tell me the truth now. Because Wendy told me you were going to kill me. Is it true?"

"Can you handle the truth?"

"I need it." His voice got deep.

She took a deep breath and sunk deeper into the chair. "When I was younger, I was a confused little girl. For the most part, I was spoiled, and my parents allowed me to do what I wanted when I wanted." She crossed her legs. "We were all so free spirited back then. Foile de trois."

"Where was Wendy?"

"She was being raised by my grandmother because she's my father's oldest daughter. He didn't claim her though. We only got close in adulthood." She sighed. "Anyway, me, my father and my mommy

144   By T. STYLES

lived a comfortable life. My mother was well known, and my father handled banking accounts for some very prestigious people. I don't know who they were. Just that they were worth a lot of money."

When a nurse stopped by to check her vitals, she paused until she collected the data she needed and bounced.

"One weekend one of his clients invited him and my mother up for a business meeting in Deep Creek. They were both so excited because the client promised to introduce daddy to his friends, which could mean millions. Then he would earn as much as mama." She shook her head.

"What did she do?"

"Entertain the world." She paused. "I don't know what happened, but I do know that when they returned, nothing was ever the same." She seemed scared and more uneasy than she was when she first started talking.

"I don't understand."

"My mother and father had marks all over them and they looked like they had been in a fight for their lives. Like they escaped death. Very bruised."

"His clients tried to kill them?"

"I don't know all the details. It's only after I got older and pregnant with you that things came into view."

He glared. "Me?"

"When they returned, I was no longer allowed to walk to my friend's house alone. I couldn't go to parties or events. Not only did my world change overnight, but I was literally locked in my room and homeschooled."

His mother never talked about the past, so he was glued to her every word.

"I was angry, Cage. I wasn't willing to give up the freedom I had been accustomed to. And just like you, I started to hate my parents."

"I never hated you."

"Says the man who murdered his father."

Silence.

"So, what you do?"

"I did what every brat does. I ran away." She paused. "I was in the world for a few days to make them miss me. And I was miserable. There's nothing like being out there when you don't know who you can trust."

He was in that predicament now.

And had he not given away Angelina, at least he would have her.

"I wanted them to miss me. And the first person I met changed my life. I remember thinking he was the most beautiful man ever when he approached me at an outdoor classic black movie event. I was sitting on the grass, by myself, with no money. Not even to buy a drink." She paused. "I was begging with my eyes for someone to have mercy.

"And he laid his quilt down beside me. Bypassing so many beautiful girls just to sit with me. As the movie played, we talked a while and I remember wanting him to touch me, but he wouldn't. Just kept saying how good I smelled. He said it was sweet like fruit."

Cage sat deeper in his chair.

He smelled fruit regularly.

He smelled fruit now.

"After that night we were inseparable. Every time he was near, he had to touch me. Smell me. But there was something else going on."

"What?"

"I got the impression that even though he cared about me, if anything changed slightly, a bad look on my part, or not doing what he desired, that he would take my life." She looked dead into his eyes. "That man was your real father."

"What...what you talking—"

"Listen, Cage. Because my thoughts come and go when I'm medicated. So, if you want them to stay, you gotta hear me out or nothing will make sense."

He knew she was being honest because the nurse just put him on to her medical history. But was everything she saying a lie?

"I'm sorry."

"This man, your father, swept me off my feet. I had everything I ever wanted and then more. Which I needed because my wealthy parents cut me off. But I was good because there was nothing I couldn't ask for that he wouldn't provide. But I noticed something."

"What?"

"We never got a chance to experience the sun."

"Ma..."

"Despite all our time together, we never spent the day in each other's arms. Only under the moon and stars."

Silence.

"But I stayed. Because he worshipped me, and I knew it. And so, the moment I got pregnant with you, for some reason I didn't tell him. Something told me to keep my secret because I felt he wasn't who I

TREASON 147

thought he was. Don't get me wrong, he treated me well, but he was still holding back a part of himself. And I was tired of being in the dark."

"Mrs. Stryker, it's time for your medicine." The nurse said.

"Can I take it later?"

"No, I have rounds and I need to get everyone before bedtime."

Lala grabbed the paper pill cup, dropped the medication in her mouth and downed the water from another paper cup.

When she left, she said, "We got fifteen minutes since I took that pill. So, if you want the truth, I suggest you not interrupt me again."

He nodded.

"The first thing I noticed was his sleeping patterns. He couldn't be awakened in the daytime and at night he stayed up for hours. But it never bothered me for some reason."

The length she was willing to take the story drove him insane.

"Well, one night I happened upon the basement after he thought I was going out with friends. What I saw shook me. There was this beautiful woman, sitting in a recliner. And she had several needles connected to various parts of her body, and they were draining her blood. She seemed calm and consenting."

"What the fuck!"

"That by itself was strange, but what he did next, caused me to run away with you in my belly. When the container that was holding the blood was full, he picked it up and drank every drop."

Cage rose.

"Sit down, Cage...please. You know I don't like a scene."

Slowly he took his seat.

"Cage, the look on his face as he devoured the liquid was something I will never forget. He seemed to be satiated in a way that made the drink look edible. And it caused me later in life to nick myself and taste my own blood."

"Why?"

"Because I needed to see if I was crazy. If blood really tasted as sweet as he put on."

"What happened?"

"It was the most disgusting thing I ever tasted in my life." She shook her head as her face began to relax, indicating she was on borrowed time because the medicine was taking hold. "So, I left him. Went to a bus stop and cried my eyes out. Knowing that I couldn't go home or return to my parents pregnant."

"Why?"

"For starters he knew where I lived, and I was afraid he would come looking for me and take you away."

He leaned back and dragged a hand down his face.

"While at the bus stop, I saw a basketball game taking place across the street from where I sat. There were a bunch of men, most without shirts and grey sweatpants. All of them had long dreads, and not to be disrespectful, but even through their sweats I could see they were heavily endowed."

He figured the medicine was starting to kick in and decided to take what she was saying from this point on with a grain of salt. "Ma, you good?"

"Son, it's late, you'll have to leave in a second," the nurse interrupted.

"I know. Just five more minutes. Please."

She nodded and walked away.

Focusing back on his mother, he tapped her face lightly when she began to close her eyes. "Ma, you gotta finish telling me."

She smiled and a tear fell from her eye. "As I stared at the men on the basketball court, I noticed their beauty seemed to be connected to nature. And one of them, Magnus, came over to me." She smiled brightly. "His friends were angry that he stopped the game to give me attention, but it was clear that he was in charge. He was alpha." She touched her own face. "He was so sweet. And he asked why such a pretty girl looked so sad."

Cage moved closer since her voice got lower.

"Something about the way he looked at me, made me feel like we would be safe. And I was, until the day you were born."

"Only for you to try and kill me."

"I was afraid. Afraid you would change into your father. Afraid you would hurt people. And I was right because you killed Magnus."

Cage felt the hate she had for him at that moment.

"There are things that go on in this world, things that people thought were folklore. Things we assumed weren't real. But I'm here to tell you that there's truth to every tale."

"Are you saying that I'm..."

"I'm saying that your genes stemmed directly from a long line of those who prefer blood. And the reason you and Magnus didn't get along, is because his genes stem from a long line of those who prefer flesh."

Cage felt dizzy. "Are you crazy? Did them...did them pills get to your head?"

"Cage, listen to me. You can't disappear or fly away or any of that stupid shit you've seen on TV. Magnus won't change to an actual Wolf with four legs or hair. That's not how it works. But the genes in both of you, have adapted to human form and that means you retain most of the traits. You crave blood. And Magnus craves flesh. This is why I stayed at the butcher, buying slabs of meat."

"But it doesn't make sense. I have been out in the daytime."

"It's true. You have been out in the daytime. But how did you feel when you were? You felt sleepy. Complained of headaches and longed for darkness. And now, due to your actions, you'll never experience sunlight again."

He glared. "Why?"

"What happened on your birthday?"

Cage looked away.

"Cage, there are two ways to become fully Vamp. The first is being born a Vamp and taking *The Fluid*. The second is being bit and taking The Fluid. If you take The Fluid, you will never experience the sun again."

"The Fluid?" He repeated. "What's that?"

"I don't know a lot, but from what I've learned from Magnus, fifty vampires have to unanimously agree to give you fluid. It comes by wet kisses, sperm, cum. They use a process called human chimerism through sex, which causes the mixing of DNA. The Fluid ceremony is not always easy, because Vamps aren't interested in increasing numbers. They're interested in survival. So, at that party you went to at Tino's, did you kiss Vampires directly? Or drink their fluid?"

Of course, he did.

"Now you understand what Magnus was trying to protect you from. And he knew immediately when he saw your face, when he picked you up from your friend's house, that you had taken The Fluid and that it was too late. It freshens the skin. Fills out the body. And some say, changes the heart. So, he decided to move you away from anybody who would take advantage of you. Even your father."

Cage was devastated...

Was his mother tripping? Did the pills take over her mind?

For answers he went to Tino's house. And to his surprise, he and JoJo were waiting out front. His arm wrapped around her waist, as if protecting her honor.

Removing his shirt, and tossing it in the grass, Cage cracked his knuckles. He may have been a punk before but these days he was prepared to fight.

"So, you lied to me?" Cage roared.

Tino laughed. "I take it you spoke to your mother."

"Answer the question!"

By T. STYLES

"If by lying you mean that I shielded you from the falsehoods your mother was intent on carrying out, the answer is yes."

"I knew you knew who I was. Why didn't you tell me?"

"Because nobody can tell you who you are." He pointed a stiff finger his way. "You have to experience it to believe it."

He was done talking.

Cage ran toward him but was stopped in his tracks when twenty men and women blocked his path. He didn't know what they planned, but he was certain that whatever happened, it would end badly for him.

Looking at JoJo Cage said, "You convinced me to kill my father." The hate he felt for her was high. "Just to do your dirty work."

"It was your life or his. What would you have me do? Let him ship you away from your own people?"

Cage felt faint. "I'm not your people!"

Everyone laughed.

"We're sure if nothing else that you know that's a lie by now." JoJo said jokingly.

"I will remember this shit," he promised.

"I hope you do," she winked.

Thinking about all he lost, he breathed in and exhaled. He felt defeated, unsure of who to fight. "Why do all of this?" He asked Tino throwing up his hands. "I don't understand."

"You're my son," Tino said plainly. "Why wouldn't I?"

Cage hated the notion. "This makes no sense."

He stepped closer. "I never knew you existed until I saw Magnus on television one night." He smiled.

"With you at his side. How you think that made me feel?"

"This was all a game to you."

"Cage, you're my son. The world can open for you in ways you can't imagine. All you must do is accept what you are, and your life will be better." He stepped closer and the men blocking him stepped out the way. "Run Affinity. And you will have more money and power than you ever dreamed of."

"Why do all of this? Why destroy my world first?"

Very simply he said, "You are Vamp. And I couldn't have you literally being raised by wolves. It's fucking embarrassing."

CHAPTER TWELVE

"Go Deeper."

When Onion and Angelina walked inside the house, giggling after having had a great time, they were surprised to see Cage sitting in the dark. His arms were on his knees with his hands clasped tightly together.

He was waiting impatiently.

"What's wrong with you, man?" Onion asked flipping on a light switch.

"Tell me what you know," Cage said plainly.

Angelina looked at Onion, and then Cage. "What's going on? Why you look mad?"

Onion knew what the source of his anger was and it was time that they talked.

"Angelina, leave us alone for a little while," he said.

"Nah, I wanna hear what happened." She tossed her purse on the end table.

"Go in the room, Angelina!" Onion yelled. "I'm not fucking around."

Cage stood up. "Hold up...fuck is you talking to her like that for?"

"She's my girl, not yours. Remember?"

Cage stomped closer. "Then treat her like it, nigga!"

With silence, Cage was letting him know that with one word, he could take his woman and destroy his dreams.

Angelina stepped between them and pushed them away from one another. This was the first time she acknowledged Cage since he broke her heart.

"We're friends and there's no need to fight," Angelina said.

They continued to stare each other down.

"I'm gone," she breathed deeply. "Okay?"

Silence.

"I'll be back." She rolled her eyes and disappeared into the house.

Onion took a deep breath. This was not what he wanted for them. "Listen, we're brothers. And I'll tell you what you wanna know but you gotta come at me differently."

Cage dragged both hands down his face. Beefing with his friends was the last thing he wanted, and yet he felt they were lying.

"What do you know?" Onion asked.

"It doesn't matter." Cage walked away and flopped on the side of the sofa. "Because I need you to be 100% with me about everything. If you ever gave a fuck about me, I need the truth. Right now! No more games!"

"Be specific."

"Do you know who Tino is? Do you know who...or what I am?"

Silence.

"Onion, please, man." He placed a hand on his heart. "Talk to me."

"Yes."

Cage shook his head. "I feel like I'm not in reality. Like nothing that's happening around me is real. I can't believe I allowed that nigga to come into my life."

He shook his head and focused on him. "So Tino set you up to do this shit? To get cool with me?"

Silence.

"Onion."

"Yeah, man. But I had my reasons. And if you knew the life I came from, you would understand."

"What about Angelina?"

"She's innocent. I was at one of Tino's dinner parties she was talking about one night. She doesn't remember me because she was high. I took her home and stayed with her all night. When she opened her eyes, and saw me in her bed, I just knew she would scream. Instead, she smiled, turned around and asked me to hold her. We've been together ever since."

"What about the sign she threw up in church? Savage season."

"I'm in Mr. Gordon's class at school. I saw you writing it on your notebook. So I gave her drugs to throw up the sign, to get your attention at church."

"You were in my class? That's a lie."

"I told you I was new."

"I can't believe this shit," he said under his breath.

"The friendship I have with you is real, Cage. I—."

"I'm not trying to hear that shit." He punched the air. "I said I want the truth! All of it!"

Onion walked up to him. "Why you mad?"

He glared. "Fuck you saying?"

"You should be happy."

"You sound stupid."

"It's the truth. We can have whatever we want. And as his son—."

"I don't want to be his son! I wanted to be with my family and now I can never do that again. Ever!"

Onion shook his head and pulled up a chair. Sitting directly in front of him he took a deep breath.

"You don't understand how amazing this is, Cage. You don't understand the power you have. Literally, if you give the word a whole society would open up to you."

Silence.

"Listen to me, if you focus on the intentions behind your words, you can get people to do anything you want. Do you hear what I'm saying? Anything. And they won't be able to resist."

Cage was finally listening to what he was saying. "Like a mind trick?"

"Kinda."

"Is that what you've been doing to me? By keeping my mind crowded up with all this talk about going to the club instead of thinking about my father. Or leaving my mother and brothers and sister alone?" He paused. "You were even in my head when I wanted to go after the niggas that killed my brother!"

"Cage..."

"I'm playing the tapes back. I remember every time I wanted to talk about my family and how you would come in and tell me it's time to forget. Is that what you've been doing? Mind tricks?"

"Don't look at it like—."

"ANSWER THE FUCKIN' QUESTION!" Cage yelled standing up.

Onion swallowed the lump in his throat. "We have the ability to seduce others in the culture. And yes, I was doing it to make you feel better. But once you stay at it long enough, you will have more power than me, because you come directly from Tino's bloodline."

Cage felt like the world was in on a joke he knew nothing about.

"This is a good thing man, I swear it." He sighed. "Let me get you a drink."

Onion walked over to the refrigerator and grabbed him a cup with a lid, and straw. Closing the fridge, he walked in his direction. Just seeing the cup come his way got Cage excited.

"This is mine," Onion said. "You can have it."

Having heard the same thing many times from him he accepted the drink and drank every drop.

Just like in the past, he felt stronger. And then, with all the liquid down his throat he paused.

Was this...

It couldn't be.

Taking the lid off, he was shocked to see the remnants of what was inside.

It was bloodshot red.

Dropping the cup on the floor, he backed away until the wall stopped his movements.

"Is...that...?"

Silence.

"What do you have me drinking, Onion?"

"You know what it is. And you must have it to survive."

"Where did you get it from?"

"Tino has supply. So, you never have to do a thing you don't want."

Cage decided at that moment that he would no longer be out of the loop. "Explain everything you know."

Onion laughed. "To remain closer to our food supply, we had to look like more enhanced versions of them. Because if we held all the traits of the past, they would have killed us a long time ago. So, we evolved by turning up the traits that appealed to Norms the most which meant getting rid of traits like shifting."

"Norms?"

"Humans."

"Go deeper, Onion."

"People are shallow. They value looks and money more than anything else. So, we look better than most, perfected the craft of seduction and are the wealthiest beings in the world."

Cage held his stomach.

This was why Magnus didn't want him wearing name brand clothing. Believing it would make him flashier and more deadly.

"How many of us are out there?"

"We're everywhere. Church. Hollywood. The blocks. But mostly where you see Social Media Influencers, you see us."

"Church?"

"When I say everywhere, I do mean everywhere. But..."

"What?"

"We have to be invited into all dwellings. Cars. Houses. The invitation can be as small as accepting our offer to take a seat or have a drink. But they *must* accept."

"What if they say no and we do it anyway?"

"Their blood can poison us. From what I heard; it tastes like turned wine or foul seafood."

By T. STYLES

Onion spent the next thirty minutes giving Cage every detail and, in the end, everything made sense. Including why Magnus tried to save him.

"Angelina," Cage said.

"What about her?"

"Did you use seduction to get her to be with you? After I broke her heart? Because she's acting like she's in love now."

Silence.

"Did you, man?"

"If I did, would it matter? She's not using anymore. I used it for that too. I take care of her, Cage. Isn't she safer with me than anybody else?

Maybe.

Maybe not.

"Let's start all over, brother." Onion said. "Just you and me. Okay?"

"I don't—"

"Cage, you are a Vamp regardless. Let me show you the new world."

Later that night, Cage and Onion went to club after club. With Onion as his guide, he finally understood the nature of the aroma that was haunting him.

It was blood and some smelled sweeter than others.

Men smelled sweet too, but more like an overcooked cookie in a microwave, and so it wasn't as appealing.

They were in the club, with the music pumping as Onion spoke in his ear. "One thing you have to remember, if a Vamp is excited or sexually aroused our dicks harden and our fangs drop. Norms don't know we exist, so most won't notice. But if they do, it could mean trouble." He sighed.

"Fangs drop?"

"It's not painful so you won't know right away. The Vampire motto is *You must control your urges. You must control your flesh.*"

Cage felt faint.

Magnus said that to him many times before.

And now he knew why.

"Do they remember after the bite?"

Onion reached in his pocket and gave him pills. "Sometimes we put this in their drinks or on their tongues while kissing. And then they forget."

"What is it?"

"A roofie." He giggled.

Cage didn't find shit funny. "Are we killing people?"

"When we bite, we can take a little or a lot. The good Vamps find people willing to give us blood. The others commit crimes just like Norms do. So there's no difference."

"Of course there is a difference."

"And yet this is your life."

For the next couple of nights, they played the darkness and Cage felt he was turning into someone else.

His anger was misdirected, and he was no longer meek and sweet.

After getting his entire body tatted with the words Magnus spoke to him on many occasions, his body healed quickly and so only the beautiful ink remained. He even placed the Vamp motto on his flesh.

He decided that the old Cage was dead, and what remained was something else.

It was time to get some pussy.

On one of their club nights, he saw a pretty girl across the room. She was wearing a yellow sundress and a smile that made him wonder if she was as innocent as she appeared.

Leaning over to Onion who went overboard with the history lesson, he said, "Enough with the Vamp talk, I gotta see what's up with her right quick."

Onion grinned when he saw the beauty. "Do you. But remember our motto."

Walking up to her, he was impressed with the smell wafting from her skin. It was a mixture of lavender and peaches and he wanted to get closer. "What's your name?"

She giggled and hid her smile. "Berry."

"That's your real name or a dance name?"

"Dance name?"

He saw the innocence behind her expression and knew she was a victim of her friends who brought her to Tino's club and not a slut. "How you find out about this place?"

"Friends of mine," she said, nodding ahead at a group of whores who were speaking loudly and looking dumb.

He focused back on her. "They don't look like your speed."

She nodded. "They're nice enough."

"Do me a favor, even if we don't get to know each other, and I want to get to know you, never come back here again. Okay?"

She giggled. "Okay."

"Now, may I buy you a drink?"

TREASON   163

She nodded. "Yes."

He got his acceptance. But he didn't want to hurt her.

They had the best time in the club. They spoke about her life, and he gave her a version of his. In the end he hoped that even though his life was dark that maybe she could be his sun.

Unlike the others he met while clubbing with Onion, who were interested in how he looked and the money in his pocket, all she wanted was conversation. And that alone had him drawn to her.

Maybe he could control his urges for her.

He at least wanted to try.

So, he invited her to his house.

They had a good time.

The next night he woke up, with her on his mind.

But when he looked to his left, he saw she was lying at his side. Completely naked, the only thing that covered her body were the marks on her neck.

Horrified, he jumped up and with a heavy breath looked at what he'd done.

The greyness of her skin let him know that he sucked the life from her body, and this put everything in perspective.

The assignment was to control his urges and control his flesh.

He failed.

He was a monster, with no purpose on earth but to murder.

Why would God make him this way?

Why did he exist?

Looking at her once more, he shuffled to the mirror.

With his reflection in view, he stared at his brown blood-stained lips. This was not who he wanted to become.

Despite the two murders under his belt, this was not who he was at heart.

And so, he determined that he had to die to save the world from his wrath.

CHAPTER THIRTEEN
"I'm Afraid Of Who I'm Becoming."

Cage knew his mother wasn't interested in talking to him again and at the same time, she was the only person he felt could answer his final questions. And so, at 7:00pm that evening, he visited her once more.

He discovered with Tino's help that she didn't tell the police that he murdered Magnus. Electing to say instead that a burglar broke into her home. This gave him hope that maybe she didn't hate him as much as she put on.

When they wheeled her out, he noticed she was spiraling deeper in the hole. This conversation could give him what he wanted to know, or nothing at all.

Basically, mama was high.

Sitting in front of her he said, "I can't live like this."

"What does that mean, Cage?" She pulled her robe together and he could tell by the way she was nodding that she had been drugged up.

He didn't have long.

"Something happened."

"Like what?"

"I can't say."

"So, you hurt someone again."

"I'm afraid of who I'm becoming."

She sat deeper in her chair. "You're talking to someone who doesn't care. About anything other than Bloom, Tatum, and Flow. I done lost two sons and a husband. Why can't you let me be?"

"Two sons?" He paused. "You still my mother. And I'm hoping that at least you can try to understand me."

"What do you want me to understand that I don't already know? Because every time I see you, every single time, I mourn Magnus and Archer all over again." She looked toward her right and he could tell she was hearing voices.

Were they talking about him?

"If you hate me so much, you'll love what I'm about to say next. Because after tonight, I plan to kill myself."

She sat up straight.

The hateful look she had moments ago turned to concern.

Maybe she cared about him after all.

"Cage, this is not the—."

"Is it easy to die? I mean, what can I do? Because I did something last night that won't happen again."

"What did you do?"

He chose against the details.

"Cage, if you want my help you have to be honest with me."

"I killed again."

She glared. "I knew this would happen."

"I'm going to take my own life. And I need to know how. Do I use a gun?"

"I don't know. Nobody knows really."

She may have claimed not to know but he believed she had some ideas.

"Tell me." His voice was powerful.

She sighed. "Cage, are you sure about this?"

"I am."

"Then I need something from you first." She leaned closer. "I need you to promise that what I ask, you'll do before you die. Because I won't get out of here. The voices are louder and I don't want them to go. So, if you want my help, you gotta promise first."

Silence.

"Cage, I need to hear the words."

"I promise."

She wiped a hand down her face. "Can I trust you?"

"I won't lie to you ever again. I won't lie to anyone ever again."

She sighed deeply. "Like I said, no one really knows how to kill a Vamp who has taken The Fluid. For a Wolf who is injured during a full moon, their death is imminent. Because it's the one-time blood pumps ferociously through their hearts and veins, causing them to bleed out. That's how Magnus died so easily."

That explained why JoJo said it had to be a specific night.

He was starting to hate her even more.

"Okay, what about me?"

"For Vamps, if they are exposed to the sun, the skin can be burned. While painful, they can live for weeks on end before death. In fact, I've heard that some are able to survive even after sun exposure."

Cage shifted a little.

She sighed. "Magnus had reason to believe Cholecalciferol would do the trick."

"Cholecalciferol?"

"Vitamin D oil. The sunshine supplement."

"Regular D from the store?" He frowned.

"Simple. The most powerful things in life usually are." She paused. "Now I need for you to see to it that my kids are protected. And away from my sister. Your father has real estate. The deeds are in a safe. I haven't told anybody where because if Wendy keeps custody, and she finds out they are wealthy, she will kill them to get to the money."

"How do you expect me to pull this off? I ain't got nothing."

Looking around she leaned closer. "I didn't tell the cops about what you did to Magnus on purpose." She whispered. "This was the purpose. I knew that before Magnus died, the voices got louder and that I couldn't make them stop. So I need you to protect your sister and brothers because I can't. Will you do that for me?"

Cage was just leaving his house in Catonsville when JoJo pulled up in her Benz. He was confused, because the plan was to check on his siblings to see what they needed, and to assess how bad the situation was with their aunt.

So, when he spotted JoJo, he was annoyed.

Fuck was she doing at his house?

After all, she was the source of all his problems.

When he walked up to the gate she said, "Tats are sexy as hell on Vamp skin."

He sighed and raised his head. "What you doing here?"

"I came to talk to you about your father."

"My father was murdered, remember? You got in my head and made me do it."

She smiled. "Cage, you can hate me all you want. But I want to talk to you about Tino. Please."

Cage took a deep breath, exited the gate, and entered her car.

Twenty minutes later, they were in a small restaurant outside of DC. Although food did nothing for Vamps, they still ate to appear like others.

Now wine was another story. Every Vamp alive could feel it's effects, despite needing high dosages to get a buzz.

"I'm here, now what?"

"There's so much you don't know, Cage. And at the risk of sounding emotional, I won't go into detail. But what I will say is this, you are Vamp. You have always been Vamp. Unlike some others, including myself, who took the bite and then The Fluid, the gene is in your blood."

He glared, having heard nothing new. "Why you telling me this?" He shrugged.

"You want to run away from your legacy. You want to pretend that savoring blood is not in you. And I'm here to tell you that you'll never be able to escape The Collective. Let your mother die in peace and accept the club Tino is trying to give you."

"You're really wasting my time now."

"If you can forgive your father and–"

When the waiter brought over two glasses of wine, Cage sat across from her and glared intensely.

When he left, he said, "I can tell you this, I will never, ever consider that man to be my father. You can tell him I said so too."

"You don't want me to do that."

"Fuck that nigga."

"Cage, you're making a big mistake. Tino will give you anything you desire. But he'll also take away what you love." She sighed and leaned across the table. "We go by two mottos. *Control your urges and you control the flesh.* And also, *blood is our bond.* This is why we don't bring just anybody into our collection."

"You think that dumb shit moves me? Now, you got five minutes and then I'm catching an Uber back to my crib. I got things to do."

"If you stay out here alone, without someone who can organize your life in the daytime, you will suffer."

"I'll take my chances."

"It doesn't have to—."

Suddenly her phone rang. "Do you mind if I take this?"

He wanted the bitch up out his face so she could do whatever. "Go."

She excused herself and walked a few feet away from the door. At that distance, Cage could see her talking, and he could tell by her mannerisms that she was likely speaking to Tino.

Five minutes later, when she was done, she returned to the table and drank all her wine.

"Everything okay?" He asked, watching the glass touch her lips.

"Like you care." She said sarcastically.

He smiled and shrugged. "I'm still asking."

"You need to give your father a chance, Cage. He can..."

Suddenly her words were paused in her throat. As he sat in front of her, he could see blood pooling from her eyes and hives rising on her skin. She looked scared and for a moment, he felt sorry for her.

He got over it quick.

Something else happened too.

Suddenly her body tensed and trembled as he watched the agony she experienced from the Vitamin D oil he placed in her drink.

His plan was to see if Vitamin D worked. At the most, he expected her to be ill. But this looked like something else.

This was vicious.

It was only supposed to be a test since he had the oil with him.

In a sense, she showed up at his house at the wrong time.

As she reeled in pain, he spotted the look of betrayal on her face. Because in that moment she saw Cage for what he really was, a man who would never fully embrace Vampirism.

And then something happened.

A headache that Cage never experienced before ripped through his forehead. It was a thundering clap that made everything around him appear blurry.

It suddenly was hard to see, and he found himself having great difficulty rising.

Afraid he would pass out in the restaurant and be vulnerable to Tino and his people once they discovered that she was hurt, he rushed to the front door to escape.

He didn't know why but when he looked through the window of the restaurant, he saw her sprawled out on the floor, gripping, and clawing at her flesh.

This is the agony he had to look forward to when he finally took his own life.

And now he had to prepare for Tino's move.

The next night, Onion rolled over in bed after experiencing one of the worst headaches of his life. Wondering what happened, he was shocked when he saw Tino sitting on the edge of his bed, his back in his direction.

Onion sat up, backed up against the headboard and asked, "Is everything okay?"

"You sleep late. Even for a Vampire."

"I...I had a bad headache. One minute I was chilling with Angelina and the next I was in so much pain I—"

"I'm not here about how you feel, nigga! I'm here because the woman I love is no longer alive!"

Onion's eyes widened. "What you mean?"

"Your friend killed JoJo last night."

Onion glared. "That's impossible. He would never do that."

"So, you calling me a liar?" He yelled.

"Of course not."

"Then if I tell you he took my wife's life, understand this is not a fucking game! She was not a game! I loved that woman and now she's gone."

Up until that moment Onion thought they were invincible.

Leave it to Cage to find a way to kill.

Tino laughed once. "You know, this is the reason Vamps aren't interested in changing others. If one person is killed and you are in The Fluid Line, you hurt too."

His heart rocked in his chest. "I'm...I'm sorry, sir. I...I don't know why he would do this. What do you need from me? What do you want me to do? Just say the word."

"I need you to bring him to me."

He frowned. "What...what will happen if I do?"

For the first time ever, Tino turned his head and looked him square in the eyes. "That's my business."

"I understand, sir. I guess...I mean, I guess I'm asking if you'll hurt him? I mean no disrespect. But I need to know."

"I have plans for him, that have nothing to do with you."

"Well, in that case, my answer is no."

Slowly, Tino rose and stood over the man. "Do you know who I am?"

"For as long as I can remember, I admired you. When I was able to help you find your son, I jumped at the chance. So, when you ask me do I know you, I idolize you."

"And having said that, you would have me demand a service and not carry it through?"

"I don't mean to, sir. It's just that he's my friend. And I can't hurt my friend."

Tino was livid but somewhat impressed.

"It's good to see you have the loyalty bone in your body. Because it's rare. But let's see how far it gets you. When I leave this room, you will no longer have access to blood. You will no longer be allowed in my clubs. And my men will follow you every day of your life. And as you do what you feel you need to do to survive, I want you to remember this day. And then, when you are miserable enough, I will take your life."

CHAPTER FOURTEEN

"I Don't Trust Myself."

After killing JoJo, Cage ditched the car Tino allowed him to use to move around on foot. It was a good thing too, because when he went to see his siblings over at his aunt Wendy's, he noticed that the house was again surrounded.

Although from the naked eye it would appear no one was watching the property, Cage had been there many times. As a result, he saw twelve men posted up in different locations.

He didn't know what he thought would happen when he poisoned and killed JoJo, but now he knew he'd gone too far. If he would have used his mind, just a little, he would have made a different decision.

Because although he felt like he was alone in the world, everything he did impacted his siblings.

Never again would he move simply by frustration. From here on out, each step would be calculated until his family was safe. And he would finally do what his father had done for many years.

Rise to the occasion.

When Onion and Angelina pulled up to the location Cage requested, he was relieved.

After all, a line had been drawn in the sand when he poisoned JoJo. And so, he didn't know who was on his side.

Hidden in a small diner, with no website or online presence, the three discussed what occurred a few nights ago. It was at this time that Angelina was made privy to who and what she was dealing with.

And still, she didn't believe her newly diamond studded ears.

It was a long conversation, but in the end, she decided to support no matter what. Because through it all, she still trusted them with her life.

"Why did you do it?" Onion asked.

"I don't know." Cage shrugged.

"That's not going to be good enough for me, man." He leaned across the table. "I fuck with you, but Tino's cutting me off! That means my moves have to be darker just for me to survive."

Cage didn't know what darker meant, but he did know he wasn't interested in hurting people to stay alive. But he could tell Onion felt differently.

At the same time, just like a baby, Cage was essentially on the bottle ever since he became Vamp. Having his blood given to him regularly.

It was hard on Vamps who weren't wealthy.

"They got into my head and had me kill my father, Onion."

Onion sighed deeply.

"And I felt like nobody gave a fuck that he was gone." He shifted a little. "To be honest, I didn't have any intentions on hurting her. The plan was to hurt myself. All I wanted was to make sure my siblings were good and find them somewhere safe to live."

"But I thought you said they were with their aunt," Onion responded.

"She's not good for them. Trust me." He paused. "Anyway, when I walked outside of the house JoJo was there. And I couldn't help myself."

"How did you do it?" Onion asked.

Cage sat back. "I prefer not to say."

Silence.

"This explains why I was bruised the last night I was at their party." She touched her neck. "I was bitten."

Cage shook his head at how everything was coming together.

"What did she want?" Angelina asked.

"She was trying to convince me to take over Tino's club. Said life would be easier if I went with the program. But I didn't want the program."

The air between the trio was thick with tension.

"I guess we gotta figure it out," Onion said. "But I'm not gonna lie, shit about to be fucked up for us out here. Tino telling anybody that sees us to bring us in. And I don't know what's gonna happen, but I hear it's torture."

"I know. I didn't think this shit through, man. I went with my emotions and now, it doesn't matter. My siblings are gonna think I abandoned them."

"They gonna know who you are," Onion said seriously. "Trust me, even if something were to happen to you, I'll make sure that they know your name. On God."

Cage nodded. "Thanks, man. But I still don't want to get you involved."

"Look around, Cage," Onion said. "We already are."

When they made it to one of Angelina's cousin's houses in Baltimore city, the plan was to stay low for a couple of days.

Angelina, now understanding that her two friends were unable to move during daylight, decided that she would run their errands.

There was one problem.

Other Vamps knew that she was an ally, and that if they wanted to find them, they needed to find her first. So, she would have to be careful, smart, and calculated with every move.

Things were going okay until the hunger pangs kicked up. Now they experienced the effects of not having Tino's blood supply.

One night, due to not feeding, Cage started experiencing a painful stomachache. Onion was slightly bad too, but he had drunk enough blood the night before to satiate him for the next day.

It didn't help that Angelina's fruity smelling ass was bouncing around the house.

At one dark moment, while Cage and Onion looked at one another across the living room, they imagined how she would taste.

Because of love they were able to control their urges and flesh.

For now.

"I don't think he looks good," Angelina said to Onion as they stood in the middle of the hallway.

"I know. Me either." Already the weight of leaving Tino came into view. It was one thing to have access to fruity blood and another to be dry. "You know what, I'll be back." He rushed to the living room.

"What you about to do?" She asked, grabbing his hand by the door.

"What I have to. I'm not going to let him be in pain. Don't worry, I know someone who can help."

Since Onion was the strongest between him and Cage and didn't care about doing what was necessary to feed, he decided to blood hunt which would mean leaving Angelina and Cage alone.

Easing into the bed with Cage, who was having a hard time she said, "Why didn't you tell me?"

He wanted her to back up. The problem was she smelled good. And the fact that he was hungry made the situation dangerous.

Control your urges. Control your flesh.

"Get away from me. I want to...I want to hurt you."

"Cage, I'm not going anywhere. I trust you."

"I don't trust myself." He sighed.

"Now why didn't you tell me you were a Vamp?"

"Listen to how that sounds? I didn't know who knew what to be honest. And I still want to believe it's not real."

"Cage, you need to understand that although I care about Onion, I care about you too. You should have never kept something so crazy from me. I could have helped a—"

"How?"

"By doing whatever I needed to help you survive."

"Angelina, months back I was a kid, living at home with my mother and father. And now everything I know has changed. Why would I want to subject you to that shit?"

She was so close that her fruity fragrance was overpowering. "I need you to back up. Please."

"Why?"

He got up and sat on the chair by the window. The man needed air. "Because you smell good enough to hurt."

"You won't hurt me. You're not that kind of person."

"You don't know what you're talking about. At the end of the day, I don't understand all this, Angelina. Shit is different. With me and Onion."

"You don't have to understand. There's nothing or anything anybody can say to make me change my mind. I care about you. I...I love you still."

Her voice was erotic and light.

She approached.

"What you doing?"

She raised her dress and removed her panties and tossed them down. "You know what I'm doing. Let me get your mind off the pain."

"We can't be—."

"Just this once, Cage," she begged. "Please."

The closer she got, the harder he grew. Within seconds his fangs dropped, and he could tell by how her eyes widened that she was shocked.

"I'm...I'm sorry you have to see me like this," he said. "I'll leave and—."

"You're beautiful," she responded, while straddling him.

Easing his thickness inside of her pussy, she was so wet his dick glided smoothly.

Experiencing the exotic smell of her flesh, coupled with the wetness of her body, his hunger ravished him.

But she was right. He was able to forget, slightly.

As she continued to move up and down, she couldn't get over how sexy he was and how good he felt.

Up and down, she moved until his shaft was completely wet with her juices. Vampire orgie withstanding, this was the best sex of his life and he wanted to rip into her flesh to taste all aspects of her body.

Having not fed, she saw what he was going through and looked him in the eyes. "If you want to taste a little, it's okay," she moaned. "I can handle it."

"What did you just say?"

"I want you to taste me."

The anger he felt in that moment was so great that even while nestled firmly in her warm body, he wrapped his hand behind her neck and looked into her eyes. "Never tell a Vampire that again! Do you hear me?"

She was literally playing with her life.

"What?"

"Never tell a Vamp he can take your blood while he's inside of you. He will never be able to control himself. And that includes Onion. And if he ever tries to hurt you, use Vitamin D oil to kill him."

Hearing the passion behind his words, only made her want him even more.

By T. STYLES

This wasn't a man who lost reason.

This was a man who cared even though his urges were out of control.

And unfortunately for them both, Onion had stepped into the room while witnessing the greatest betrayal of his life.

When they both saw him hanging in the doorway, with the Styrofoam cup in hand, they knew this act would never be forgiven.

He was so hurt that the cup dropped from his grip. Leaving blood splatters along the carpet and wall.

The pain in his eyes, the way his body trembled, all made it known that he loved Cage, only for him to do him a foul.

"You just had to have her didn't you?"

Angelina jumped up as Cage tucked his dick back into his boxers. "It wasn't about that, Onion. I swear."

"Is that why your fangs and dick are out, nigga?" He shook his head.

"I didn't mean for you to see this shit."

"Is that right, Cage?"

"All I can say is I'm sorry, man. And I never wanted to hurt you like this. Angelina didn't either. Please forgive—."

"Don't tell me what she wants!" He raged. "You don't speak for her!"

Seeing the pain in his eyes, Cage was suddenly concerned for Angelina.

Of course he knew they were wrong. And yes, he felt bad that he hurt his friend, but Angelina was the love of his life.

He already lost his father, was losing his mother and was concerned about his siblings. He wasn't about to lose her too.

"Angelina, come with me," Cage said softly.

Her eyes widened and she was about to run to him until Onion snatched her by the hair and bent her neck to the side.

"I will drain her first." His fangs dropped. "Get out. Now."

The fact that he bowed out of a relationship with her for this made him hate all his decisions.

"Angelina, come..." His statement was cut short when he saw the look in Onion's eyes.

He'd never seen this type of hate in all their friendship.

And he knew if he pressed the matter, that he would kill her before he allowed them to be together.

"I'm gone," Cage said, raising his hands. "Just...just let her go."

Onion lowered his mouth to her neck.

"Please, man!" Tears rolled down his face. "I know you care about her too. Don't do this. I'm leaving."

"Go. Now!"

When Onion released her, Angelina dropped and wept quietly on the floor.

"You have less than twenty-four hours to get out of this city," Onion said. "Because if I ever see you again. I will kill you and drain her dry."

By T. STYLES

Defeated and embarrassed for trusting Cage, two days later Onion showed up on Tino's doorstep.

Unlike in the past, he wasn't allowed inside, but that was to be expected. After all, Onion had chosen Cage thereby sealing his fate with The Collective. "I'm sorry." He said under his breath.

"I can't hear you."

He stepped closer and cleared his throat. "I...I said I'm sorry," he said louder.

"I have no use for sorry men."

"I'm willing to do whatever necessary to make things right."

"I need you to be clearer."

Onion took a deep breath, because even thinking the words he was about to say still felt like betrayal. Despite seeing two people he cared about engrossed in sex as he went to get blood for him to stay alive.

"I will bring you Cage. I will make this right."

Tino grinned sinisterly. "If you ever go against me or The Collective again, you're done. There will be no coming back next time. I promise."

CHAPTER FIFTEEN
"We Are Capable Of So Much More."

The moon was high, and Gordon was sitting in his classroom grading papers when suddenly he felt he wasn't alone. Normally, he would work during daytime hours, but he held secrets that caused him to operate better at night.

Turning his head, he wasn't surprised when he saw Cage in the doorway.

"You're Vamp, aren't you?"

The teacher gazed at him with a look of disappointment. He could see the change in his body, his aura, and his eyes. "You didn't, Cage. Tell me you didn't take The Fluid."

Silence.

"Follow me." He closed the folder on his desk.

Five minutes later, they were in the darkest portion of the school in the hallway. There Cage told him about everything he experienced over the past few months. And when he was done, Gordon's head hung low.

He had high hopes for the kid and now he realized his dreams were crushed. "This is not what I wanted for you."

He frowned. "Hold up, you knew this whole time?"

"Of course, I did. Your father brought you here, to this school, for me to look after."

Cage was shaken. "Why?"

"Because he knew what you would have to go through, being a Vamp who walked during the day.

By T. STYLES

We go through a lot. Sun sensitivity. Rage. It's hard, but we get by."

Cage looked down and steadied his breath. "Why didn't you tell me before?"

"It wasn't my place. Your father, who is respected by Vamps and Wolves alike, asked me to do him a favor. And that's exactly what I did. When you needed to talk, I was there. If I felt you leaving the path, I nudged you the right way."

"But I thought Wolves, and Vampires didn't get along."

"Who told you that?" Gordon frowned. "There is a world out there with many rules. But within these rules lies the heart of what keeps everything running. And that's respect. And Magnus had a lot of it." He looked at his neck. "And I can tell by the tattoos of his philosophy on your body, that you realize that now."

The more he learned about how great Magnus was, the worse he felt. He killed a king among kings. And he wondered what possible plan could God have for him other than death.

"When did you take The Fluid?" Gordon asked.

"A few months back."

"Was it worth it?"

Silence.

"What do I do now?" Cage asked. "My mother is drugged up most of the time. And she wants me to help my siblings, but I don't know where to start."

"First let me make clear what you probably do or don't know. Vamps and Wolves have been able to exist due to staying out each other's way. And since you are Magnus' son, both sides will want you even more now that he's gone."

"What do I do now? Because I'm alone, man."

"You have to be smart. You must think five steps ahead of everyone. If you want to make a move, predict your opponent's moves first. And never underestimate what you're worth. People will claim to want to help you, only to hurt you. You must learn the art of detecting deceit." He moved closer. "We are more perfect versions of Norms physically. Clearer skin. Heightened senses. Having taken The Fluid, you also have your sense of smell. Fruit for the blood of a woman. A burnt cookie-like scent for the blood of a man."

"How do we tell each other apart?"

"Most run-in collections. But there's a better way. Vamps smell like the earth before the rain. However, the newer generation never develops the skill to detect their own. In fact, the only skill ever developed with the new generation is the scent of blood to feed. But with the right leader, we are capable of so much more. Even harmony."

Cage stepped closer. "I need your help."

"What is it?"

"My siblings are in danger. I gotta get them out of my aunt's house. But at the same time, it's being watched."

"Why?"

"Because I killed JoJo."

The look of horror on Gordon's face said it all. "You killed JoJo?"

He nodded.

"That should've been quite painful for you, especially if she was in your fluid line."

"It was. Took me out for a day."

"You're young. For the older Vamps killing someone in the fluid line can take them out for weeks."

Once again, something he didn't know.

When he saw Cage's youth and naivety shining through, Gordon felt partially responsible for not telling him the truth.

So he took a deep breath and said, "Okay. I'll go get your siblings. I have an aunt in the mountains, who will allow you to stay with her until you come up with a plan. She hasn't taken The Fluid and can be snappy in the daytime. But that's okay because she'll give you all you need to survive."

"How do I reach her?"

"You don't. She'll reach you when she thinks you're ready."

"And that's all she'll do? Give me a place to live."

"Someone who's able to watch your back in the daytime when you can't watch yourself is priceless. You'll learn that too. You need to find someone you can trust later in life. Either a Vamp who hasn't taken The Fluid or a younger woman. When you do, marry her, that way she'll be protected. But never bring her into The Collective. Ever."

He nodded and looked down.

Gordon placed a hand on his shoulder. "Cage, this happened for a reason. I feel it. And I know people think a lot of weird shit about us. But it's not true. We're just another species trying to survive. Create a code for yourself. Stand on that code, and you can be used for good."

"I don't want to be used for good. I want to—."

"You'll either be used for good or evil. Your choice." He paused. "In the meantime, here are the keys to my house. Go there and wait. I'll be there when I can."

Cage went to Gordon's house as instructed.

It was neat with no frills although everything was in place. What he liked most was that it was clean and comfortable enough for him to stay at least one night.

He also felt safe due to the security cameras surrounding the property.

Realizing it was getting early, he locked himself in the bathroom and barricaded the doors. The home was built for a Vamp because there were no windows in the bathroom. And hardly any around the house. As a result, it was dark and cozy.

A perfect place for him to hide.

Needing some rest, he laid down on the cold bathroom floor.

Within seconds he was asleep.

The next night, when he woke up, he was surprised he was still alone.

Gordon could move in the daytime, so he should have been there when he walked into the living room. Instead, he was shocked to see Gordon's girlfriend, Amelia, sitting on the couch with her back in his direction.

"Why did you come here?" She asked in a low voice.

"Excuse me?" He said.

"Why did you come here? Why did you get him involved?" She turned around and looked at him. Her eyes were bloodshot red, evident from someone who had been crying all day.

"Who are you?"

"They killed him. They killed him because he was trying to help you."

"But why? He...he..."

Upon hearing the news, he stumbled backwards, just as the phone in his pocket rang. Slowly he removed it after seeing an unknown number. "Who is this?"

"You should have never touched her. She was the one thing off limits, and you couldn't give me that."

It was Onion.

"Brother, I'm sorry. I—."

"Never call me brother again," he interrupted. "It's because of you the teacher is dead, nigga. And since you wanna be his student, you're next."

CHAPTER SIXTEEN
"They Will Use It Against You."

Tatum, Bloom and Flow sat in the living room looking at one another. They just got off the phone with their mother, and she sounded worse than she ever had.

"Mom is going to leave us, isn't she?" Bloom asked.

"I don't know." Flow responded. "I want things to go back to normal. Before dad was killed. And Archer was killed."

"Why can't we go back home? Why does this have to be our story?" Bloom continued.

"We gotta go through this because it's Cage's fault."

"No, it's not," Flow said.

"Then why doesn't he come get us?"

The siblings were beside themselves with grief. They were too young to understand a lot but what they did know was that this was quite possibly the end.

The end of their childhood.

The end of their happiness.

And if their mean aunt continued to carry on as she did, it could mean the end of their family too.

Because it was said that if they couldn't get along with her, then they would be taken into the foster care system, never to see each other again.

They were still staring at one another until there was a knock at the door. Afraid, they looked at one another in fear. Wendy made it clear that she didn't want anyone answering her door.

KNOCK. KNOCK. KNOCK.

"What we gonna do?" Tatum whispered.

"I'm going to answer it." Bloom said.

"No." Tatum said. "You heard what she said last time. Not to mess with her door. If you do, you're going to get us in trouble and separated."

"I don't care." Bloom said.

When she opened the door, they saw a kid on the other side. "Cage said to follow me."

A smile stretched across Bloom's face. Looking back at her siblings she said, "Let's go."

The kid walked through their house and out the back door. Jumping over two more fences, they found Cage on another street waiting.

The moment Bloom saw him, she wrapped her arms around him and inhaled.

"Where is Wendy?" Cage asked.

"She's not home."

"Good, you're coming with me." He looked at Tatum and Flow. Let's go. Now!"

An hour later, they were inside a small decrepit motel room.

There was one king size bed. And as they sat on the edge of it, they knew that someone would have to sleep on the nastiest rug they'd ever seen in their lives.

"Don't worry about it," Cage laughed once. "I'll sleep on the floor."

Bloom and Flow nodded.

"What's going on?" Tatum asked. "Why did you bring us here?"

"I can't get into all of that right now. But I want you to know that I'm not going to let anything happen to you."

"Why you lying?" Tatum asked. "You can't protect us. Aunt Wendy told us already."

"I understand why you're upset. I do. But you're my family. And—."

"Did you do it? Did you kill dad?"

"No."

Although he had, he chose lying, for fear they wouldn't follow along with his plan.

"Told you so!" Flow said to his siblings.

"Listen to me, all of you." He paused. "You have to be smart. If you're separated for any reason, you must blend in with the rest. You can't let people think you're different, in any way. Or they will use it against you."

"Why would we be different?" Flow asked.

Cage looked at him. "For starters, you do this weird thing where you sniff people's seats. I've also seen you get violent with animals. If you're separated, that would give them all the reason they need to put you away." He looked at Bloom. "And you'll have to stop marking up your body."

"I don't do that."

He walked up to her, pushed her legs apart and pointed out the tiny cut marks on her inner thigh.

"This will be the reason they'll use to lock you up. To convince you that you're suicidal." He looked at Tatum. "And your popularity, coupled with your arrogance will give people a reason to hate you, just to see you fall. So, you'll have to work on your personality now."

Tatum rolled his eyes.

He took a deep breath. "I don't mean to scare you all, but this is what we're facing. And—."

"I'm hungry." Tatum said. "Can you get me some rare burgers?"

"Me too!" Bloom and Flow added.

Cage nodded. "Okay, I'll go get you something to eat. Stay here and stay away from that door."

Before leaving, he looked back at them once. "I will spend the rest of my life making sure you're safe. Even if we aren't together, remember my words."

Bloom smiled.

Leaving the motel room, he walked towards the car that he had stolen earlier that day. When he spotted Dewey, and another one of Tino's men, his heart thumped wildly in his chest.

He didn't know how they knew where he was.

But he knew he had to get his siblings to safety, or they could be exposed to real harm.

Busting into the room, he yelled, "It's time to go!"

"But I'm hungry." Tatum said. "Where's the food?"

"Now! We aren't safe and I won't say it again."

Catching his fear, the foursome ran toward the car. Luckily, they were able to get inside, right before Dewey spotted them.

In a hurry, Cage pulled out of the parking lot with extreme speed.

When Dewey saw where they were going, he followed just as fast. The way he handled that car let Cage know that he had done this many times before.

While they maneuvered down the road, on a wild Vamp chase, Cage went faster, pushing the limits of a car he didn't own.

Despite his best efforts, they still managed to keep up. Closer than ever, the two men with Dewey rolled down the windows and fired toward the vehicle. The first bullet went right over Bloom's head.

He missed.

"Duck!" Cage yelled.

The second bullet was aimed in the backseat at both Tatum and Flow. And Cage felt rage like he hadn't since learning that JoJo played him.

Because at that moment, it was apparent that they weren't trying to hurt Cage. They were trying to break his heart by taking out his entire family.

He had to work harder to keep them safe.

Cage went faster and it looked like he was about to get away.

But once again they gained up on him and he had to replan. Looking at the road to his right, he noticed it was a one-way street. Taking it could be dangerous due to the fast, heavy traffic. But there was nothing else to do.

"They're going to kill us," Bloom cried.

"Slow down!" Tatum yelled. "You're going to get us hurt!"

Flow was the only one who chose to remain silent, but it didn't mean he wasn't frightened.

Desperate times called for desperate maneuvers.

When the moment was right, and he was sure that Dewey would think he was going straight ahead, he yanked the wheel to the one-way street.

By the time Dewey knew what was happening, it was too late.

Cage continued at high speed down this road until he was out of their sight.

For now, everyone was okay.

Everyone was safe.

But where could they go?

Later on that night, Cage had broken into an abandoned house. Because his family had grown up in luxury, the surroundings were enough to make them want to throw up.

But Cage didn't care about the beauty of the space.

He wanted them safe.

Sitting on a wooden floor with mouse traps in the corners of the walls, the siblings looked at one another in fear.

They had fallen from grace.

"You have to tell us what's going on?" Tatum said. "We're old enough to know the truth."

Cage swallowed the lump in his throat. "They're trying to kill me. And because I care about you, they're trying to kill you too."

Bloom peed on herself.

"But why?" Flow asked.

"I can't tell you that right now." He looked at them all. "But I'm not going to let them hurt you."

"But you can't make that promise." Tatum said.

"Yes, he can," Flow added. "He's our big brother. He'll protect us."

Cage felt guilt, like he never had before. Needing to get away from their sad eyes, he said, "Um, go get cleaned up Bloom. I'll get you some fresh clothing and something to eat. Stay away from this living room window. Don't answer the door for anyone. Do you understand?"

They nodded.

The weight of his world was obvious.

They had placed their entire lives in his hands. And he realized becoming a man was harder than he thought.

After making sure the coast was clear, Cage went to buy Bloom some pants and then to the butchers. He picked up four rare burgers, some fries, and soft drinks.

As he continued to think about what was ahead of him, he also thought about Gordon. His words really connected with him, and he knew making sporadic moves, even if his heart was in the right place, was dangerous.

Going back to the place, he watched them eat in silence.

What was he going to do with them?

How was he going to keep them safe with the world hunting him and barely no money?

As they looked at him without saying another word, he felt they didn't trust him. But he realized trust had to be earned.

And then he felt the sun coming...

Exhaustion was taking over.

"I have to get some sleep. Whatever you try to do, don't wake me."

They nodded in agreement.

He wanted to stay up with them all night long, in the hopes of easing their fears. But he had chosen the dark side when he went to the Ledger's. And as a result, when the sun was nearer, the exhaustion that came over Cage was similar to being drugged.

But he had to sleep away from them, unsure of what he looked like during the morning hours.

After a brief hunt, he found a closet in the basement.

Walking inside, he closed the door and sat down after shooing away a big mouse.

Once as comfortable as possible, there he stayed.

When the moon came out the next night, Cage woke up and exited the closet.

Things were eerily silent.

Why?

Rushing through the house, he went to find his siblings. What he saw made his heart stop.

They were gone.

Their shoes, still sitting in the corner of the room.

CHAPTER SEVENTEEN

"Remember What I Told You. Don't Forget A Word."

Cage sat in another stolen car while thinking about what happened.

In less than 48 hours, he lost his siblings, and was sure that Onion and Tino were going to hurt them.

He was clearly out of his league.

And at the same time, he couldn't give in because he was all they had left.

Remembering Gordon and Magnus' wise words, he thought clearly about his opponents. In that moment there was something that didn't connect with him.

The day they took his siblings, why did they leave him alive? And why didn't they take him?

That's because it wasn't Tino's people.

He knew where they were now.

Twenty-five minutes later, he was in front of Wendy's house. When he saw none of Tino's men were there, he knew he was correct. They weren't there because they thought they were with him.

Knocking firmly, within a few seconds Wendy opened the door.

"Can I come in?"

She smiled and opened it wide. "Yes."

Cage rushed inside, and there were his siblings.

By T. STYLES

He sighed in relief until he realized they looked afraid and confused.

"I told you I had friends in the grimiest of places." Wendy bragged. "Friends that see all and know more. And one nigga with three kids stands out like a dick in a playground."

"Wendy, I--"

"Why did you take them?" She asked. "You don't have custody of them. I do!"

"You're right," he took a deep breath because it was important that he connected with her in a different way.

Because although he didn't want to admit it, he needed her to keep them safe. He couldn't do it alone. And at the same time, she was one of the evilest people he had ever met in his life.

And he realized, even if they stayed with her for a short time this could never be a permanent situation.

Ever.

"Wendy, you have to leave this house. You have to take them with you."

"I don't have to do anything."

"If you don't get them out of here, they will be back."

"Who's they?"

"People who are after me."

"That sounds like a personal problem. And like I said before, this is my house, and I'm not going anywhere."

Cage tried to reason with her, but he could tell it was of no use. "Get up." He told his siblings. "You're coming with me."

Suddenly, she pulled a gun from the back of her jeans and aimed at him.

He remained still, although his siblings began to cry.

"What you doing?" Cage asked, looking at her and then his family. "Why would you scare them like this?"

"Get out," Wendy said.

"I'm not going anywhere."

She cocked her weapon. "And I'm not going to tell you again."

He stepped closer.

The confident way he moved made her believe that he wasn't afraid of being shot.

But why?

And so, she put the gun to Bloom's head.

He was afraid now.

He stopped walking.

"Get out of my house. I won't say it again."

Cage hated feeling useless. And he made a promise that he would get himself to a position where no one would ever have power over him ever again.

Looking at his siblings he said, "Remember what I told you. Don't forget a word."

"If I tell you to get out again, somebody will die."

Cage stared her down for what seemed like forever before storming out the door.

He would kill her soon.

By T. STYLES

Cage could no longer avoid the obvious.

He needed to feed.

His mind was swirling with the next steps to take, and he didn't have enough energy for the long haul.

Driving down the street, he wondered what he was going to do after placing the lives of his siblings in danger.

There were no smart moves entering his mind.

He was still wondering when he saw a couple arguing in front of a strip club. He figured whatever went down inside was enough to make the woman uneasy.

He was about to keep driving past until he looked out of the rearview mirror and saw him grab her by the arm.

Pulling over he clutched the steering wheel before getting out. He needed to be sure this is what he had to do.

He realized he had no choice.

When he was ready, he pushed open the car door and approached the couple.

"Is everything okay here?"

"Nigga, get the fuck out my face."

Cage focused on the woman who smelled of fruit. "Are you okay?"

She was crying and her stare alternated between Cage's, and her boyfriend. That was all the answer he needed.

"Is this your car?"

She nodded yes.

"Go home."

"You don't tell her what to—." Cage punched him in the gut and watched him double over.

"Go home."

The woman quickly got into her car and sped away.

When she was out of sight, he grabbed the man by the arm. He was still hunched over after having lost wind. Dragging him into the alley, he shoved him against the wall.

"What you doing?" He coughed, as he tried desperately to catch his breath.

Cage straightened him up and punched him in the stomach once more. Weakened, he knew that the man could do nothing to fight against his wills.

And since they weren't in a dwelling, an invitation wasn't needed.

Although he wasn't aroused erotically, he was excited. And that was enough to make his fangs drop.

The moment the stranger saw them, he said, "What are you?"

Cage didn't feel like answering. Instead, he bit down into his neck and sucked. Deeper he went before sucking harder.

He didn't stop until he was strong. And since he didn't want to have to do this for at least a couple of days, he drained him dry.

When he was fed, he wiped his mouth with the back of his hand and bopped away.

Whether or not the man survived was not his problem.

He didn't care.

He had to save his siblings. And now he had the strength to do that.

He didn't realize that Onion was watching him from afar.

CHAPTER EIGHTEEN

"Invite Me In, Bloom."

Bloom was sitting on the porch when Onion walked up. Over the weeks, he was really getting into his Vampirism. And so, he had a way with him. A way that would be irresistible to a young girl.

Even a young wolf.

"Where your brothers?" He asked from the outside of the gate.

A van behind him.

"Hi, Onion," she smiled, having always had a crush on him in the past. "How did you know we were here?"

Since they were at Wendy's friend's house, after she surprisingly took Cage's advice and left her home, the little girl was confused on how anybody found them.

"I got some friends around here. Plus, Cage told me you were here."

"He did?"

"Yep. Where your brothers?"

"They in the house."

He nodded. "Like I said, Cage sent me here to get y'all."

Her eyes widened.

"You know he don't fuck with your aunt, so he was concerned something would happen to you."

"Yeah, he doesn't like her. We don't either."

"I know. That's why he said he wanted you to come with me. To make sure you were safe over here.

Since so much is going on. And you know I always looked at you like a little sister." He gazed down at the gate. "Are you going to invite me in? It's hard to hear you from here."

It was a dwelling.

So he needed permission.

She smiled. "You're silly."

He chuckled. "Why you say that?"

"I can't invite you in."

"I don't get it."

"I was told to never invite you inside."

Hearing her words caused the fake smile on his face to disappear like ice on a hot sunny day. "What you talking about?"

"You know what I'm talking about, Onion."

"Invite me in, Bloom." He said firmly.

"No," she said, ditching her smile in lieu of a glare.

Within seconds, Flow rushed out the front door. "Hey, Onion!"

Bloom popped up. "Go back in the house."

"I don't wanna. Auntie is taking a nap and she stinks." He sighed and looked at Onion. "Onion...Why you out there? Come inside."

Damn.

The fear on Bloom's face was opposite from the smile on Onion's.

All he needed was an invite.

And just that quickly, he got what he came for.

By T. STYLES

Cage stood in the center of a store, looking at nothing. He called his aunt's phone many times. So many times that the pressure he used as he tapped the screen, caused small fractures throughout the device.

But his mind was wrecked. He needed to know where his brothers and sister were, and he wasn't getting answers.

Finally, after what seemed like forever, a woman answered the phone. "Who is this?" She asked in an anxious tone.

"I'm looking for my aunt and my siblings." He said as his chest rose and fell. "Flow, Tatum and Bloom."

"Son, I'm sorry. But I let her stay with me for a little while. When I came home everything was ransacked. I don't see any signs of anyone anywhere. I don't know what to tell you."

CHAPTER NINETEEN

"Never Trust Me. Never Trust Him."

Cage had to take a chance. After all, she was literally all he had left.

And so, in the mental institution that held his mother, he met Angelina in a supply closet in the back. The moment she entered he was knocked over by her fruity fragrance again.

Good thing he fed already.

But Angelina was so happy to see him that she rushed him, before planting small kisses all over his face. It took everything in his power, which wasn't much, to resist. And to his surprise, when she was done, she handed him a Styrofoam cup.

Now understanding what it was, he devoured the drink. And when he was done, he wiped his mouth with the back of his hand.

"Where did you get this?" He sat the cup down.

"I took it from the house. He's, he's working for Tino again."

He frowned and shook his head. "He'll know it's missing."

"I don't care. You probably haven't fed, and I wanted to make sure you were good." She stepped closer. "Are you good?"

He crossed his arms over his chest. "Angelina, I hate to put you in the middle of this."

"Cage, can you please stop saying that?" She sighed. "If I didn't care about you, I wouldn't be here. When are we leaving? I'm ready to go."

Unfortunately, at the moment anyway, he wasn't there for the romance.

"Do you know where Onion has my sister and brothers?"

She stepped back. "Wait...he has them?"

He could tell by the look in her eyes that she didn't know anything. And his heart dropped.

"If he wanted me, why not come at me? Why take them?" Wiping his hand down his face he said, "I'm going to have to leave for a while. To come up with a plan. And I don't know when I'll return." He paused. "But I want to say something before I go. I don't want you to trust me and Onion, ever again."

"Cage, I—."

He placed a warm hand on the side of her face. "Listen! Tonight, I saw what I was willing to do to survive. And until I get a hold of things, and whatever this is, I want you to escape. Because over the years me and Onion may seem the same. But we will be very different." He looked down. "I'm told we'll get slightly older in some ways but not physically. But I want you to remember the words I'm saying. Never trust me. Never trust him. Ever again."

Cage spent his last five minutes talking to his mother after he spoke with Angelina.

They were completely alone.

Ever since she lost her kids to her jealous sister, her health spiraled out of control. As a result, the voices were more frequent, so they kept her drugged so she could have a clearer mind.

That often meant she stayed high.

Sitting in front of his mother, and realizing he was responsible for it all, he vowed to do what was necessary to get them back.

"I welcome death, Cage."

"Don't talk like that."

"It's true."

He scratched his head. "I won't be able to come back," he sat directly in front of her.

Her gaze was far off. "Why?"

"I made things worse. But—."

"I don't care. Get my kids away from my sister."

He nodded and lowered his head.

She lifted his chin. "You promised. And you've broken a lot of promises. This is one that I need you to keep."

He nodded. "I have to go to the bathroom."

"Hurry back. There's something else I want to say."

He trudged away.

After peeing and washing his hands, he looked at himself in the mirror. While his body was getting more defined, he wondered if his mind would ever catch up because he still felt young as fuck. He felt alone and needed more information on Tino if he was going to be able to save his family.

Suddenly he heard his mother yell, "Come in!"

Running out the bathroom to see what was up, he saw Dewey and four other men at his side.

Quickly he ran toward the side door, hoping he could guide them out of the facility and away from his mother. "Dewey, I'm over here!" He pushed the door open.

Dewey looked at him.

But instead of chasing him, they walked over to Lala, who was nodding off.

Helping her out of the chair, Dewey pulled her closely to his body. In fear, Cage was frozen, as he wondered how far he would go.

Smiling at Cage, he saw his fangs drop as he bit into the side of his mother's neck.

Instead of crying, she smiled.

And Cage knew why.

She wanted to die.

With rage coursing through his veins, he was preparing to run into their direction. He was tired of playing it cool, not wanting to make things worse. But watching them kill his mother had him ready to risk it all.

Right before the door closed that he was holding, he was yanked out and a bag was placed over his head.

Cage kicked and punched but it didn't matter.

He was eventually overtaken and thrown in the back of a van.

PRESENT DAY

When Abuela closed her eyes, Violet stood up and walked toward the window. As rain poured down on the institution, she looked at the reporters who had set up shop outside of the hospital.

It was just a matter of time.

After all, Abuela was a very famous woman.

Instead of looking at them, she focused on a couple running toward their car. Neither had an umbrella, but she could tell by their laughter that they were in love and didn't care.

For the first time in months, due to watching them, she smiled.

How she wished she could be as carefree.

Her life was in pieces, not peace.

She had broken up with her boyfriend after ten years, due to spending all her time with Abuela and him 'not showing enough compassion'. And now she was going through the toughest period of her life, alone.

Because if her grandmother died, she would be nothing, she was certain.

She needed something to change in her life.

Or someone good to enter.

Suddenly, the door opened, and Jeanette and Chloe came through.

That's not what she had in mind.

When Violet saw their faces and breathed in their unwashed bodies, she grew irritated.

"What do you want?" She walked from the window and sat on the chair next to her Abuela.

By T. STYLES

"You see the reporters out there?" Chloe said excitedly.

"This is so cool," Jeannette added, looking out the window too.

"The doctor and grandmother's lawyer are ready." Chloe smeared more glossy lipstick on her recently injected mouth. "Are you coming to this meeting? Because they won't tell us shit without you."

"Don't talk like that in front of her!" Violet warned. "Ever."

Chloe and Jeanette looked at her and busted out into laughter.

"This bitch will be dead within a few minutes." Jeannette said, flipping the collar of her jacket. "She ain't even making sense no more, and yet you spend all your time here, talking to a wall. Her rich ass ain't gonna give you no more money than she gives us."

"Exactly, so you doing all of this for no reason." Chloe continued, dropping her lipstick into her purse.

"You're wrong. She talks to me. She lets me know she's awake and she may not even die. So if you waiting for a payout, you may be waiting for the rest of your lives."

Chloe shook her head. "You know what, since you wanna do the meeting in here, I'ma tell them to come to the room. Because you won't waste no more of my time delaying the obvious." Chloe rushed out the door.

Jeannette sighed. "I know you love her, Violet."

She frowned. "Why are you always nicer to me when she's not around?"

"That's not true."

Thunder clapped the sky.

"It is. When we're alone, you're the perfect sister. But when she comes back you're different."

She sat down. "I don't know. Maybe it's because she gets me. We're from the same world. But it doesn't mean I don't love you too." She paused. "But you gotta stop all of this. She's dying. But death is the end of life. Not love."

Violet smiled, after just hearing those words from Abuela.

"She talks to me." She cried softly. "You believe me right?"

"I believe you believe. Can't that be enough?"

PART TWO

CHAPTER TWENTY

"God Has Beings In All Walks Of Life."

Cage was asleep until he was awakened with a shove and a push.

"Get up, nigga!" A beefy man with black bushy hair on top and a white beard in front yelled. "Ain't no free rides around here."

Cage popped his eyes open and noticed he was in a room built for five people. Jumping up he yelled, "When is somebody gonna tell me what the fuck is going on? I've been here for days. And where's my cell phone?"

"We tossed it. There was a tracker on it."

That explained how they always knew his whereabouts.

"Now calm down," the man laughed. "The name's Shane but they call me Pigsty."

"I ain't asking. I need to know what's up with my mother." He paused. "So I can—."

He tossed a newspaper in his lap. The headline read: WOMAN STABBED IN THE NECK AND KILLED.

Stabbed? But I saw him bite her.

Immediately his eyes moved to the section about her massacre at the mental institution.

What drew him next were the comments from people who knew Lala. *"She was a lovely woman. Just sick for a long time."* One person said.

"I knew her from church and she was very kind. I'm not sure what happened, but she didn't deserve to be killed like this."

As he continued to read, the quotes were suddenly about him. *"I hope Cage is okay. He was always so playful."*

Another said, *"On his birthday, he said no matter what he got, he only wanted peace. Such a pleasant child."*

When he read that quote, the newspaper fell from his hand. Because now he understood why Magnus wanted him to utter such strange words at his church.

He knew darkness was coming.

And he was buying his son's character witnesses.

"That's enough reading." He snatched the paper from him. "I'm gonna take you to Miss Savannah." He walked to the door but Cage remained where he was. Shane turned around. "Are you coming or not?"

Five minutes later he walked into an older woman's room. He knew it belonged to an older female because there were five wig racks standing in front of the window. On top of each were grey short curly bushes, each not much different from the other.

All the furniture was wooden including the dresser and a queen-sized bed which had an oxygen tank next to it.

But where was she?

Cage turned and looked back at Shane who was too happy for a nigga probably involved with his kidnapping.

"Where is she?"

"I'm right here," a woman yelled before he could see her face. "Give me a moment!"

"She's in the bathroom," Shane said.

A few seconds later she came into view. She was compact, with precise features, and beautiful long soft black hair. Why was she wearing older wigs? Her eyes were thoughtful and grey, but she looked wary.

Was she Vamp?

He didn't smell fruit or burnt cookies.

But when she laid her eyes on Cage she relaxed and smiled, which made her look far younger than her forty-five-year-old tenure.

"Excuse the oxygen tanks, Cage. I get a little breathy sometimes but I'm happy to have you," she winked. "I'm Savannah."

"Why did you yank me? Who are you? And what the fuck do you want with me?"

Slowly she frowned, and suddenly she looked ninety-six years old. "Who the fuck are you talking to? Huh? Do you realize the entire world is looking for you? And that I'm doing you a favor. You should be on your knees eating my pussy right about now."

Cage glared and stepped back. "What you just—."

"There is a hit on you. A million. And—."

"I gotta get my sister and—."

"Just being around them places their lives in danger. Don't you see what happened? Tino's men killed your mother because they knew that would hurt you most. Which also means that anybody who cares about you, or who you care about, is in danger."

Cage felt sick as his siblings and Angelina came to mind.

"So, the best thing you can do is stay here."

"I don't even know where the fuck I am."

"You're in Maryland. A secluded part where no one knows who you are."

"You...you do know what I am right?"

She smiled. "You're a Vamp who has taken The Fluid."

"Then why help me?"

"When I was younger, I lived in a house with my grandparents who didn't believe in using a bank." She sat on the side of her bed. "So we were burglarized once a month. After some time, I found a dog in an abandoned house. Brought him home, I liked him so much. Under my roof, he would kiss my face every time he saw me. Got along with my grandparents too. But with everybody else, even our guests, he would lunge at and try to bite."

"What's your point?"

"He was a mean dog, but after we got him nobody broke into our house anymore. Was the dog barking due to being untamed? Or did he know our "so called friends" were the ones taking advantage? I'll never know. But I do know this, I firmly believe God has beings in all walks of life. And He uses everything and everybody to His end. Even the wicked."

He felt the woman talked too much but he decided against letting her know.

"So what do you want?"

"Work," Shane said in a serious tone, much different than he presented from the first time he met him. "We all work around here."

"Doing what?"

"You'll see," Savannah said excitedly. She snatched a wig off the rack, stuffed her hair inside and grinned.

"Why do you wear that thing?"

"When I take it off it makes me feel younger." She shrugged. "For now, it's time to eat. I gotta introduce you to the other misfits."

A few minutes later they were in a large dining room. Sitting at the table was Ellison, a short black 23-year-old man who had a hazy cornea. Which made his eye appear as if it was covered with a pearl.

On the left of him was Brandon, a beautiful black man of 27 years of age with sadness in his eyes. He had a patch of bleach kinky hair on top of his head. And when Cage looked at him, he felt as if he was as fucked up in the head as he was.

And finally, there was Ian, a 33-year-old man who looked at Cage with disgust. He wore cornrows down the back and a scowl on his face.

Savannah and Shane sat at the table and Cage plopped in the only available seat.

"Are you all Vamp?" Cage asked.

They looked at one another and all but Brandon laughed.

"Fuck is so funny?"

"We don't call ourselves Vamps."

"Then what do you call yourself?"

"Bevvies," Ian said.

"What are Bevvies?"

"Look it up."

Cage rolled his eyes. "Are all of you able to move around in the daytime? Because I need somebody to check on my siblings and—."

"We all have the gene but none of us have taken The Fluid, but you. And we aren't your personal servants anyway." Savannah said. "Now enough with your questions." She clapped her hands when a group of women holding platefuls of fried chicken and rice for them, and a cup for Cage entered. "Eat and drink up. You'll need your energy."

Weeks had passed and it was time for Cage to leave the house. Savannah would have put him to work earlier, but since they had to go close to those who wanted to kill him, she wanted to wait to make sure the coast was clear.

On the way to work, the van smelled of old cigarettes and wet sneakers and Cage was annoyed.

Outside of saying he had to work to earn his keep, Savannah didn't tell him what else she wanted. That didn't stop him from questioning everyone who looked his way for answers.

Most spoke to him as if he were too young to understand.

Brandon was the only one who he believed wanted to give him more detail. But he didn't.

Sitting in the deepest part of the vehicle, he couldn't help but feel their stares upon him.

Ian drove the van and Ellison, Brandon, and Shane, were also present.

"So, tell me, rich boy...what you doing out here slumming with us?" Ian asked.

Cage shook his head and looked out the window. "So, I'm supposed to forget the fact that you kidnapped me?"

"It wasn't a kidnap. It was a rescue. There's a difference."

"I'm still waiting on the part that makes you believe I want to be here."

"You can leave anytime you want," Ellison said, his pearl eye looking in his direction. "Ain't nobody holding you hostage."

"Knowing you, you'll probably get in the way, anyway." Ian continued. "Especially when you find out what you gotta do."

"He's not going to run," Brandon said. "He's Tino's son."

That was the first time that Cage was certain that they grabbed him for a reason, other than search and rescue. Although he was smart enough to realize it before, confirming that they kept him close because of Tino was now a fact.

"There's nothing you can put in front of me at this point that I can't handle."

"We'll see about that," Ian said. "Especially on the first of the month."

They all laughed, and he wondered what the joke was about. He also knew enough to realize that within time, he would soon find out.

When the van finally stopped, they were in a district Cage had never seen before.

There were many tall buildings, most unfinished, that appeared abandoned.

"What is this place?" Cage asked, looking around.

"It's owned by Raymond Teller," Brandon whispered. "He didn't have enough money to finish his vision, so the streets took it over."

Cage nodded.

When they drove to what appeared to be the center of the property, there were no cars. Just construction vehicles with so much dust on them they appeared hidden.

Toward the left, was a road that led directly to and from the beltway.

Ian grabbed a bag from the seat and handed them individual sacks. Inside of each were small bags containing roofies.

Cage finally knew what was happening.

They were drug dealers.

At this point he didn't care. Doing something besides staying in the house with Savannah's weird stares was better than nothing. So, he would ride the plan out.

For now.

"We're only doing $50 bags," Ian said with authority.

Cage couldn't stand him.

"No divides." He continued. "So, if they want one and a half, they have to buy two."

Everyone but Cage nodded.

"Shane and Ellison, you're in the front," He continued. "Brandon, you're in the rear, and I'll do my walk arounds." He paused. "New kid, you're in the basement."

They're jaws dropped.

"You're putting him in the basement?" Brandon asked with great concern.

"Yeah. You have a problem with that?"

Brandon shifted a little. "I think that's a bit much, even for Tino's son. Since you know what goes—."

"Well, when you're called to run the shop, then you can have a mothafucking opinion. For now, get ready to work."

Ian entered the duffle again and handed each of them weapons.

Cage was given nothing.

"So, I can't protect myself now?"

"You can protect yourself. Just use your hands if you can box."

He couldn't.

"Otherwise, like I said, I'll be doing my rounds."

"I'm confused on what I'm supposed to do," Cage said.

"Hustle mothafucka." Ellison answered.

"Shane and Ellison serve their customers in the front, Brandon in the rear and I'll be walking around." Ian continued. "And like I said, you'll get the basement. It's pretty smooth. But very rarely, we have two people coming down at the same time. But if they do, I'll be there to sort it out."

"I got one question."

"What?"

"Am I getting paid for this shit?"

"Yeah, we all do."

Cage had a feeling that he wasn't telling him something else.

And he felt like it was a setup.

But what could he do if this was going to be his life? He had better get used to staying in the dark to keep with his plan.

To save his siblings and now, if he were being honest, Angelina.

So, all he had to do was collect enough money to put them in a safe place until they became eighteen and got access to Magnus' money.

In the meantime, he had a date with karma.

The basement was worse than Cage thought...

It was cold and dank. And what made matters worse, with the exception of the window across the way, that gave a spotlight effect in the center of the room, it was pitch black.

There was no direct door, instead customers walked in from the outside, through a short tunnel and up to him.

At first, he thought they were keeping him in the dark as a joke. And he went about the walls, in total darkness looking for a light switch. For his effort he was rewarded by the remnants of rust, mold, and wetness on his palms.

When Ian did his rounds and came down the stairs, Cage asked, "Where the lights? I can't see."

"What you talking about? The light is over there."

So basically, they want me to die, Cage thought.

"This don't make no sense. How can anybody hustle here?"

"Miss Savannah wants you down here. But if you scared, say that."

So, he stood in the middle of the floor, and waited. This meant that with him staying in the light, whoever came to be serviced was out of view.

Before Ian left, he gave him instructions. He was given specific orders to keep the drugs in his left pocket and the money in the right. And with that information, it was time to get to work in the darkness.

The first person, a man, entered and sounded jittery. And just as he expected, he could barely see him in view.

"What you want?" Cage asked.

"Two."

"Pay me first."

He was handed a $100 bill. After examining the cash to make sure it was authentic, he stuffed it into his right pocket and removed two sacks from his left. Once he got his product, the man scurried away.

The next person that entered was a woman with a high-pitched voice. She sounded nervous, almost as if it was her first time.

He sold her one.

The traffic was pretty steady, and surprisingly he felt like he could handle the job. For some reason, he wasn't even concerned about the police.

Perhaps the fact that they were in an abandoned district, away from prying eyes gave him an unearned feeling of safety. The less eyes on him, the better.

The only thing he had trouble with was the scent of fruit and cookies that bombarded his senses. But he chanted the motto several times...

Control your urges and you control the flesh.

By T. STYLES

If things continued to be undramatic, he could see doing this until he stacked up enough money to make his escape.

He was almost out of sacks, and was going to ask for more, when another person entered. Like the others, he couldn't see his face.

His voice was deep and far away, and Cage felt like he was deliberately trying to stay out the light.

"What do you want?"

"Four."

"I don't have it."

"So, you had a good night, huh? Made a lot of money?"

Cage was uneasy. "Shop is closed. Ain't no—."

Before Cage could respond, he was struck in the face with a closed fist. Despite being Vamp, the pain was still strong enough to cause him discomfort.

Lying on the cold wet floor, the stranger picked him up by the shirt and hit him in the center of the face again.

Since Cage's body was halfway in the spotlight, he was dragged a few feet away and deeper into the darkness. Within seconds, his pockets were emptied of everything he had which included money and drugs.

Having gotten all he came for, the thief scurried through the tunnel and into the night.

TREASON 227

When Cage awoke in his bed, he saw an eerie sight...

Savannah was lying in front of him with her hand on his dick. The grey wig on top of her head.

"What are you—."

She yanked him silent.

Breathing slowly, he said, "Savannah, what's going on?"

"That's one of the things I like about those of you who took The Fluid. Those of us who obsess over you, get to watch you in the daytime, when you're sleeping."

"Can you please let me—."

"All we have to do is make sure the sun is up, and we can have our way with you all day." She giggled softly. "Did you know The Fluids go to sleep naturally erect?"

He didn't.

He was shocked and embarrassed.

"You probably don't know a lot about The Collective. But that's okay because I'm going to teach you everything you need to know, and more."

"Why are you touching me?"

"You lost a lot of my money," she jerked him passionately and slowly. "And you're going to have to make that back."

Hating that he was being turned on, he decided to say fuck her and get up. Luckily her blood didn't appeal to him, or he would've sucked her dry. But when she nodded across the room, where a cup sat on his dresser, he remained still.

He didn't know where she was getting her blood. But the fact that she supplied him prevented him from doing anything violent.

By T. STYLES

He needed to feed.

And for now, he needed her help.

"Do you find me beautiful?"

Ironically, Cage didn't find her hard on the eyes. He just wasn't interested. "What do you want from me?"

"Like I said, you made a mistake, and cost me money. So, I'm going to take it out of your cash until I'm paid in full. Plus interest. But if you make another mistake in the future, you will be in my bed. And you will do anything I ask."

"You want something else from me, Savannah. What is it?"

She smiled. "You're getting smarter. And when the right time comes, I'll let you know what else I need. For now, get up." She continued to jerk him until he ejaculated into her palm. "It's time to go to work."

Although his bruises had healed, his ego was still impacted.

He couldn't believe that the night before he was robbed. And he knew he wasn't willing to be taken advantage of on a repetitive basis.

He would have to get smarter if he was going to survive.

Weeks passed and he continued to do his job most nights without incident.

And now it was the dreaded first of the month that he heard about.

Customers came for their orders, and he supplied them with what they needed. But he would be lying if he didn't say that his nerves weren't on edge every time he made a sale.

It was almost time for him to get off when he heard one set of feet. Before he knew it, he heard another.

"Who is that?" He yelled with authority.

Silence.

This wouldn't end well for him, he was sure.

Tucking the drugs in his pocket, he stepped out of the light. The moment he did, he heard feet moving towards him. He was being surrounded and he reasoned that it was time for combat.

He wished he had a weapon, but for whatever reason, Savannah didn't allow him to have one.

He was prepared to battle to the end, when unlike the last time, suddenly gunfire blasted in the small space. Due to the orange flash of light, he could see Brandon, standing over the body of the perpetrator.

The other one ran down the tunnel and away from the scene.

When the footsteps were gone, Brandon reached into his pocket and grabbed a lighter. When he flicked it, it partially lit up the room. Cage wondered why he hadn't thought of that before.

"Thank you."

"You know they're going to continue to play with you right?"

"Why y'all letting people down here without checking to see if I'm busy?"

"You mean besides the fact that cell phones are the best way to get caught?" He laughed. "This a trap house, nigga. And you being tested. And until they can make sure that you are who you say you are they—."

"I don't want to be tested. I want to be left alone. Why they playing these games anyway?"

"The *whys* don't matter. The only thing that matters is if you'll survive when this is all said and done. Because I'm sure you know by now, Fluids can be hurt and killed."

That was a slight to what he did to JoJo. He was certain.

Brandon turned off the light.

"Cut it back on," Cage said, finding comfort under the blaze.

"You're Vamp. Find ease in the darkness." He paused. "Now tell me what you smell."

Cage was annoyed at this point, feeling as if the world was against him. "I don't know what you talking about."

"Listen to me!" Brandon yelled. "Now tell me what you smell?"

"Nastiness and shit."

"If you aren't even going to try, why you here? I thought you wanted to find your siblings and your bitch. How you gonna do that as a broke ass, scary ass nigga?"

Realizing he appeared to be the only person on his side, he took a deep breath.

"Now what do you smell?"

Cage inhaled deeply. "Mold."

"What else?"

"Old water."

"And what else?"

"This is going to sound crazy, and I don't know why, but I smell roaches. It's a funky sweet odor that I smelled...that I smelled..."

"What?"

"When I was a baby." He paused, suddenly remembering his time with Wendy as an infant. "How do I know that?"

"You will gain memories of when you were a child the longer you live." He shifted. "Now finish."

"I smell lotion that you're probably wearing. And, rain. Recently fallen rain. It's not as strong as I've smelled before when I was around JoJo, but still."

That was the scent that Gordon told him would let him know who was Vamp and who was a Norm.

He smelled rain, which he had before because Brandon was a Vamp who had yet to take The Fluid.

Brandon flicked the light on and smiled. "Good." Cutting it back off he said, "I want you to tell me what you hear."

He walked away, footsteps scurrying across the floor.

"You're leaving."

"Where am I," he said firmer.

"You're in the right corner, in front of me."

He heard more footsteps.

"What am I doing now?"

Cage listened closely. "You're leaving." He paused. "Now you're behind me."

More footsteps.

"What about now?"

"You're behind me. On the left side." Cage was surprised at how well his senses were doing and he couldn't help but smile.

"What about now?"

There were more footsteps this time, so he figured he was further away.

"You're on the left, on the furthest side of the basement."

"Good."

Suddenly he didn't hear any footsteps. And he was overcome with that same eerie feeling he had before he was robbed.

Be calm. He told himself.

Instead of being scared, he sensed the air. The temperature of the room. And the smell.

Without waiting on Brandon to ask he said, "You're directly behind me. I can feel your body heat."

Brandon flicked on the lighter.

He was right.

Walking in front of him he said, "This is what you're going to have to do in this basement. You're better at it than we are because you're fully Vamp."

"I thought we weren't allowed to say Vamps."

"We don't say that word in public because we don't want to freak people out. But if you put half of the work we do into sharpening your senses, you will be dangerous. And no one will ever take advantage of you ever again."

"Thanks, man."

Brandon flipped off the lighter. "I'll tell Ian what happened, so he can collect this body."

CHAPTER TWENTY-ONE
THREE YEARS LATER
"I'm Done."

Cage walked into the kitchen and grabbed his cup out of the refrigerator to feed. He just finished scanning the paper for any news on his siblings and Angelina. Although he knew it meant nothing, he found comfort that for now, no news meant they were safe.

If only he was allowed to leave the house like the others, he could look around. But Savannah convinced him that things were still dangerous.

And so he remained.

After two women fixed up extra plates with burgers and left the kitchen, Cage sipped his drink. For some reason he thought about what or who had to be hurt for him to drink. When he realized the thought didn't serve him, he decided to put that out of his mind.

"How you doing?" Brandon asked.

"I'm cool."

Brandon nodded and Cage could tell he seemed sadder than normal. And although they weren't into getting into each other's feelings, he figured he might as well since Brandon had been solid with him over the years. If he were going to have another friend, it would be him.

Even though they couldn't be further apart.

By T. STYLES

Brandon preferred to spend his nights outside, looking at the large land surrounding the property.

Sleeping the entire day, Cage, on the other hand, preferred to spend his time thinking about the next moves he would make before getting his siblings and Angelina.

But tonight he had time for a possible friend.

"You good?" Cage asked Brandon.

He grabbed a plate out of the refrigerator and put it in the microwave. "Not really."

Cage cleared his throat. "Listen, I'm not the sort of person to get in someone's business but if you want to talk, I'm listening."

He sighed deeply. "I just found out I have a kid."

"That's good news!" He said excitedly. "I mean, why you here? With Savannah?"

He chuckled once. "The same reason most of us are. We're outcasts. And I made some wrong decisions that caught up with me." He shrugged. "Savannah agreed to help me out. And the rest is history."

"Will you ever be able to leave?"

"Eventually, when I'm able to pay them back."

"Pay *them* back? You owe?"

"Let's just say I had a thing for the dice, and it ruined my life." Brandon took a deep breath, grabbed his plate, and walked toward the exit.

Before leaving, and with his back in Cage's direction he said, "Thanks for listening. That doesn't happen much around here."

He walked away.

After Cage drank his fill he was about to leave when Ian entered.

"If it's not the precious Cage Stryker."

TREASON   235

Although years passed, one thing was certain. He couldn't stand him.

"Why you always sound like a jealous ass nigga?"

"That's funny. I didn't know the great heir had jokes."

"What you want?"

"Nothing." He grabbed his plate. "All I can say is you trust the wrong people."

Cage didn't know what he was talking about.

For starters, everyone knew he was the person least to be trusted. He stole people's food, cozied up to Savannah when he thought it would get him what he wanted, and gossiped like a blogger.

The only positive thing about Ian was that at least you knew where he was coming from.

"I can handle myself."

"I hope you're right."

Although years passed, and Cage was better at working from the basement, he was still angry.

If he was supposed to be respected as Tino's son, why was it that he was forced to work out of such horrific conditions? The good thing was, he had managed to pay back Savannah and created a hefty nest egg that he hid in a strategic place under a tree by the house.

By T. STYLES

Originally, he kept his money in his room. But when he heard Ian liked to circle his spot when he was asleep, he changed up his position.

In the basement, Cage had successfully finished one batch and was about to tuck his money and get another when he heard someone enter.

One of the things that Cage changed over the years was that he no longer stood in the spotlight. Instead, he directed whoever wanted an order to stand there.

From his new position, he was able to see their faces clearly. And if they had ill will in their hearts, he could deal with it accordingly.

"Step into the light," Cage said from the darkness.

The person remained silent.

"Who in here?"

He heard another set of feet. Unlike the times before, where he was almost ambushed, this time he closed his eyes.

The smells were sharper and sweet.

The sounds were crisper.

And he could feel body heat with a slight temperature change in the room. In fact, from this position, he felt someone to the right and left of him. And they were getting closer.

How they knew where he was since he was in the dark, he wasn't certain.

Truthfully it didn't matter.

At the end of the day, he would have to fight for his life because he was certain that although he knew of only one way to kill a Vamp who had taken The Fluid, that they were many more unknown to him.

When he felt the body heat of a person on the right, he stepped back.

TREASON   237

They moved closer.

This time Cage remained still.

When the person was upon him, Cage stabbed them in the stomach multiple times.

"Ahhhhhh!" He screamed out in pain.

When they dropped, he closed his eyes tighter and listened for the second.

Technically Cage was not supposed to have a knife, which he never knew why, but he was tired of having to defend himself with his hands. So he removed one from the kitchen years ago.

With the first on the ground moaning, when he heard the other person running, he went after him. Cage's speed was faster than normal, and, in that moment, he realized there was another talent available to him.

In under three seconds, he rushed behind the final perpetrator and stabbed him twenty times, just as Ellison and Shane rushed inside holding lighters, which also weren't allowed.

"What happened?" Shane asked, shining the light around.

"They tried to rob me."

The man he had just stabbed was lying face down as he dug through his pocket. Removing the hoodie from over his face, he was surprised at what he found.

"Wait, is that..."

"Brandon," Shane said, cutting Ellison off.

To say Cage was devastated was an understatement.

He had gotten closer to Brandon from a distance and now he realized how rare real niggas were.

This made him miss Onion even more.

Upon witnessing a great betrayal, the three looked at one another in disbelief.

"Sorry, Cage," Ellison said. "I know you fucked with him."

"Go get Ian," he grabbed the money and work out of Brandon's pocket. "It's time to bounce."

A few minutes later, Cage, Ian, Ellison, and Shane were in the van.

They would've left earlier, but they all had to wait for the bodies to be removed from the building.

When it was done, they all sat in silence.

"So whenever we kill, someone removes the bodies?" Cage asked in a low voice.

"Yeah," Shane said. "It's the reason for the majority of adult missing persons."

"I'm done," Cage said.

Shane nodded. "I know."

The next night, while sitting around the dinner table, with Savannah, Ian, Shane and Ellison, Cage said, "I'm leaving."

She had already been made aware that he was done, and he was at the point where she couldn't hold him anymore.

She always feared this moment, and at the same time she knew she couldn't keep him caged up forever.

"Well, you've learned all you can from us, so I'm not surprised," Savannah said. "You're stronger and smarter than you were before you got here and—."

"Why did Brandon do it?" Cage interrupted. "I thought he was...cool."

"It was the first of the month and you had become one of my best workers. And he knew you had money on you. So, he made a decision that he would do whatever he could to help his family." She paused. "I know you're angry, but ask yourself, who would you have hurt to get back to yours?"

The world and everybody in it. He thought.

"I'm going with you," Ellison said. "They're still looking for you and you can't be out there alone."

Cage wanted to dispute, but he needed someone watching his back in the daytime.

"I'm going too," Shane responded.

Hearing that they both were leaving, Savannah was shook. "You can't go." She said to them. "I—."

"We all know what you want," Shane said.

"And we also know that Cage is the only way to get it."

Cage frowned. "What they talking about?"

"Tell him," Ellison said.

Savannah took a deep breath, preparing to say what she held back for years. Looking into Cage's eyes she said, "I want to take The Fluid."

He shrugged. "So do it."

"I don't have enough. You need fifty."

Cage thought about how he was converted and sat back on his chair. "Why would you want this life? Why would you want to go to sleep, only to be afraid that someone will violate you in the daytime?"

"At my age, I wish somebody would violate me in the morning. In fact, I would welcome it. Because I'm getting older," she said. "And unless I get it soon, even if I take The Fluid, I will be too old to like myself. I don't want to be frozen at fifty. I want to be frozen in time now."

"You've helped a lot of people. How come they don't get together and give you the numbers for—
."

"They think I'm reckless. They think I'm high risk due to my line of work. And despite everybody I help, they never come back like they promise once they get accepted into a line."

Cage sighed.

He had no time for her worries.

It was all about his sister and brothers. And of course, Angelina. But he liked her.

"Cage, will you come back for me?"

He could've told her anything she wanted to hear, but he wanted to make his words worth something. And despite her raunchy behavior, he saw something in her he could fuck with.

He heard the conversations at night when she would provide motherly advice to those who needed her the most. He saw her give money to members who were a little short for providing for their families.

And he finally understood why she kept him in the basement.

It wasn't to hurt him.

It was to sharpen his skills. And as a result, she had literally made him dangerous to his enemies.

"Why didn't you give me a weapon? Everyone else had one."

"Because you can't be killed. Not in the way Norms or Bevvies can. So, for you, even if you're feeding, murder should be a last resort."

"Well, what about the blood you get for me?"

"Every ounce of blood I received was bartered. I may be a dirty old lady, but I never hurt anyone unless I had to." She sighed. "As a matter of fact, since you've been working with me, I've seen more people die than I ever had in my lifetime. None of them were under my watch."

Suddenly he looked at her differently.

"Will you give me The Fluid?"

He took a deep breath and looked dead into her eyes. "I don't know what my future holds, because the only thing in my mind is finding my family and girl. But if it's in my power, I will help you."

She exhaled. "Thank you. Now all we gotta do is keep you safe."

"What's your plan?" Shane asked.

"I'm going to disrupt shit. But I want to give them a chance to tell me where my family is."

"What are you saying?" Savannah asked.

"Set up a meeting with *daddy*." He said sarcastically. "And then do what you said you would do. Protect me."

Affinity Nightclub was filled to capacity...

By T. STYLES

The music pounded the speakers as sexy Norms vied for the attention of the Vamps, who they only knew as the most powerful men and women, in the room. Just being in their presence had many of them feeling like Gods. And every one of them were ready to give their lives to be chosen.

And before the end of the night, most of them would.

Tino sat in the back of his nightclub in VIP, overlooking the crowd that came to frequent the hottest place in the city.

Norms weren't the only beings doing the most.

Gorgeous Vamps hung around Tino each vying to become the next Mrs. Ledger. But he wasn't interested in a new wife.

He had other things on his mind.

Glancing around the scene he took a deep breath as he looked at his people.

Vamps were perfect. They knew what to wear. What to say. And the ones who followed Tino's lead, also had extreme wealth, which made them more alluring.

Which meant more blood.

By Tino's side, as usual, was Onion.

Who over the years had become more powerful than ever. Once a man considered too ugly to get a bitch, Onion was now so attractive that Vamps and Norms couldn't keep their hands off him.

Cage always said with age and money he would be alright.

He was correct.

Throughout it all, despite his indiscretions he was still very much in love with Angelina.

But there was one problem.

Last month he asked her to be his wife. And she turned him down cold. This brought out a darker side in him that she hadn't expected because if they were nothing else, they started out as friends.

"You've done well." Tino said as he continued to scan the club.

"Thank you, sir." He pulled on a cigar.

"What have you done with your money? Because I don't understand why you still live in that house I bought Cage."

"Been stacking my paper to tell you the truth. But we're moving into a new house next week."

"Well like I said, good job with the club. We're bringing in more money and more blood than ever."

"Thank you. I took your advice and me and Angelina made sure we connected with the most powerful influencers."

Tino nodded. "With her beauty and your smarts, it was bound to happen. You're like a son to me." Tino paused. "Tell me, Onion, where's your father?"

Onion looked away. "He's dead." He cleared his throat. "Sir, I hate to push things, but lately, despite the success you seem sad."

"Not sad. I just don't understand why Cage has yet to be brought to me. As you promised."

Onion felt hollow.

"It's not for lack of trying. I've looked all over and it's like he vanished."

"No one ever truly vanishes. You just have to know where to look." He inhaled. "And pretty soon, I'm going to need you to make good on your promise or –."

Before he could finish his sentence Dewey walked up to him in a hurry. He was holding a phone with the look of urgency on his face.

"What is it?" Tino asked.

"You're going to want to take this call." He extended the phone.

"Who is it?"

"Cage. He wants a meeting."

Glaring, Onion rose slowly.

While Tino smiled. "The prodigal son has returned."

Tino immediately left the club to go to the location he was given.

Despite the elders warning against this move because he was their leader. He went anyway with one demand.

"Protect me at all costs."

And as a result, every Vamp in Maryland converged on the abandoned building district where Cage had worked for years. They hid in the darkness, but Cage knew they were there.

With five elders following him, Tino entered the building and then the basement. Unlike the newer generation Tino perfected his senses a long time ago, and so the darkness didn't bother him.

Once inside, Tino stood in the light. His men hung behind him, electing to remain in the shadows.

"Cage, I know you're here. I can smell my own blood."

"I'm not hiding. There's only room for one in the spotlight."

"It's very dangerous for you to invite me here. I could have so many things done to you. Things you can't imagine."

"And yet I'm still here. Because I don't give a fuck." He paused. "Besides, I'm not alone either."

"Why did you want to see me?"

"Where are they?" He said from the darkness.

Tino was enraged. "How many times are you going to ask me about you're fucking brothers and sister?"

"For the rest of my life, nigga!" He yelled. "I searched everywhere. And so, I'm giving you an opportunity to let me have them before I begin the breakdown of everything you love. The destruction of The Collective."

"Threatening me too?"

"I'm even willing to turn myself over to you if you agree to release them."

"What?" Shane yelled from the darkness, making it known he was there too. "That wasn't the arrangement!"

"I see you have people surrounding you who don't know when to remain silent. Picking the wrong people to have on your team is dangerous."

"My family doesn't have anything to do with this." Cage said, bringing the subject back to the Stryker's. "They're innocent. Give them to me."

"Okay, let's do this. Turn yourself over to me, tonight, and I will give them to you."

246 **By T. STYLES**

"So, you're telling me your answer is no? Because I'm not dumb enough to come to you without verifying they alive."

"I'm telling you I make the rules. And as my son, you fall under my rule. And if you don't come with me now, I will kill everything you love later. That includes your brothers and sister."

Cage was heated.

"Remember that whatever happens next is on you." Cage sighed. "You can leave. And tell your other men to go. The smell of rain is overpowering."

"Despite the fact that your world will soon be over I will say this, you've never made me prouder. Let the games begin."

PRESENT DAY

Against her wishes, the meeting was held in Abuela's room.

Sitting in mismatched chairs, the doctor stood in front of them and took a deep breath. "Mrs. Maria Cano will most likely not survive the weekend."

Jeanette and Chloe cheered excitedly, while Violet's heart banged within the walls of her chest.

Looking up at him, Violet said, "But how can you be sure? She spoke to me today. She told me she was tired. She told me she was weak. But used her voice."

"Violet, listen," the doctor said, moving closer. "You are an amazing woman. And if I were going to have a grandchild, I would want her to embody every trait you possess." He paused. "You moved her when you were concerned she wasn't getting the best of care and the paparazzi were getting closer. You even slept here every night, often to the point of the staff having to put you out."

Chloe rolled her eyes.

Jeanette looked down in shame.

"So destroying your hope is not something I want to do. And still, I would be remiss if I didn't tell you that it's impossible for her to speak to you. She suffered from schizophrenia, which over the years led to dementia. But lately she's been in a coma. For weeks."

The Attorney cleared his throat. "So let me get this straight, are you saying she's brain dead?"

"Yes."

Chloe exclaimed in glee.

"In my opinion, Mrs. Cano will no longer inhabit her body."

The Attorney cleared his throat again. "Well as you all know, I'm here to handle her estate."

"She's not dead yet," Violet said. "Be respectful!"

"Understood, but as you know your grandmother is a very wealthy woman. In the event she does pass, I need to speak to you directly, Violet. Because--."

"Violet? What about us?" Chloe interrupted.

He frowned. "What about you?"

"We came here to see what we were going to get. We want our money!"

The doctor was confused. "I called you because I thought you wanted to know your grandmother's status."

"Nah, fuck that shit! I want to talk to the lawyer."

The Attorney sat back and then sat forward. "Let me be clear, the only reason I'm here is because I handle your grandmother's affairs. And in doing so, I was summoned by the doctor, by law, as I'm on the record. But regarding her affairs, in the event of her death, the only one I am authorized to speak to is Violet Cano."

Chloe was pissed.

Removing her sweaty jacket, stained with cum, she tossed it to the floor, and stomped up to him. "This woman has written about me since I was a child." She pointed at Abuela. "And I don't know what's going on, but I will get what's coming to me, even if I have to take it."

"So you're going to steal from her?" He asked. "Because as an officer of the court, I have to record that threat."

"Call it what you will. But I'ma get my money!" She grabbed Jeanette's hand. "Come on. We gotta go."

By T. STYLES

PART THREE

CHAPTER TWENTY-TWO
ONE YEAR LATER
"What Brings You Out Tonight?"

This was a luxurious club.

The type of spot, people went to when they had money, and wanted to flaunt hard.

Franklin sat at the bar, gawking at everything with exposed skin and hair down the middle of their backs.

He wasn't looking for love.

He was looking for an experience.

He needed a female to remind him daily of how powerful he was, even though he was fully aware that he was falling short in one way or another. He wanted to be perceived as successful, rich, and intelligent. All while realizing he was not.

"What you drinking?" Cage asked, sitting next to him at the bar.

The years and the V Swag had done Cage well, and as a result his body was fit in all the right places. Hair had touched his face lightly, and instead of shaving it off, tonight he decided on a five o'clock shadow.

The man was giving big dick energy.

This did nothing but drive the women who had spotted him the moment he walked into the club wild. Wearing a long black sleeve shirt, black jeans and a watch, a chain that read MAGNUS also hung from his neck.

252   **By T. STYLES**

Unlike the wide-eyed kid of yesteryear, he knew who he was today.

"My usual." He raised the glass and allowed the ice to knock against one another. "Vodka straight up."

Cage flagged the bartender over. "Give me what he's having. And I got his next round too."

Franklin didn't know what was going on, but he did know he wasn't homosexual, so he wanted to be clear. "I don't go that way."

Cage laughed. "I'm not gay. But even if I was, what makes you think I would pick you?"

Franklin stared at him for a moment and busted out in laughter. After all, it was presumptuous to assume a man wanted dick instead of conversation.

"The name's Franklin," he said, extending his hand.

"Cage." He shook it and released quickly.

"Want a drink?"

"Yeah, why not."

While Cage handled business, he smiled as a pretty girl walked up to him and did her best to knock against him softly, in a freak whore attempt to get his attention.

And it was easy to see why.

"Hey," she said, whispering in his face. Her breath smelled like mint. Her body smelled like fruit.

But the woman standing next to her, gave off no such odor. And she glared his way. "I'll be over there." She looked at Cage once more and strutted away.

Who was she?

Snapping her fingers to return his focus, the girl said, "Feel like buying a girl a drink?"

"Maybe later." He winked at the pretty thing, as he pretended to be interested in anything other than the man on his right. "I'll get up with you, beautiful."

"Do that." She grinned before walking away.

Focusing back on Franklin he said, "So, what brings you out tonight?"

"Actually, I got into a fight with my girlfriend, so I decided to get some fresh air and ended up here." He paused. "What 'bout you?"

"Looking for something sweet."

Franklin nodded. "Is that why you let that sweet thing get away?"

Cage laughed and ignored the question. "You smoke?"

"Who doesn't?" He giggled.

"A lot of people."

"Well, I ain't one of them."

"I have one in the car if you want to fire up," Cage suggested.

"Cool with me." He drank the rest of his liquor.

Cage looked him square in the eyes. "Are you saying you're accepting the invitation to my car?"

Per usual this had to be specified. Because when entering all dwellings, including cars, Norms had to agree.

"Pretty much. Show me to your ride."

"I need you to say yes or no."

"Yes." He frowned. "I gave you an answer."

An hour later, they were sitting in Cage's car. Powder cloud after powder cloud danced in the air. Before long, Franklin was so high, he could hardly see straight.

But when the smoke cleared, he noticed Cage was no longer smiling. The mood suddenly felt dark and

By T. STYLES

ominous. Where was the gracious man who bought him a drink an hour earlier? Had he not gotten so sloppy drunk, he may have seen.

"You don't remember me?" Cage asked.

"Should I?"

"I don't know...you killed my brother."

"I killed a lot of people."

Cage's jaw twitched. His careless attitude would make it easy to do what would come next.

"My little brother jumped your fence in your backyard. And you fired. Your bullet was the one that killed him."

Now he remembered.

"What you want?"

"It doesn't matter," Cage smiled and allowed his fangs to drop.

Pulling him close, he bent his head to the right and bit into his neck.

Tasting sweetness, he sucked until every ounce of blood was removed from his flesh and he was grey.

Cage pulled up in front of a brick house in Baltimore County.

Thanks to the man who killed Archer, he was full and a few couple hundred dollars richer.

Because he was smarter, and his senses were perfected, Cage could feel and smell when Onion or

Tino or his people were near. And he would shift and move, all while maintaining his plan.

That's why they could never catch him.

While he looked for his family, it led to a lonely life because he realized as long as Tino and Onion survived, that he would forever be single because he couldn't risk someone he loved getting hurt.

When his phone rang, he looked down at it and answered. "What's up?"

It was Ellison. "We found out where she lives. We also found out a few of her habits."

Cage sunk deeper in his seat. "How...how does she...?"

He wanted to ask how she looked. And if she was as beautiful as he remembered. But the only thing he told Ellison and Shane was that he wanted to know her address and if she were safe.

So being superficial was weak.

"Cage, you good?"

"How did you find her?"

"It took us a while, but we found out where her man lives first."

His jaw twitched.

"And where is that?"

"In this big ass house in Potomac, Maryland. Once we had the address, from afar we watched the location. And she came out one morning."

The fact that Ellison could still move in the day because he hadn't taken The Fluid made him somewhat jealous. But he pushed that feeling aside because jealousy eroded the soul.

"Thanks."

"No problem, man. But when you coming home?"

"Yeah, because we need to keep our eyes on you," Shane yelled in the background.

Cage laughed once. "Look, enjoy the view from the penthouse and I'll see you when I can. Until I get the Stryker's back, there's still work to be done. Stand by though."

"You know it."

Walking into the gate and down the steps leading into a basement, when he opened the door, he was surprised to see Old Man Dick in his basement apartment instead of his own place upstairs.

"Why you in my spot?" Cage closed the door.

"This my house." He tugged on his suspenders, and they popped against the side of his protruding belly. He resembled Fred Sanford except he was meaner and uglier. "And I can be wherever I want."

"No, the fuck you can't either," Cage said playfully. "Unless you wanna box."

He knew the man was old and nosey, so he liked to fuck with him every now and again.

"For your information, I was checking to see if you needed toilet paper. But I guess you don't wipe your ass 'round here so it don't make me no never mind." He looked at him closer. "Why are you here? Living with me?" His tone was serious. "Because I know money when I see it. And you got it don't you?"

He wasn't wrong.

With Ellison, Shane and Savannah's help, Cage did accumulate wealth but unlike when he was a kid, he didn't care to show it.

After all, he was in hiding and hunted.

Cage laughed and opened the door that led upstairs. "Go home."

"Fuck you too."

When he walked out, Cage locked his door and moved towards his bedroom. There he lifted the floorboard and tucked the money he got from his victim into a box.

With the new addition, he had over $90,000 in pocket cash, all of which he planned to use when the time was right. That said nothing about the wealth he generated with Savannah's help.

On his empire shit, he was considered a millionaire.

And no one knew.

One day he could live like a king.

But not yet.

With thoughts of the future on his mind, he went to his closet which held a bed on the floor and a pillow. Once he was lying down, he locked the door from the inside.

There he slept through the morning.

CHAPTER TWENTY-THREE
"He's Threatening Your Life."

The stars sparkled on Cage's black Audi as he sat in the driver's seat in a mall's parking lot. Staring at his phone, he waited impatiently for it to ring. When it finally did, he answered quickly.

"What took you so long?"

Shane sighed. "Me and Ell been here for fifteen minutes. But we wanted to make sure the coast was clear before you walked inside. Or did you forget you got a price on your head?"

Cage realized he was being inconsiderate and took a deep breath. "My bad, man. It just seems like there ain't enough hours at night for me to do what I gotta do and—."

"No apologies necessary. Let us protect you. That's why we're here. Now go. We're watching."

He quickly exited his car, rushed toward the mall, and entered a cell phone store.

"I need the phone with a good camera."

The young cashier looked at his current gadget. "Like that one? I mean, how many phones do you fucking need?"

Cage glared. "You smell like cookies."

"What does that mean?"

Cage smiled.

For some reason, now, the man feared him greatly. "Um, I...I have a few ideas."

After being recommended the best phone for what he needed, he grabbed some accessories, a couple of chargers and a case. All while looking out of the large window that looked out into the mall periodically.

When he was ready, he walked out the store and "fake accidently" ran into Angelina.

When she saw his handsome face, she looked as if she'd just seen a ghost. "Cage, is that you?" She placed a hand over her beating heart.

Fruit.

Although he had a plan, that he, Ellison, Shane, and Savannah had gone over many times, seeing her face to face fucked up his head.

It had been years.

Her skin glowed and her hair had gotten thicker and cascaded down her back. She was wearing jeans that hugged her curves and a white top that cut low enough for him to remember the last time they fucked. She also chose to wear two diamond cuff bracelets and a black designer scarf which she tied around her neck that seemed off season.

Still, she looked amazing.

And he could tell that she was no longer using drugs.

"Cage," she looked around and into Ellison's face, who was staring from afar. She didn't know he was with Cage, but she did know he was watching. Focusing back on him she said, "What are you...what are you doing here? This is dangerous."

"Living."

"Cage, I...I don't understand. Where were you all these years? What...what happened to you?" She touched his arm as she spoke and feeling his chiseled body had her wanting to do the forbidden things again.

"I've been around."

"What does that mean? You don't know how scared I was for you. I know your mother was killed and..."

"Leave it."

"Cage..."

"What about you?" He said, choosing to skip the subject ASAP. "What you been up to?"

"I've been doing the same. But there's not a day that goes by where I don't imagine how you are. And..."

Suddenly she got quiet.

"What is it?"

"I'm...I'm just wondering if you ever think about me."

Of course he did.

In fact, the wealth he accumulated, the plan he had in mind was always to bring them together.

As a family.

But first things first.

"I been too busy to be honest," he said. "You know, I been worried about my sister and brothers so..."

"Of course,"

Shane, who was within ear hustle distance, shook his head. Believing he was doing too much.

"But since you are here, I wanna know if you took my advice."

Fruit.

"What advice?"

"About Onion."

She looked away and he could tell she didn't. Of course, he already knew the answer. He just wanted to hear her say the words.

"I wanted to. I meant to but...all I have ever known was you and Onion. You know my story. Who else in the world would want me?"

After seeing the beautiful woman Cage went on and on about, Ellison and Shane raised their hands in their minds.

They would give her the dick for sure.

She was stunning.

"You know what, we shouldn't be talking. I don't want you to get hurt." He walked down the mall and she followed. It may have seemed abrupt, but everything Cage was doing at this point was necessary.

"Cage, where you going?"

Concerned he would get away, she ran faster and looped her arm through his as if she belonged to him. Just a few minutes ago she was worried that one of the men she believed Onion had following her would see them together.

But in the moment, she didn't give a fuck.

She couldn't let him get away.

"So, who has been keeping you fed?" She asked, "Because you look healthy."

"I make do."

She wiped her hair behind her ear. "We talk about you. Both of us. I miss you. I think he does too."

His jaw twitched because he believed in his heart that either Onion, or Tino knew where his siblings were. And despite all the money he accrued, he hadn't made any headway on their location. And he was growing impatient.

And desperate.

"Is that right?"

She stopped walking. "Why do you always do that, Cage? I make a statement and then you answer with a question. As if I'm going to forget."

"I don't think you're going to forget." He touched her face and felt her tremble. "I repeat what you said so I can understand. Because my mind moves differently than it did when we were kids. I just wanna be sure. That's it."

She nodded. "Onion and I are a couple."

He knew.

"But he hasn't converted you?"

"He doesn't want to."

"But what do you want?"

In a wispy tone she said, "To be happy."

He examined her a bit closer and now focused on the scarf and the cuffs again. He knew what was going on.

Anger boiled in his body.

Grabbing her by the arm, he snatched off a cuff and saw the teeth marks. Wanting answers, he pulled her into a public men's bathroom, leaving Shane and Ellison confused.

This wasn't the plan.

They followed, while immediately going into stalls, pretending not to be listening.

"You letting that nigga drink from you?" Cage whispered.

Silence.

"Is he drinking from—."

"Yes."

He sighed. "Why didn't you leave him? Like I told you to."

"He needed me."

"That's not needing you!" He ripped the scarf off her neck, revealing more teeth marks. It floated to the wet floor. "He has access to blood. He doesn't have to use you. He's threatening your life. Reminding you each day what will happen if you left him for me."

"Cage, don't!"

He stepped closer. "The way he is now, he needs no one. He won't even turn you because in our culture, turning someone is dumb. All we want is to feed."

"*Our culture*?" She questioned.

He heard himself talking but what could he do? It was best to be honest. "Angelina, listen, I'm a part of this now." He held her hands into his. "And unlike Onion, I didn't ask to be in this world. But there's no turning back. There is for you."

"He said he will always control his urge when it comes to me. And I believe him."

He hated that nigga from the bottom of his heart. If he could have gone back in time, he would've never given her up.

It was one of his biggest mistakes.

"Cage, I don't want to talk about him."

"Awww," Shane said too loudly, in the stall.

Cage frowned.

"Do you think they're listening," she whispered.

"No, go ahead."

She took a deep breath. "All I know is I literally prayed for this moment. To be able to lay eyes on you. To know you're safe."

Cage's plan was to ask her about his family at a later time after she grew comfortable. But looking at how much it was apparent she adored him, he decided to ask now.

264   **By T. STYLES**

"Angelina, I wanna ask you something. Do you—."

"OUCH!" Shane yelled from behind the stall. It was obvious it was deliberate.

Cage glared due to being interrupted.

"What do you wanna ask me?"

Shane and Ellison exited the bathroom, stopping all conversation.

Pulling him closer, she grabbed the phone in his pocket and stored her number inside. "Call me when you settle. It doesn't have to be right now. It doesn't even have to be tomorrow; I just need to know you're good."

With that she left.

When she was gone Shane said, "You know you can't do it this soon right?"

Cage continued to focus on the door she exited, as if he could still see her beautiful face.

"Cage," Ellison yelled. "You know you have to be careful right?"

He nodded. "I know."

"Stick with the plan," Ellison begged. "And then even if she don't know where they are, when you say the right things and give her that dick, she will find them for you."

CHAPTER TWENTY-FOUR

"You Better Be Careful Where You Open Up Your Body."

Using his new cell phone. Cage consumed over five hours of social media nonstop. About his business, he researched the top influencers of the game, particularly men who had a way with women.

They were mostly Vamps but the Norms didn't know.

He studied their mannerisms.

He studied how they dressed, what they said, and even flashes of the homes they claimed to possess.

He didn't just look at the videos for the sake of consuming. He took copious notes too. He didn't want to miss a thing because if he did, his plans would be fucked up.

When there was a knock at the door, he started not to answer because he specifically told the Old Man to leave him alone. But then again, the Old Man always did what he wanted.

"Come in!" Cage yelled. The door opened and squeaked a little. "What do you want? I told you I'll be busy tonight."

"Dinner is almost ready."

Cage looked at his phone and turned it face down on his desk. "I keep telling you, you don't have to cook for me."

"I'm not cooking for you. I made enough for everybody. Now do you want some or not?"

He didn't.

266 **By T. STYLES**

But he knew, like all Vamps, it was best to consume every now and again to avoid suspicion. Because although Norms didn't know anything about them yet, they didn't want the day to arrive in the future, where they were finally discovered, only for Norms to play the tapes back in their minds. Essentially remembering who ate and who didn't.

They were sitting in front of plates of spaghetti until Cage decided to break silence. "Do you have a son?" He forked the meal around and placed small amounts in his mouth.

"Yes. How do you know?"

"Saw a picture of a dude on your wall. He looked kind of young, so I figured he was your son."

He glared. "What are you, the FBI or something?"

"You don't mind getting into my business so I figured I might as well return the favor."

"My son was killed."

Cage frowned. "I need more."

"The phrase you use...*I need more*... has to be the most narcissistic statement I ever heard."

"Are you going to tell me or not?"

"He was murdered for a seat on the bus." He paused. "They thought he hadn't paid after everybody returned from a rest stop. But he had. And was on his way to see me."

"Sorry to hear that."

"Well, that's not gonna bring him back now is it?"

Cage sat back and allowed the man to grieve.

"Losing him was the hardest thing I've ever had to experience. Losing a child in that way guarantees you'll never recover."

Cage nodded, thinking about his mother and father. "I guess that explains why you latch on to me so hard."

He slammed his fork down. "I don't latch on to you."

Cage laughed, which angered the Old Man.

"But I'm going to give you some advice, son."

"Nah, I'm good." Cage waved the air.

"Well, I'm going to give it to you anyway." He paused. "A man your age shouldn't be alone. Now I'm an old geezer, and we're thrown away the moment we can't produce enough sperm or make enough money. But you have your youth going for you. So why are you living in my basement?"

The Old Man grabbed a steak knife in preparation to butter his bread.

"I have my reasons."

"Well as long as your reasons don't conflict with mine, we good."

Cage chuckled. "Got it, Old Man. I'm not about to fight with you."

"Good, because you won't win."

When the Old Man buttered his bread, he accidentally cut his finger in the process.

Burnt cookies was stronger than ever in the air.

First, he shouldn't have used such a sharp knife, but none of that mattered at the moment, because he unknowingly opened his flesh across the table from a Vampire.

Smelling his fragrant blood, Cage immediately jumped up and grabbed the Old Man by his shirt. Slamming him against the wall, he was deciding at that moment if he should drain him dry or let him be.

By T. STYLES

Since Cage lived with him, he had been subjected to repeated conversations about how the world hated older people. Maybe Cage could do him a favor and put him out of his misery.

While feeding at the same time.

Instead, he heard his father's voice.

Control your urges and control the flesh.

He remembered that this would do nothing for his plan to reconnect his family.

"You better be careful where you open up your body, Old Man." Cage warned. "People like you could be eaten alive."

CHAPTER TWENTY-FIVE

"Hurts Less That Way."

Days later, sitting on his couch, Cage's thoughts ran crazily in his mind. One of the hardest things he had to contend with, was whether Bloom, Tatum and Flow were still alive.

The other major thought was if Onion was hurting Angelina, and if he would have to put a man who was once a good friend to death.

For now he couldn't be sure.

It was important to stay on plan.

Grabbing his cell phone, he made a call. "Hey Sexy."

Savannah giggled. "You don't have to seduce me with your words. Unless you want to finally give me some dick."

He laughed. "You already know the answer."

"Cage, when you rule The Collective, what are your plans?"

"I told you, I'm not interested in ruling shit. I just want my family safe."

"So...so how will you convert me?"

"You have to trust me. I gave you my word. You can stand on it." He paused. "Listen, I'm hungry and I was wondering if the supplier you used is still—."

"She died. Yesterday."

Cage's eyes grew.

"Right now, I'm still working on someone else to help you but—."

"Don't worry about it." Cage said. "I'll...I'll find someone."

"Cage, listen. To live like this, you must stay on brand. You don't have to hurt people to get blood. There are ways—."

"What if there are people in the world, who are better off not here? People who, if they remain alive, would do more harm than good?"

"So, you're playing God now?"

"No. But if this is going to be my life, at least until I find my family, I don't have a choice."

She sighed. "Okay, but I'll have someone else for you. I promise."

"Tell Ellis and Shane when you do."

He couldn't wait.

It was time to feed.

Ending the call, he maneuvered to an app on his phone. He could have made his selection from anybody, but he was looking for a *certain type of girl*. And so far, he had yet to find her.

Lying on the cot in his closet, he frowned when suddenly his phone dinged.

He had been chosen.

It was time.

He checked out her message.

Hey, future bae.

He shook his head and continued to read.

Your profile caught my eye and I decided to give you a heart. I don't know what you're doing tonight, but if you're free, so am I.

He sure hoped she meant it.

An hour later Cage was at the motel.

He told his guest that he would leave the door open, and if she wanted to enter, to just walk inside.

That would be the invitation.

He was pleasantly surprised to see she was punctual. Because he didn't have much time to waste.

When the door opened, he examined her for a second. She was a cute brown skin twenty-four-year-old with an adorable face, a button nose and doe eyes. And she was wearing a tight red dress that attacked the curves of her body.

It was giving WHORE.

But it smelled like FRUIT.

Closing the door behind herself she smiled when she saw him sitting on the edge of the bed.

He was wearing a black beanie hat, rolled tight and a white t-shirt that allowed her to see the many tatts caressing his body. Per usual, the chain Magnus never left his neck.

"What does Magnus mean?"

"In Latin, it means *great*."

"You're perfect," she said. "Like moving art."

"You gonna frame me?"

She giggled once. "Not unless you want me to."

"Is that right?"

"I ain't lying." She looked as if she could eat him alive as she read the passages on his dark skin.

By T. STYLES

The good thing was, Cage liked to bite too.

"You fine as shit." He told her.

Walking inside, she sat on the only chair in the room. Removing her jacket, she crossed her legs and smiled at him as if he were a succulent piece of dessert.

"I can't believe you're single," she said.

"I never said I was single."

She sighed deeply. It was obvious she was done with the small talk and shit. "Are we going to play this game all night? I mean what do you want? Because we're here for a reason."

That was true.

He chuckled. "Okay, I'm on the app because I'm looking for something as sweet as you."

"Guess you got your wish." She threw her hands up.

"Only time will tell."

She nodded and looked around the room. When she spotted what she was looking for she walked towards it. On the only shelf present sat a bottle of liquor and plastic cups.

"Thirsty?" He asked.

"I was thinking it would be okay considering you made a big deal about alcohol on the profile."

"What you talking about?"

He knew what she meant. But due to boredom, he was in the mood for games.

"Is it true that you can't handle your liquor?" She grinned. "But you still like the taste?"

"Yeah, when it comes to my guts I can't hold up." On some trap shit, he removed a sack of one-hundred-dollar bills from his pocket, counted them and stuffed them back.

She didn't miss a beat.

Saw every dollar.

But remained mum.

"I'm talking about the drunk sex part," her eyes twinkled. "Because you mentioned that too."

"Oh yeah. Ain't nothing like fucking while you high. You ever try it?"

"No but I'll do anything once."

I bet you would.

He nodded. "Well, I guess you in the right place." He winked. "So, help yourself to a drink and then get over here."

"Don't mind if I do."

She tore off the seal to the liquor while Cage sat across the room and gazed at her. She smelled sweet like a peach. And it took everything in his power to prevent his fangs from dropping too early.

After pouring herself a cup, she poured him one too.

Except, he had a little more.

He drank cup after cup. And although he felt a little buzz, a Vamp's tolerance was way higher than Norms.

That didn't stop him from faking drunk.

After three glasses, his head bobbed up and down and his eyes closed. And that was all she needed.

"You gonna be able to give me some of that D?" She asked, groping his dick.

While his head wobbled and bopped, he said, "Yeah...I...I got you, ma."

She felt he was too fine to be so sloppy but that was his problem not hers.

She was about her paper.

Within minutes she was digging into his pockets preparing to rob him blind. Thinking he was out for the count, when she finally found the money stack he flaunted, she grinned. "I swear I love me some green ass niggas. Learn how to handle your liquor."

With the cash firmly in her grasp, she was on her way out the door until he grabbed her by the wrist from behind.

How did his fine ass move so fast?

Turning around slowly, her eyes widened because she thought he was out for the count.

She thought wrong.

Fully aware and alert, he pulled her toward the bed before placing her in the middle as if she were on the center of his plate.

Kissing her with a roofie on his tongue he said, "Swallow."

She did.

"Stay there."

With his eyes on her the entire time, he locked the door and returned to the bed. Crawling on top of her, his dick stiffened as he continued to inhale her scent.

"What are you gonna do to me?"

"Do you really wanna know?"

She swallowed the lump in her throat. "Are you still gonna make love to me?"

"Is that what you want?"

"Will whatever you do hurt?"

"I can be easy. Hurts less that way."

She nodded. "Please."

Removing her panties first, he took off his jeans and boxers next. Pushing her legs apart, he entered her slowly. Why she was wet he couldn't understand.

But it felt so good.

TREASON   275

Still, he was there for other reasons.

"I'm going to bite you now, but I don't want you to scream."

She nodded, as she continued to be seduced by his long dick strokes. Preparing for the worst, her body heated up as he bit into her flesh. The harder he sucked, the wetter she got, and she found herself aroused.

That would be short lived.

Because soon, due to the pill and blood loss, she would be delirious.

And to think, she could have avoided this all if she wasn't out here scamming.

He bit down further and drank his fill.

But he would leave her with the rest.

Later, that night, Cage returned home after feasting.

He would be good for the next two days because unlike some who drank for sport, he drank to survive.

Feeding only when hungry.

As a result, his body was ripped because just like Norms, Vamps could overindulge, which would cause their bodies to fill out unnecessarily.

After taking a shower, he looked at himself in the mirror. He reasoned he was clean enough to look the part for what had to happen next.

Once dressed, he logged on to his social media account to prepare for the games. There was soft rap music in the background, and although he didn't need it, he placed a ring light not too far from his face, which caused his skin to illuminate even more.

When he was ready, he tapped the live button once and cleared his throat.

"My name is Raheem Holm and I'm here for one reason. To let the ladies know that you deserve more..." is how he started. "I'm a man, but I also have a little sister who I want to hear the truth about these niggas out here."

His tone was passionate and strong.

"Some men will take from you what you give and what you aren't prepared to let go of. They will do this without caring about how you feel. It's all about the games. Tonight, I'm going to give you 10 ways to avoid the wrong man from entering your life."

On and on Cage went listing point after point. He studied other influencers a lot, so he knew what to say and how to say it.

He was charismatic and had the perfect mashup of all the top influencers that he watched over the months. Being Vamp, he automatically had an appeal that most women couldn't resist.

After he was done seducing, he logged out and removed his clothes to put on something a bit more comfortable.

When he saw his phone light up several times on the desk, he was shocked.

"Who the fuck is that?" He said out loud.

From what he was told from Ellison and Shane, it took six months to a year to develop a following on social media. And so his plan to find his siblings was detailed, as he prepared for the long con. But what he forgot to understand was that Vamps were so seductive; they could say the least with the most effort.

When it was all said and done, after going live for the first time, over 200 women liked his post, and followed the fake account.

This was the beginning of his plan.

And it was working.

By T. STYLES

CHAPTER TWENTY-SIX

"Can I Trust You?"

The next night, Cage loaded the final box that was sitting in his kitchen.

Once it was filled, he taped it and put it next to the other boxes by the door. It didn't take long to pack everything he owned. Because his real crib was a penthouse overlooking Baltimore city and Cage knew per his plan, he needed to be ready to move at the drop of a dime.

When there was a knock at the connecting door, Cage walked over and opened it wide. On the other side was Old Man Dick.

"I guess I'm finally going to be free of you." He said, with the look of sadness on his face.

He could front all he wanted. Cage knew he cared about him. "Yep, I'm finally giving you back your crib."

"You didn't have to give me back shit. I don't be down here no ways. So, you're wasting time if you're leaving for me."

Cage could still smell the dried blood on his wound.

And he actively controlled his urges.

Reaching into his pocket, he pulled out $500 from a stack. Handing it to the Old Man, he said, "Thank you for everything. And remember what I said."

He frowned. "What's this for? You paid me three months in advance already."

"I know. Use it in case you have some repairs that need to be done."

When he felt himself getting emotional, he said, "Well, I don't need no charity. What I need you to do is get out my house since you want to get out so bad."

"You don't have to do it like this, Old Man. You—."

"Get out!" He shoved him. "Now!"

"You—."

"Leave!"

Knowing he was in pain; Cage placed the money on the table anyway. Touching him softly on the back, he said, "Thank you for everything. You still got some life in you. Don't count yourself out yet."

The Old Man nodded, not having enough fight in him to respond.

When Cage was on the other side of town, he opened the door to his new basement apartment. This was the type of thing he did. He never got comfortable in one spot, preferring to keep moving to prevent his whereabouts from being known.

There was no being on planet Earth, with a longer memory than a Vampire.

And he knew Onion was waiting.

Looking at his new temporary apartment that was recently furnished, he pushed most of the boxes

By T. STYLES

against the wall, electing only to unload the one that mattered.

It included his camera stand and lighting.

Grabbing his cell, he dialed a number and waited. Flopping in a chair, he ran his hand down his face and said, "Angelina..."

"Cage?" Her tone was breathy and alluring.

"What's up with you?"

"I...I thought you were going to run away again."

"Maybe I did and now I'm back. For you."

She laughed.

"I need to see you."

"Don't play games with me, Cage."

"Where's the joke? Can you get away from him or not?"

"Give me the location."

He gave her the address which she recorded diligently.

"I'll be there in five," she said.

"Can I trust you?"

"If you have to ask..."

"Can I trust you, Angelina?" He said firmer.

"Of course, you can."

"Then come alone."

The moment he hung up his cell phone rang again. It was the Old Man. "What's up?"

"They came. Just like you said."

"Are you safe?"

"Yep. Faked senile like you told me. So they left me alone."

The fireplace crackled as Onion sat in his lounge.

Feeling like a failure, he was waiting for an important phone call when suddenly he saw Angelina rush out of the bedroom. Her long hair ran down her back and the tight jeans she wore sexually assaulted her curves.

Damn she fine. He thought.

"You look beautiful," he grinned. "Are you still mine?"

She looked over at him and quickly looked away. "Forever and always."

He stood up and walked over to her. "Have you rethought my marriage proposal?"

She grabbed her purse. "I thought you said you were going to wait until I asked you this time."

He glared. "Don't play games. You'll either be my wife or you'll be nothing."

She looked up into his chocolate face. Over the years, he got even finer. "Give me a little more time."

"I'm getting impatient. Don't make me have to hurt people."

She stepped back. "What does that mean?"

"You know."

She stood on her tiptoes and kissed his lips, just as his phone rang. Rushing over to it, he answered.

"I'll be home soon," she ran out the door.

"What's the word?" He asked on the cell phone.

"He got away again," Cheddar said. "Some old man answered the door. But he was half crazy."

"Fuck! How do we keep missing him?"

"I'm not sure, but he may have perfected his senses. And can feel us before we get there."

"Nah, that nigga can't do all of that. We just gotta be smarter that's all."

"Maybe you're right. But Tino's getting impatient too. He's tired of what he says are excuses from you. Says he wants Cage now."

"Well he's gonna have to wait."

"Do you really want me to tell him that?"

Onion walked up to the fireplace. "Nah...tell him I'm close."

Cage and Angelina were sitting in a park next to what was referred to as the Lover's tunnel. They had been there for fifteen minutes and if someone were to glance upon them, they would think they were in love.

"I can't believe all of the stupid shit we did when we were kids." Angelina said, remembering their free-spirited days.

"I don't know why." Cage shrugged. "But it's all a blur to me."

"Well I remember everything. We didn't have a care in the world. Like nothing mattered." She looked into his eyes before looking away. He had gotten so much more attractive that his looks had her questioning her own beauty. "I miss those days."

Cage examined her closely. "Are you taking care of yourself?"

"Why?" She looked down. "You gonna come rescue me?"

"Do you need to be rescued?"

"The only thing I need is an understanding of the questions that I have. And for you to finally talk to me."

"I've kept it one hundred with you, Angelina."

"That's not what I feel."

"I want to say something, but I don't want you to take it the wrong way." He said skipping the subject.

"Okay, now I'm worried."

"I don't want you to be scared either."

"Then what do you want?" She glared.

"I know I broke your heart in the shower that day, and to be honest, I will answer to that for the rest of my life. But I did that because--."

"You felt sorry for Onion."

"Not just that. I thought I didn't deserve you. Because of what I did to my father."

She looked away.

"What is it?" He asked.

"Don't do this, Cage. Not now."

"Don't do what? Express how I feel? Because I'm tired of lying. Will you give me a chance? A real chance to make you happy?"

"Do you have a death wish?"

"Meaning?" He glared.

"Cage, don't be stupid. You and I both know if he found us together, he would murder you, and suck me dry. He told us that to our faces."

"Let me worry about Onion."

She looked at him closer. "This is really about your sister and brothers, isn't it?"

Standing up she looked down at him.

He rose too.

"You are still as beautiful as the first day I saw you in my father's church." He kissed her on the forehead, the cheeks, and lips. "Be my woman, Angelina. I'm begging you."

"I'm not giving you an invitation over my soul."

"Fuck your soul. I'm after your heart."

"Cage, don't—."

"Do you want me or not?" He said louder, causing a few people walking by to stop what they were doing and listen.

"You picked the wrong time to ask, Cage. And I'm sorry, but I can't. Because I don't want to be responsible for him...for him..."

"For him what?"

"Hurting you and your family." She ran away.

He got the answer he wanted.

Onion did know where they were.

And more importantly, they were alive.

Now he could proceed as planned.

The next night Cage was sitting in front of his cell phone.

In a matter of days, he accumulated over 500,000 followers on social media, and they were devoted to him in a way that felt cult-like.

On the surface it looked as if he was simply giving advice to women who needed him the most. A little like his father, except instead of opening it up to the world, Cage was ministering to women only.

But he had other motives.

Standing in front of a window, he held the phone against his ear. "Are you ready for the next move?" Shane asked.

"I am." Cage said.

"But are you sure nobody will—."

"I thought about this plan for years at Savannah's crib. It will work." Cage said strongly. "Now look, I gotta go."

After hanging up with him and getting situated in front of his camera, he took a deep breath. "Good evening, ladies. First, I want to say thank you for your support and loyalty. I don't know what I would do without you, and I do mean each one of you."

The hearts and flowers rained on his screen from the love he was receiving.

"As I mentioned last week, I have an announcement to make. Talking to you from the video seems so impersonal. It's important to me that you know who I am physically. That way you can see I speak from the heart. Because each one of you deserves happiness. So I'm hosting an event just for you. Just for us."

More hearts rained and even coins which were virtual money.

"I want you all to come to this event. I want to see your faces. I want to tell you what you've meant to

286   By T. STYLES

me over these past weeks. It'll be an event with just us." He chuckled lightly. "And it's free." So many hearts covered the side that it looked like a thick red line. "Click the link in my bio. It leads directly to an invitation you must accept. And when you do, I'll see you that night."

CHAPTER TWENTY-SEVEN

"Fruit From The Street."

The hole in the wall that held Cage's event was epic.

He hired the best caterers, and the decorations were top notch. Although it was supposed to be his introduction to the world party, Cage had other plans.

As Shane and Ellison ushered in beautiful women after beautiful women, they were all giddy with excitement to meet their fearless leader. Not only did they attend on time per his request, but they also wore his signature color.

Red.

With every woman in attendance, there was one thing that became clear, not a single man was invited.

But you could smell the fruit from the street.

Some ladies wondered why it was women only, although they should not have been shocked since he said it would be a night for just them.

As the waiters kept their glasses overflowing with champagne, they whispered to one another, while the music boomed from the speakers.

"Where is he?" They asked.

"Do you think he's as handsome as he looks on social media? Or did he use a filter?"

"Do you think he'll like me?"

By T. STYLES

Question after question was piled on one another, although as the night went on, without Cage, there were no answers.

Truthfully, they didn't care if there were answers or not because the anticipation alone was enough to make them wait.

After all, they have been following Cage for weeks.

His advice had some of them breaking up with their boyfriends and others demanding more in their relationships.

So, to them he was everything.

And then something happened...

The uninvited came.

Damn, the Vamps were fine!

They stood out like diamonds atop a recently paved black road. They were perfect, and not one had a scar anywhere on their bodies.

They knew how to speak, had shiny cars on the curb, money in their pockets and could seduce easily.

Their weapon was Norms' vanity.

Superficiality.

With extreme confidence after being given an invitation by the hosts they piled into the hall.

They too were dressed for the occasion, in mostly red.

After much speculation, some of the women thought that perhaps Cage brought them there so that the broken-hearted could find love. Maybe he tricked them to come so he could introduce them to the perfect men who were on their level.

You see these weren't average looking men.

They came in an array of colors from Vanilla to Dark Chocolate Cherry. So there was somebody for everybody. And as long as you had blood in your body, be it fat, short or skinny, they found you attractive.

The plan was going better than Cage ever could have hoped.

But nothing good came without pain.

Back at his temporary apartment, Cage stood in the middle of his living room on the phone.

He was bracing for the worst.

"You were right," Shane said. "They piled inside and we're ready."

Cage nodded. "I knew it would work. I remember being at Affinity club when I just took The Fluid. So many women were in the club that they could smell fruit from the street. I just needed to put my event in the right place. Amongst Onion's men."

"How did you know they would come?"

"Because they're young. And greedy. A Vamps' flaw. Now proceed with the plan."

"This is going to be a hard night. Will you be okay?"

"I will. Just make sure you—"

"We'll take care of the ladies. They will be unharmed." He paused. "But take care of yourself. We can't risk anything happening to you."

"Shane..."

"Yes?"

"Thanks for riding."

"Til' the end."

Cage nodded and hung up.

After closing the windows in his hideaway apartment, he laid down. Because he knew in a matter of moments, things would change.

To say that he was prepared was an understatement.

And still, it would undoubtedly be one of the most painful nights of his life.

And yet he didn't give a fuck.

If he couldn't have his family, The Collective could suck his dick.

Face up in his closet looking at the ceiling, he took a deep breath. The pain came on soft at first, and then heavier. Unable to deal, he released a moan when suddenly his head rocked. It was the kind of pain that one couldn't escape from even if they tried.

To balance the agony, he placed a palm on each side of his face as he attempted to squeeze the sensation away.

But it would do no good.

Because in his party there were flutes circulating with champagne tainted with Vitamin D.

And every vampire in the building, in an effort to fit in, took a glass with hefty sips.

And since many were in Cage's Fluid line, he felt pain like he couldn't imagine as each met their death. The sensation became so excruciating that squeezing his head would do no good.

He would have to deal.

But at least Onion would be fucked up too.

In the end, he succumbed to the torture and passed out.

By T. STYLES

CHAPTER TWENTY-EIGHT
"It's The Choice You'll Have To Make Alone."

Something was wrong with Onion and Angelina was worried.

Since she thought he was invincible, she was shocked to see him in bed in a tortured state of being. Most of the men at his side went down too.

Tino, who was higher in the fluid line, was not impacted because the elders, who were in his line, were not at the party.

They would never fall for such frivolous traps.

Angelina was clueless.

When her phone rang, she started not to answer, but decided that stepping away from Onion for a few moments would do her some good. After all, since he was feeling so bad, the rage he exhibited toward her was great.

She was his punching bag.

From telling her how worthless she was, to refusing to talk to her, she felt like there was nothing she could do to help. Even at night, when they used to stay up, since daytime was out of the question, Onion chose to shut her out instead.

Taking a deep breath she said, "Hello."

"Angelina...it's Cage." His voice was weak.

She looked behind her once. "I can't talk right—."

"I know this is a bad time."

"It's actually *the* worst time ever."

"I get it. But I need you to come see me."

She thought about Onion. "I'm sorry. But the answer is no. Onion is doing so badly and—."

"Please. I need you. Will you come to me?"

Who was she fooling?

He was the love of her life, and the reason she said no to Onion's proposal.

She took a deep breath. "I'm on my way."

Twenty-five minutes later, Angelina had entered Cage's apartment through an unlocked door. He was in the bedroom, under the sheets.

For some reason, Cage looked worse than Onion.

His skin was dry and didn't have its sheen that she had been accustomed to since he took the fluid and reentered her life.

"What has happened to you? I'm confused. Onion is down. His friends are down. What's going on?"

"I can't involve you."

She placed her purse down on the side table. "Wait, you can't involve me, but you invite me over?"

"Angelina, please."

"Don't *Angelina please* me! I need to know what happened and I need to know now. Why are you and Onion ill?"

"I'll explain to you later. I promise."

Suddenly, she received a text message.

By T. STYLES

**I know I ain't been shit. And I get why you needed to leave tonight. Just come back home. Please.
I have to tell you...**

"Is everything okay?" Cage asked, interrupting her before she could finish reading.

She sighed. "Yes. It's Onion. He just hit my phone."

He sat up in bed and shifted a little. "What does he want?"

Returning to the message it said...

Cage put a hit on us. If you see him anywhere, just know you can't trust him. Be safe. And come home soon.

Looking up from her screen she asked, "Is it true?"

He looked down. "He told you?"

"That's not answering my question." She dropped her phone into her purse. "Is it true or not?"

"What did he say?"

"Why would you hurt your own people?" She stepped closer to the bed. "And what happened to the culture talk? And all that shit."

Despite still being weak, he sat up. "For years, I begged someone to tell me where my brothers and sister were. And I been met with nothing but disrespect while they attempted to kill me and ruin my life. And I'm tired. So, at this point I'll do whatever I gotta do, even if it means wiping all these niggas off the planet."

TREASON   295

"Cage, if you do this you won't win. How will you find them if you're incapacitated? It doesn't make sense."

"A lot of things don't make sense. It took some time, but I've come to understand that this is my fault and I just wanna make things right. I should have never killed my father. I should have never gone over the Ledgers' house. But there's nothing I can do about that now. What's done is done. But I can save you. I can save my siblings."

"Cage...I...what if they...what if they are dead?"

He lowered his brow. "I know you know that they're alive. You all but told me the other day."

She looked down and flopped in her chair. "I discovered something one night, when he was drinking from me."

He leaned closer. "What?"

"Whenever you drink directly from a body, and a question is asked, Vamps have a tendency to tell the truth. At first I thought it was a fluke, but since he likes to have sex with me, while drinking from my body, I asked him a different question at a later time. This time it was about your family."

"What...what did he say?"

"He told me they were alive. But that was a year ago."

Cage sighed in relief.

"I knew it." He smiled. "Look, good friends of mine are missing."

"Who?"

"Their names are Savannah, Shane and Ellison. So, I need you to help me so I can find out where my brothers and sister are."

She was disappointed. "Cage..."

296   By T. STYLES

"Will you help me? Please, baby."

"Of course, I will help you. You know that. What do you need?"

Silence.

"Cage..."

"I need blood. I'm too weak to hunt."

She rose slowly from her seat. "Blood? I don't have access to any. Onion guard's his so much that..."

Angelina focused on him a bit harder.

"Wait, you want to drink from...from me?" She whispered.

"Ordinarily I would never ask you to do this, but I can tell that you've become accustomed to giving of yourself in this way."

"What does that mean?"

"The marks on your neck and wrists."

"But you told me to never trust you." She backed up slowly.

"I did. So, it's the choice you will have to make alone."

She walked around the room and looked at him. "If I do this, no more poisonings. No more hurting your own. Because if you do, I will leave you forever."

"I'm not saying I'll do it again, but if I do, why would it bother you?"

"Because I...I..." She sat down. "I don't understand how all of this works. I don't fully get the fluid line or any of it. All I know is I care about you and I care about Onion, too. So if I do this, you have to promise no more attacks."

Silence.

"Cage, promise me."

He sighed. "Since my mother died, I said I would never make a promise I wouldn't keep."

"So say the words."

"I don't know who else I'll kill to find them, but I promise you that for now, there will be no more attacks."

One by one she kicked off her shoes. Next she removed her jeans, followed by her shirt.

He looked at her body and exhaled. "What are you doing?"

She removed her bra and presented her full breasts. Nipples erect, they were perfect in every way. And although she was across the room, he longed to touch her.

To lick her.

To taste her.

To drink her sweetness.

Almost naked, she removed her panties and crawled into bed. "I want you to make love to me...and then you can--"

"No!" He said firmly. "It's too dangerous."

"These are my rules." She kissed him on the chest. "All or nothing. Finish what you started."

Softly, she kissed his neck, chin, face and lips. She smelled so juicy he could no longer play games.

Pushing her down, he eased on top of her warm body. His dick was rock hard as he moved toward her wet pussy. Looking into her eyes, he tried his best to gain control of his urges.

"I feel your heart pounding," she said. "And still I trust you." She raised her chin and exposed her neck.

Gliding in and out of her body, he lowered his head and opened his mouth, within seconds he pressed his fangs deep, while sucking the fruit from her.

Because he was fucking her slow, she felt little to no pain. And when he went faster, deeper, and longer with the dick strokes, she could feel nothing.

Snaking his hands up under her ass, he lifted her closer to his body. Now he was so far inside of her, there was nowhere else to go.

"Cage, I love you," she said.

But he couldn't hear her.

He was in a trance.

The juice from her body tasted so sweet that he was taking his fill. At this rate if he didn't stop soon, he would undoubtedly kill the love of his life.

"Cage..." She whispered, feeling herself being brought closer to an orgasm. "Cage..."

He continued to fuck and suck, until his heartrate slowed down.

She was no longer Angelina, she was a feast.

Suddenly he came and splashed his cum deeply into her body. And then he smelled the scent of cocoa butter on her skin.

This was not food.

This was his one true love.

Removing his fangs from her neck, he quickly looked down at her. Blood drops dripped on her cheek.

What had he done?

Her eyes were shut and he felt dizzy. If she was dead, he would kill himself within the hour.

"Ange...Angelina."

Her eyes remained closed.

"Angelina...baby...are you okay?"

Slowly she opened her lids and looked at him. With a smile on her face she said, "I'm good. How do you feel?"

Relieved, he kissed her deeply, before holding her in his arms.

By T. STYLES

CHAPTER TWENTY-NINE

"I Don't Require Love."

Onion was focused on his phone, with great intensity.

Why hadn't Angelina called or come home?

Since the fiasco that Cage orchestrated with his LADIES ONLY EVENT, that lured vamps in his fluid line, he wasn't himself.

The good thing about it was, not many members of their fluid line remained anymore, so they weren't as vulnerable.

His body was weak, and he wasn't sure when the pain would go away. Plus when he realized Angelina had yet to return, the betrayal he felt in that moment was very great.

Still in his thoughts, he was hopeful that he could get through to her when there was a knock at the door. But when it opened and he saw Tino, the air was pressed from his lungs.

Now that he thought about it, it could only be the boss. No one else would dare open the door without authorization.

"How are you holding up?" Onion asked.

"As good as to be expected," Tino admitted. "I can't believe Cage went this far."

Onion frowned. "Why can't you believe it? He's been holding a vendetta against us for the longest."

Tino shook his head. "Do you understand the hate and commitment you must have to kill over fifty vampires in one night? Many of them in his own

TREASON   301

line?" He sat on the edge of his bed. "He's making it clear that he would go to any lengths to find his family."

"Forgive me for my disrespect but you sound like you admire him."

"I wouldn't say I admire him. But the further he goes to find his siblings makes me proud he's of my bloodline. I just wish I knew where they were." He turned to face him. "So I can handle them myself. Do you know where they are? Do you have his family?"

"Sir, I told you I didn't."

Tino nodded.

"But I do have to tell you something, and it's something I've been holding on to for this moment," Onion continued.

"I'm listening."

"I can have Cage taken out tonight."

"Taken out?" He frowned.

"Murdered."

Tino glared. "What are you talking about? Where is he?"

"I think he's with a friend."

"I told you he's never to be touched. I want him brought to me. Tonight."

This enraged him. "How can you say you don't want him taken out?" He spoke louder than he ever had. "I mean look at everything he did. Look at all the people he killed. Doesn't he deserve to get what's coming to him?"

"Onion, I have come to care for you like a son. But I don't know how else to tell you because at this point, we've spoken about this at great lengths. But I will try once more, in the hopes that you never ask me again."

"Yes, sir."

"Cage is never to be touched. Ever. Not under any circumstances. He's my family. He's my son. And I still believe that at some point he will come around when it's clear we are all he has left."

"He will never love you as a father like I do."

"I don't require love. I require those of my bloodline, to fall in line. And he will. Eventually. Because if he doesn't, I will make things very hard for him. It's already working. He can never rest his head in peace. He has to move regularly."

"So, you going to let him get away with killing fifty of his own people?"

"He'll pay. He's paying now. Because nothing living can survive the guilt from harming their own."

Onion was consumed with jealousy. "Well, what's your plan? Now that he's come out in the open."

Tino sighed. "You asked me before what I wanted done to him. And I told you at that time that my plan is my own. So why are you asking me again?"

"You're right, sir."

Tino focused on him. "But I will say this, until he acts right, everything he loves will die."

Onion felt sick. Because he knew Cage was in love with Angelina.

Would he kill her too?

"Whoever she is, will be my target." Tino continued. "As a matter of fact, where's your girl? I hear he favors her."

Onion rose and poured two glasses of wine. Handing one to Tino, he held the other one himself. "Probably out shopping. You know how these women are."

"I do. Have her contact me when she returns."

"Of course."

"Cage is a creature of habit and habit gets a lot of people hemmed up." Tino took a deep sip. "I've waited for this moment for a long time. And I'm going to see to it that things go—."

Suddenly Tino's eyes widened, and the glass fell from his hand before shattering against the floor.

It wasn't until that moment that Tino realized that Cage wasn't the only one willing to go through pain to get revenge.

"I'm sorry," Onion said, placing down the glass he did not drink from. "And I hope you will come to respect my decision, as you do Cage's."

Tino's eyes widened in fear due to having drank the Vitamin D oil, which Onion placed in the bottle just for this night.

But Tino wasn't the only person in agony.

Onion grabbed the sides of his head to relieve some of the pressure. The torture he felt was so great, due to being in Tino's direct fluid line that his knees buckled.

"Why would you do this?" Tino muttered, as he writhed in pain.

Unfortunately for him, he got no response as Onion became a victim of his own revenge and dropped to the floor.

CHAPTER THIRTY
"And When You Do, I'll Be There To Help."

After going down again in pain, Cage wished he could go back to the moment when his mother begged him not to go to the Ledger's house. But hindsight ain't help shit because he had taken the journey of no return.

To make matters worse, he spent days trying to locate Ellison, Shane, and Savannah, for fear that they were caught up due to participating in his LADIES ONLY EVENT. Having no one on his team complicated things more, because he lost three people he knew he could trust.

People who could walk in the daytime.

When his phone rang, he yanked it but saw a number he didn't recognize.

Sitting on the edge of his bed, he asked, "Who is this?"

"A friend of a friend."

"Just because you a friend of a friend don't mean you not my enemy. Now how did you get my number?"

She laughed. "I'm a friend of your teacher. Gordon."

Cage stood up and sat back down, due to not having his full strength.

Gordon said someone would be reaching out when the time was right. Was this it?

Because up until that moment, he always assumed it was Savannah.

"He was going to have me help you when you first went on the run. And if I had, perhaps you wouldn't have done some of the stupid shit I've seen you do since."

"Be careful how you talk to me."

"No, son, you should've been careful. Because I can't believe you went as far as to harm your own people. Just to get revenge."

The hairs on the back of Cage's neck rose. "What do you know about it?"

"I know more than I should. I know that you are of Tino's direct bloodline. And I know that's the only reason you survived after all of these years."

Caged laughed. "I survived because I was smart at—."

"You survived because even though you are hunted with orders to bring you to Tino, they were also told that you were not to be harmed. But that's changed now."

He frowned, "What?"

"Have you wondered why you were weakened a second time?"

Cage thought about her question. The first time he was weakened, he prepared for it. Even buckled down in his closet for the long ride since his event was created to harm Vampires.

But the second time he went weak he didn't understand what was happening. He figured someone major had died in his line. To be honest he didn't care.

But this woman, whoever she was, seemed to have the answers.

"I'm listening."

"Tino is dead."

Cage stumbled a bit. "That's not true."

"You sound upset. I thought you hated him."

"I'm not upset. I just don't believe you."

"Believe what you will, it's of no consequence to me. But what I want you to know is this...you are the rightful successor. And hurting your own will only drive a wedge between us."

"Us?" He laughed. "All I want are my brothers and sister to come back to me. And if it's true that Tino's gone, all of this is for nothing."

"If that's truly your goal, you're going about it the wrong way."

"They went about it the wrong way, the moment they decided to take them from me. And I'm just finishing what they started."

"At some point, you'll stop being so arrogant. And when you do, I'll be there to help. Until then, the name is Arabia. I'll be in contact."

Cage walked out of the room and looked over at the recliner at Angelina.

When he went down the second time, he required so much blood from her that it weakened her in ways he hadn't prepared for.

As a result, her skin was grainy, and her body was fragile.

And if he didn't do something right away, he feared she would be dead in under an hour.

"Did you tell Onion about the oil? To kill Vampires."

"No. Of course not." She paused. "Who was on the phone?" She asked.

He wanted to tell her the truth, but he knew she would blame him for killing Tino. Since he killed fifty vampires and JoJo.

Kneeling he touched her leg, "Nobody you know."

"Are you lying to me?"

"No, Angelina." He despised her weakened state. "I thought I said don't trust me?" He felt like shit.

She giggled. "That's what you want to say to me on my dying day?"

"I'm not going to let you die." He rubbed her leg feeling like shit for using her in such a way. "I have someone coming to help you. They're going to put an IV in your arm and give you some fluids. But you have to eat too."

"What about you Cage? You aren't strong enough right now without blood. And I can't give it to you."

"I'm going to do what I have to do. But there's no way I can see taking from you anymore. You'll be fine. I'm sure of it."

By T. STYLES

After learning that Tino was dead, Cage needed to think clearly. And to do that, he needed blood. So he went to a district that he frequented in the past when he wanted to find answers about his siblings.

After researching for years and speaking to those who were willing to talk in Onion's squad, he learned that at least one of the Vamps close to Tino's line was gay.

But now he was back in the district, not to find answers.

But to find blood.

And he knew exactly who to get it from.

Dressed in a trench coat with the collars popped, Cage walked down the street with his hands tucked in his pockets. After some time, he happened upon Ziggy. He was muscular but wore a blonde wig and high heels that didn't make him feminine in the least.

Still, he saved him for last.

Back in the day he bullied Cage daily in high school.

And my, had the tables turned.

For Cage's purposes, to drink fully, he would do. Especially since he had fallen so far down the drug hole that he didn't recognize Cage's face.

"You see something you like?" Ziggy asked.

"Do you remember me?"

"No. Should I?"

Cage smiled.

"Now do you like what you see or what?" Ziggy asked.

"That depends."

"On what?"

"On if you're my type."

Ziggy giggled. "Look at me." He raised his arms. "I'm everybody's type."

Cage nodded.

Still, it was time for the invitation.

"Would you like to take a drive with me?" Cage asked.

It took a moment.

Ziggy had yet to accept the invitation.

"A drive huh? That's different."

He stepped closer. "Do you accept or not?"

Finally, he said, "Yes."

Once he was in his car, while remembering every torturous thing he did to him as a child, Cage sucked him dry.

By T. STYLES

CHAPTER THIRTY-ONE
"The Elders Have All Left."

When Onion woke up after his coma-like pain session, due to having murdered Tino, he learned that once again, Angelina never returned home. The rage he felt was compounded with the fact that he wasn't in full health.

He needed to get strong soon if he would get revenge.

And then he would kill her.

Going to his refrigerator, the first thing he did was down three cups of blood. With every drop he felt stronger and more like himself. Unlike so many who weren't wealthy enough to feast right away, due to the physical damage caused by Tino's death, he had all he could drink.

Sitting in the kitchen, he was about to go for another cup until Cheddar walked up to him. He was a trusted general in Tino's clan.

Now he worked for him. "I have to talk to you."

"Sure, you do." Onion sighed, walking to the fridge to get another. "What is it this time?"

"Half of The Collective has left."

He sat the cup on the table. "Again?"

Cheddar frowned.

"What do you mean half of the squad left?" He took his seat.

"They're angry with you for killing Tino, and from what I'm told, they're conversations taking place about your death."

Onion situated to the left in his chair. "Are you a part of these conversations?"

"If I was, I wouldn't be here."

He took a sip and wiped his mouth with the back of his hand. "Well, we all know with Tino dead that a hit can't be placed on my head. I'm in charge." He was arrogant to the Gods.

"That's not true."

Onion frowned.

"Although no Vampire can kill you, someone with the direct bloodline to Tino can."

Onion glared. "And who would that be?"

"You know, sir."

He knew but still said his name, "My childhood friend. Cage."

"At this point, I have to tell you something else...the elders have all left."

Now Onion was worried.

Without their influence things could get out of hand. "Why?"

"They say you're young and reckless. And they won't witness the demise of the generation."

Onion shook his head. "What does that mean?"

"Anyone with respect and honor is no longer on your side. The only ones that remain are the darkest. They have no code. They have no morals, and that makes them dangerous."

He smirked, not seeing the issue.

"As long as I have them, where's the problem?" Onion smiled. "Sounds like the weak have fled leaving me with the best. Set up a meeting with all those on my side. I want to talk to them. Now."

By T. STYLES

In a closed east Baltimore restaurant, the rain pounded from the sky as Onion walked into a room full of Vamps who were tired of the old way of thinking that the elders possessed.

Since he was Tino's right hand, they were eager to hear his plan.

"As you all know, Tino is gone." He said plainly, as he looked around at Vamps who were seated as if they were waiting to be served. "And with him, the old ways went too." He beat his chest once. "Now I'm in charge. And the only thing that will change, is that with me in charge, I won't be the only Vamp making money. With my plan we feed and drink together."

"But what about Cage?" West Coast, a new aged pimp who sold women off the net asked.

"This is why I invited you all here. If we gonna be in control, he must die. We can't have two kings. And we have to do it tonight. Before the elders find him and try to take me out."

"Where do we start?"

"Wake up your best men! Wake up the streets! Kill that nigga. Tonight. A blood bounty is officially on his head!"

TREASON   313

Cage's phone rang off the hook nonstop.

And from what he was told, he would be dead within the hour.

He was back in his car when he received a call from an ally he hired. He needed to know about Angelina who was on the I.V. "She looks good sir. The fluids are flowing and she's drinking Ensure."

"Don't let her die."

"We aren't anywhere near that stage. But, sir, there's something else."

Cage shifted in his seat. "What?"

"I don't know if she told you, but we aren't at your house anymore. We're at a hotel."

"Why was she moved?" He frowned.

"I don't wanna get involved. But she said she heard you killed Tino. And you broke your promise."

He shook his head, not believing they were blaming him for the one crime he didn't commit. But he was a Vampire killer.

Technically, the accusation was on brand.

"But I'm the one paying you." Cage said. "So where is she?"

"Maybe you should call her."

Hanging up with him, he hit Angelina's phone immediately.

She didn't answer.

And he was devastated.

With Ellison, Shane and Savannah gone, he was alone. He couldn't lose her too.

What was he to do?

A half-moon sat on top of Baltimore city as he drove down the street going well under the speed limit. The leather seat was as soft as his completely tatted body and his chocolate skin illuminated in such a way, it made him look as if he were brushed with a filter.

But nah.

This man was perfection.

And still, there were many who wanted him dead. Snuffed out.

He was on borrowed time.

Calling Angelina again, he breathed a sigh of relief when she answered. "You done with me?"

"Cage, I have to get well."

He sank deeper. Scratched his muscular chest and sighed. "And you know I want that for you. Can I come to where you are?"

"Why?"

"Because I may not make it tonight."

"Don't say that."

"It's true. You know I'm a dead man."

Silence.

"Can I come over to wherever you are, baby?"

"So you can hurt me too? Like you did Tino? Because the only people you care about is your family. I won't fall for the trap."

"You're family. And I'll leave if you say so."

"Since when do you do what someone else asks?"

"Yes or—."

Suddenly three dark blue Jeeps pulled in front of his truck. When he tried to back up, he saw three more.

Shaking his head, he smiled.

"Cage, what's happening?"

"I'm probably about to die."

In each truck, four men exited. In the end, twenty-four men surrounded his Audi and all but two had weapons.

They were spectacles to behold.

Every one of them stood well over six feet. They were shirtless, wearing grey sweatpants and from any distance the dick prints showed through clearly.

Long locs dripped down most of their backs. While the others chose to wear theirs up in buns.

"Cage..." Angelina said.

"Hey, beautiful," He was calm despite seeing his life flash before his gaze.

The men moved closer, in sync, pack like.

"Yes." She said.

"Yes what?"

"Yes you can come see me."

He laughed softly at the irony. "You would give me the okay at the worst time."

He heard her crying.

"Head up, shawty. Because I need you to hear me."

She sniffled. "O...okay."

"It wasn't me. I would never do what was said. And I didn't kill Tino. I didn't lie to you. This had to be Onion."

The leader raised his hand.

Cage knew when his hand dropped, it would be over.

Under his silent command, each man outside aimed squarely in Cage's direction. At that distance, and with the number of bullets having his name on them, he would be severely injured in twenty seconds at best. And after that, one injection of Vitamin D would take him out forever.

316   By T. STYLES

"If something happens to me, I don't want you with him," Cage said. "He's dangerous. So promise me."

Slowly the leader's hand began to drop and he reminded him of Magnus.

But why?

"Never." She said. "I will never be with Onion again."

Guns aimed.

And he braced for the worst.

They fired.

But instead of the glass shattering under the weight of bullets, he saw they were being shot over the car instead. Whipping his head around, he noticed a fleet of cars behind him.

He could tell by the rain smell in the air, that they were his people.

That they were Vamp.

And that Onion had placed a blood bounty on his head.

Focusing back on the men ahead, he squinted to see them clearer. He didn't recognize their odor, but he would never forget it.

And then something happened.

He recognized them.

They had shown up to his father's church long ago, before Magnus had them escorted out.

Confused, Cage exited the car and walked toward the back. He needed to see who just tried to kill him first. There he bared witness to Vampires laying out on the ground in agony.

The men who fired weren't trying to kill him.

They were saving his life.

Slowly the men in front of the car all walked over to Cage. "I take it you don't know them, because you're well."

Cage frowned. "I don't understand."

"Had they been in your fluid line, you would be in pain."

Now he got it. And it proved even more that Onion was involved. Because he never would've sent people in his line to do the dirty work.

"How did you shoot them?"

"With bullets."

"We don't die from bullets."

"You do if they're laced with D."

Cage glared. "How did you know about that?"

"Most of the powerful Vamps in town have been down for weeks. It didn't take us long to find out that Tino was dead. After a little more research, we learned what you did with the Vitamin D at your LADIES ONLY event, and how you killed JoJo. In doing that, you exposed yourself, son. And your people too."

"Then what is your business with me?"

"The only thing I'm interested in is Bloom, Flow and Tatum."

Cage saw red. "Why are you so interested in my family?"

"Son, how much do you know about your father?"

He glared. "Don't come at me about Tino."

"I'm talking about Magnus."

Cage crossed his arms over his chest. "Who sent you?"

"Arabia. She heard about this hit. Now come with us."

"I have to be careful." Cage said, dropping his hands. "If they think I killed Tino, the city will be looking for me."

"You're safe with us." They all raised guns laced with D bullets. "Trust."

CHAPTER THIRTY-TWO
"With Us, They Are Safe."

Cage was in a library that was closed for the night. He felt it was strange meeting there and at the same time it seemed to work. The many books prevented sound from resonating throughout which made it perfect for a serious private conversation.

"Did you kill him?" Row asked Cage. "Did you murder Magnus?"

Cage took a deep breath and glanced around the library. They all looked powerful, and he reasoned telling the truth could get him killed.

"I did."

Canelo and Shannon, growled. But Row raised his hand, silencing them instantly.

"You were seduced, weren't you?" Row asked. "By Tino or JoJo?"

"JoJo." Cage was surprised that he wasn't angrier. "I didn't know I was being seduced at first although it's no excuse. Had I known who Tino, and JoJo were, I would've stayed the fuck away. But I was a kid, and I was...I was young and dumb."

"You're young and dumb now." Row responded.

Cage glared. "If you want my support, you better be careful with how you come at me."

"I'm not here for your support. I'm here to find my niece and nephews."

"Niece and nephews?"

"Yes."

"I need more."

By T. STYLES

"Magnus was my brother, and your siblings are related to me by blood."

Cage glared. "So, you found them?"

"We tried. While the Vamps were down after Tino was murdered we were all over town. All of you were weakened so it was easy to check every hole. Every building. And every closet. But through all our efforts, we still came up short. And then I learned from Arabia that there was a hit on your head."

He now saw how powerful the strange caller was.

"Listen, all we want are your brothers and sister. Their absence doesn't affect you. But it affects us."

"I'm not interested in this shit between the Wolves, or Vamps. I'm interested in my siblings who share my blood." He beat his chest "And if you want to convince me to hand them over you better start by making clear what your intentions are."

"Your father was alpha. When he was younger, even as a child, he was excellent at keeping us together. Although most of us dabbled in every industry in the world...from corporate America to the streets, he was respected by all, and his respect kept honor amongst us. But when he fell in love with your mother, everything changed."

"Why?"

"First of all, I'm not sure if you know much about our culture but women go through quite a painful scenario when we breed. Our penises are long, not because they're used for pleasure, but the length allows us to increase our chances of getting our women pregnant by 100%. A wolf's female's body will remain molded to the man she has chosen for life, making her his forever."

"Why are you telling me about your dicks?" He frowned.

"Because a Norm, like your mother, every time she has sex with a wolf, runs the possibility of not only destroying her organs, but also of killing her. So, we didn't understand why he was so dead set on being with Lala. When the act of making love could take her life alone."

"No wonder he didn't want you around." Cage said to Row.

"He took our questioning of his logic as disrespect and ran away with her while she was pregnant with you." Canelo said.

"And that's not all," Shannon said. "We knew him being with your mother would anger Tino." Shannon added. "And we were right."

"I still don't get your concern. There are enough of you. Why do you need my siblings?"

"Lately a shift has been happening. Our younger Wolves are being seduced by Vamp culture. And we're afraid if the younger generation of Vamps connect with the younger generation of Wolves things will get violent."

"I can't believe this is happening," Cage said. "I also know there's something you aren't telling me. They just kids."

"Kids now. Leaders later."

Cage shook his head.

"I'm sorry I had to subject you to the truth, but it's best you know now. Let us protect them. You're alone. You're hunted. But with us, they are safe. Think about it." He looked at the others.

Cage nodded. "I need time on this."

"We need an answer tonight. So stay here, we're going to get some burgers for--"

Suddenly Cage's eyes widened.

"What is it?"

Cage's mind went back to the past. He thought about Magnus' words of wisdom. He thought about his mother's and more importantly, in this moment, Gordon's.

One of the last things Gordon said to him was, *"People will claim to want to help you, only to hurt you. You must learn the art of detecting deceit."*

"What is it, Cage?"

"I fucked up. I know where they are."

They walked up to him with weapons cocked. "Let's go!"

CHAPTER THIRTY-THREE
"I Don't Drink Trash."

Savannah was floating around the kitchen.

She had twenty bracelets on her left and right wrist, and so many chains around her neck she looked like a slave.

Although she wasn't in the cooking mood, after hearing some good news from Onion, she realized that maybe luck was coming for her after all.

For her betrayal, Onion would finally give her The Fluid ceremony she desired. His only demand was that she make sure that Cage's siblings would remain there, until he gave orders.

She didn't have a problem.

Because she snatched the kids long ago after learning who Cage was. She knew at some point she would be able to barter for their lives, and she was right.

The worst part is, they were in the same house Cage slept in every night when he worked for Savannah. Right in the basement. So when Ian was telling him not to trust someone, he was talking about her, not Brandon.

Taking the bowls of oatmeal and bacon downstairs she nodded at one of the men who was put there to help her keep order. Quickly he unlocked and opened the door, allowing her to step inside with a fake smile on her face.

Looking at the young ones she said, "Hungry?"

It had been a long road since their father died and their mother lost what was left of her mind. Savannah was evil and at the same time, after learning that their mother was killed and Wendy was possibly murdered too, the stranger was all they had.

Placing the food down on the table they walked toward it. They were growing teenagers now so at this point, they needed meat. She provided them with that every now and again, but she didn't want them getting too comfortable tasting flesh.

For fear they would want hers next.

So those treats were few and far between.

As she watched them eat the meal, she waited with her hands clasped tightly in front of her for an ego stroke. "Am I missing anything?"

They looked at one another. And it was Tatum, who decided to speak.

"Thank you, Miss Savannah."

She nodded and walked out, making sure the door was locked securely.

When she sauntered back upstairs her blood literally ran cold when she saw Cage standing in the living room with Row and family behind him.

"How did you know?"

"A while ago, Brandon taught me the importance of smells. Tonight, when I met them," he looked back at Row and the gang, "I remember smelling their scent before. In this house. And then the burgers."

She looked down and back at him.

"It wasn't personal."

"You took the only people I cared about, bitch. Don't tell me it wasn't personal. Now how did you get them?"

TREASON   325

"Onion led them out the house, and we overpowered him and put them in our van." She shrugged. "I promised to get back in contact with him if you broke your promise."

"But I didn't."

"You said you didn't want to rule. And I couldn't wait."

"Are you that pressed for The Fluid that you would do this to my family?" Cage asked. "I told you I had you covered."

"I'll be fifty soon. Onion offered to change me tonight. Why would I wait until later when you don't even want to run The Collective?"

"I can see why nobody wants to fuck with you."

At first, she was embarrassed but then realized this was probably the last time she would be alive, so she might as well speak what was on her mind.

"You killed your own father. You killed fifty vamps and you kill to survive every time you taste blood. And yet you're judging me?"

"All you had to do was give me time."

"Look at my face, Cage! I don't have time. And Onion was offering me now if I gave them up tonight."

"Where are Ellison and Shane?"

"I don't know. That's the truth. You can believe it or not."

He rushed up to her, grabbed her around her neck and slammed her against the wall. "Where are they?"

"What are you going to do now, drink my blood too?" She laughed, knowing it would make him violently ill.

"Nah, I don't drink trash."

He looked behind himself at the oldest of the uncles who walked up to her. And with one grip, he twisted and snapped her neck.

Going down to the basement the worker who was in charge, looked at Cage and the company and shook his head. He didn't want any problems which is why when he heard Tino was dead and that Cage was the successor the Elders respected, he started talking quickly to let them know they were there.

"Sir, I want you to know that I had nothing to do with this. I was only doing what I was instructed."

Cage nodded. "I'll investigate later. We'll leave it at that for now."

Opening the door, when he saw the condition of his brothers and sister, his knees buckled. They didn't have the glow that they were accustomed to, and they looked like they'd been through hell.

The smell of urine and feces was rampant, and it was obvious they hadn't been taken care of in years.

Upon seeing Cage, Bloom dropped her spoon and quickly rushed over to him, wrapping her arms around his body.

Tatum did the same.

But it was Flow who gave him the look of disgust.

He didn't want to have anything else to do with him. That was obvious. And so, he put down his spoon, walked up to his brother and spit at his feet.

When they were upstairs, Cage said, "These are your uncle's. And although my plan was to have you all live with me, things are hot. And I can't risk something happening to you right now."

"But how do you know they are related to us?" Bloom asked.

"Mom told me before she died." He took a deep breath. "So, they're going to take you. They're going to protect you and I'll be helping."

"Why can't we stay with you?" Bloom begged.

"How much do you know about who you are?"

"I'm your sister, and they're your brothers," she continued looking back at Tatum and Flow. "And we have the same mother and father and—."

"Okay, okay, 'lil sis."

It was obvious she didn't know anything of value.

"I'm going to explain things deeper. When the time is right. Now, I wanna get you to safety."

"You don't have to tell us later." Flow said. "We not kids anymore. Tatum is 19, Bloom is 17 and I'm 15. We know what happened. Wendy told us before she went missing. You killed Pops and now you gonna abandon us again."

"Flow, you don't have to do this. I'm--."

"You're useless." He said. "Don't worry though." He looked at his uncles. "I'll go with them and wait for my money from dad's estate. Because we can't count on you anyway." Flow stormed out.

Tatum and Bloom followed.

Canelo walked up to Cage and placed a hand on his shoulder. "Don't worry. I'll talk to him."

"He used to look up to me. I don't get it."

The others laughed and Cage grew heated.

"Fuck is so funny?"

"He's just like Magnus when he was young. I mean look at his name."

"What about it?"

"Flow spelled backwards is wolf. Didn't you know?"

Cage sat on Savannah's porch thinking about his life...

He couldn't believe his siblings were in the same house he stayed in, and he didn't know.

He felt hateful and stupid and he wished he could kill Savannah again.

When suddenly he smelled rain, despite the night sky being clear.

Jumping up, he was surprised when he turned around and saw a beautiful thick black woman with large breasts and red rimmed glasses staring at him. Surrounding her were five men.

"You're Arabia aren't you? And Magnus was going to send me to live with you wasn't he?"

She smiled and sat on the porch. "Sit with me. Please."

Slowly, he sat down. "How did you know where I was?"

"I've always known. But I wanted to wait for the perfect time." She sighed and looked out into the land. "This is such a beautiful property. If Savannah is good for anything, it's teaching a young Vamp how to survive."

"I feel stupid. They were in this house the entire time and I didn't know."

She giggled and said, "Listen, I'll be around more often, but I want to explain a few things that you need to know."

"Why am I like this? I don't get it."

"In the jungle, the lion is at the top of the food chain. And because of his hunting ability, everything remains in harmony. No species grows out of control. All is in order." She smiled. "We are here for balance, and we're only connected to the most superficial, or those who continue to look outward for things that they have inside. You will know them because their bodies smell the ripest. Like sweet fruit.

"On the other hand, because God makes sure every being is equipped for battle, all of the animals in the jungle have instincts. This allows them to sense the lion many feet away." She looked at him. "So that brings me to those, who know who they are and look inward for answers. You will also know them because they will give no odor."

Cage recalled the girl in the club who, unlike her friend, had no scent.

"So, we, the Vamps, with our perfect skin and attractive features, reflect back to Norms those things they value the most. Feeding only on those who connect with us. While the others remain safe."

"But why?"

"So that humans, or Norms, can remember who they are."

Cage looked down and back at her. "So, we're the lions?"

"I never said that."

He glared. "So, who are the fucking lions?"

"The Wolves, Cage. They will eventually become attracted to our flesh. Which will protect the Norms when it's time."

Cage was shocked. "Do the Wolves know?"

"No, but Magnus did. It was the reason your mother locked you in your room once you took The Fluid. She didn't want your siblings harming you." She exhaled. "Did you notice how they inhaled the air when you were around?"

Silence.

"Even Magnus craved you, which is why when you took The Fluid, he had to hold back, to prevent from hurting you. It's also the reason if the young Wolves connect with the young Vamps, there will be problems. So, we need you to step up, Cage."

"And do what?"

"There will come a time when those who took The Fluid must die. And you will have to help with this process, to keep the order, even if it means your life."

"Go against my own people? That's treason."

"I know." She touched him on the shoulder, rose and walked away.

By T. STYLES

CHAPTER THIRTY-FOUR

ONE YEAR LATER

The Worst

A year had passed, and Cage was standing in front of Angelina, at a night wedding, giving vows.

He was surrounded by beautiful Vampires who at the moment Tino died professed their loyalty to him. Bloom and Tatum were also present.

But Flow was nowhere to be found.

Over time, it had become harder for Cage to connect with his youngest brother. Although he would never give up hope, it was obvious the hate he had toward him was sincere.

At the end of the day Flow blamed him for killing their father and destroying their family. It was even whispered that the moment he got a chance he would take his brother's life with his own hands.

But for anyone trying to harm Cage it would be easier said than done. For the best of the best had vowed to protect him at all costs and so far, it was working.

They were strong.

But not everybody from the other side hated him, because also at the wedding were the uncles who agreed to be in his corner.

While all realizing things were about to get bad.

As the wedding proceeded, in the far, far distance, someone was watching with malice in his heart, and he was surrounded by goons.

But the king was clueless.

For him, it was a good day.

He manifested what he always wanted.

At his reception, Cage was sitting at the Bride and Groom table with his beautiful new wife and friends.

As everyone danced and enjoyed the celebration, she looked over at him. "You really made me your wife."

Cage knew they didn't have forever after talking to Arabia, so he relished in the now.

"I want you to know that my only focus is you, Angelina. I'm done with fighting. I'm done with the violence. Just you and my sister and brothers."

She wanted to believe him badly and smiled. "What about Flow? Because he seems so angry."

"I'm gonna work on him." He kissed her lips. "He'll come around."

"What about Onion?"

"I'm letting it go."

"You promise?"

Suddenly his phone rang. When he picked it up, he saw a number he didn't recognize. And since he wanted to be on call for all of his siblings, he answered.

"Hello."

"Cage, its Onion."

He jumped up.

"Sit down. We don't want to alarm your beautiful new bride."

"Cage, is everything okay?" Angelina asked, looking up at him.

He scanned the room for Onion, and so far all he saw were friendly faces.

"Yes, baby," he said. "Everything good." He took his seat and squeezed her hand.

"That's right. Keep her happy."

"What do you want?" He whispered.

"I want to give you your wedding gift. For starters, I won't do anything tonight. But I also want you to know something. The night Magnus died, it was my bullet that killed him. I shot him through your open window. Remember your words to me? The window's always open."

Cage was so angry he grabbed a glass and it shattered. "You're a liar."

"I'm not. JoJo and Tino were afraid you wouldn't pull the trigger, so they sent me."

"Why?" Cage said in a low voice. "We were friends."

"'Cause there were things that I wanted too. And they were in a position to give 'em to me."

Cage turned his head away from Angelina so that only he heard his next words. "I will find you and I will kill you slow."

"I'm looking forward to the challenge. But remember, I taught you everything you know."

"Not everything my nigga."

PRESENT DAY

The moon was out when Violet and the Attorney walked into Her grandmother's estate.

Her home was magnificent.

Golden chandeliers.

White marble floors and staircase.

It was the home reminiscent of a New York Times bestselling author. Although it was a spectacle to behold, neither was there to bask in its glory.

They were there because of the business that needed to be handled.

Business that Violet wasn't interested in dealing with just yet.

But after learning from the doctor that her grandmother was being pronounced brain dead, he felt it important to carry out her wishes that night. And since the greedy sister's left after realizing they would get next to nothing, he felt it wasn't necessary to be done in the hospital.

Sitting in the kitchen with a pot of coffee and two cups between them she took a deep breath.

"I'm listening."

"Okay, as you know your grandmother is worth millions. Her books generate between 500 to $600,000 a year alone. And she's giving it all to you."

"I don't care about any of that."

"She knew that too, which made her want to take care of you even more. But she does have a request."

"Okay. What is it?"

"She wants you to see to it that her book is finished."

By T. STYLES

"What book?"

"The book that she claims is based on her life."

"You mean the series?"

"Yes."

She giggled. "But it's impossible to be based on her life. She made her living and wealth off Vampire novels."

"I understand. But she hated that she never got to finish her saga. Believing that if a writer dies without completing their work, the world remains open. And since your mother died and her oldest daughter left long ago, it's up to you."

She frowned. "Her oldest?"

"She had a daughter named Lalasha. I believe she got married but your grandmother never saw her again. So, you're all she has."

"But I'm not a writer. I don't even know where to start."

"I have all the files you need. They're locked away in a safe. But she wants me to tell you this. You can't let anyone know you're finishing her book."

"I don't even know if I'm going to accept this challenge. But if I did, why the secrecy?"

"She wouldn't say. Just led me to believe that there are people who don't want this story completed. She always felt as if things went on in the world, that most of us were clueless about. And she poured these ideas into her characters--."

"Cage and Onion," she interrupted.

"So you've read the books?"

She smiled. "Of course. I love them. And it was our favorite pastime. Once the books were done, I would read them to her."

He smiled. "That explains even more why she chose you." He placed a warm hand on her arm, and she felt his kindness despite her views of lawyers. "She believed that the moment she created these characters, she pulled them into this world. And now she wants to close those doors with her final tale."

"Or they will take over?" Violet giggled. "She can't be serious."

"Your grandmother was ill and took medication for the majority of her life for schizophrenia. Some believe this is the reason Lalasha ran away."

Violet felt sick.

"If you are willing to proceed with your grandmother's request, the royalties will be yours, as well as the proceeds from this current book which will generate millions upon release."

She sighed.

"If you are not willing, she wants me to burn the records and you'll still be taken care of for the rest of your life."

"I'm not saying yes. But did she tell you what she wanted the name of the book to be called?"

"She said *Oignon.*"

"What is an Oignon?"

"I don't know."

She sighed. "I'm sorry, but I need to think." Grabbing her keys, she got in her car and drove to a store.

Waiting in line, she ordered iced coffee loving a caffeine buzz. It was a weird night drink but she wanted it all the same.

While she waited for it to be completed, and stood up against the wall, she was mesmerized when a tall dark-skinned man entered.

By T. STYLES

All eyes were on his fine ass.

Walking up to the counter to get his drink, he stood next to her and waited for his order.

"You been here long?"

She grinned. This was the type of man who usually didn't give her the time of day. So she was nervous. "K...kinda."

He smiled. "Why you talking under your breath?"

"No reason."

"There's a reason for everything isn't there?"

"My grandmother thinks so."

He nodded. "So listen, I don't want coffee anymore. You wanna grab a drink with me instead?"

"That's kind of forward. I really don't know you."

"But that can change."

Something about him was so seductive, it had her weak at the knees. When she saw a faint scar on his face, she was curious. It was barely visible, and at the same time, in her opinion added to his appeal.

"What's your name?" She asked.

"Pierre." He extended his hand. "And yours?"

"Violet." She shook it softly.

"What a beautiful name."

"I like yours more. Have always liked the name Pierre."

He sighed. "Unfortunately for me, it holds some pretty dark memories."

She focused deeply. "Well, we still haven't gotten our coffees yet. I can listen if you want to share."

"You know what, I do think it's time." He placed a hand on the small of her back and led her to a table and chairs.

"Thank you."

He sat next to her and took a deep breath.

"My mother grew up on a rural farm with her father. There were many dogs, to help with the livestock and to keep out prey. When her mother died, she soon found out that there was no bigger prey than him. And he began to look at her in ways that were unnatural. Needless to say, after fighting him off as best she could, I was born. And my father, also my grandfather, became obsessed with her and keeping his secret."

"I'm sorry, I didn't realize it was so private. I--."

"No, it's okay. Really." He paused. "I haven't told anyone this story before but I feel comfortable telling you."

She nodded.

"When I was twelve, my twenty-seven-year-old mother overheard him plotting to kill both her and I with his friend. She wasn't certain, but she believed mauling by dogs would be involved because she saw my father letting the animals sniff our clothing."

A few people passed by and he paused.

He looked at her with kind eyes. "One night, she woke me up and told me I had to run. She had just made love to him, something she stopped doing because she was strong enough to fight back. But she did it to put him to sleep. There were a lot of things said, most I can't remember outside of these words, 'run for your life'."

Violet leaned closer.

"But before doing so, she recalled a story she heard about the photo of a slave named Whipped Peter. It was only later that she realized that Pierre in French translated to Peter in English. Anyway, in this story he rubbed onions all over his body to conceal his smell from the bloodhounds meant to capture him and return him to his master. And my dear, Violet, that night, my mother did the same to me. Removing the onions that we grew on our farm, she rubbed them all over me. Not having enough for herself. So she stayed back."

She was captivated by his voice, and the way he told such a horrendous tale.

"Under the moonlight, I ran through cornfields larger than me, with the smell of onion so strong on my skin, I vomited several times. The stalks whipped my face, causing cuts throughout my cheeks."

That's how he got the marks. She thought.

"In the end, since I told no one my real name, I was placed in foster care. The man in the family worked for a powerful man. And I vowed that when I was old enough, I would work for this powerful man too."

"Why?"

"So I could return home and save my mother."

"Did you?"

"After an opportunity came my way, I was employed by this man. And I did return home. Older. Stronger. Richer. And more importantly, no longer afraid." He shook his head. "He spoke to me as if I didn't remember the past because we spoke in the present. Put on as if things were sweet on that farm. The thing was, I remembered everything he did to her. And what he wanted to do to me."

"Where was your mother?"

"He claimed she left. But when I looked out into the fields, I knew she was there."

"What did you do to him?"

"Let's just say I sucked him dry, of everything he loved. And now, I own that farm. So whether my mother returns, or if her body is in the fields, no matter what, we will always be together."

Touching her heart she said, "You are officially the most interesting man I ever met in my life."

The barista called their numbers.

With coffee cups in hand, Pierre said, "Well, Violet, I have bared all to you. May I take you out? I promise despite my sad story, it will be a good time."

She smiled. "I wouldn't want to be anywhere else."

He stepped closer. "I'm a gentleman. So before you get in my car, I need you to accept."

She thought his tone serious but took a deep breath. After all, he was fine, looked like money and she was lonely. "Yes. I will go with you. Besides, what do I have to lose?"

Make sure you follow:

T. Styles' Twisted Babies Readers –

The Exclusive Edition

Reading Group on Facebook!

By T. STYLES

CARTEL PUBLICATIONS

PRESENTS

The Cartel Publications Order Form

www.thecartelpublications.com

Inmates **ONLY** receive novels for $10.00 per book **PLUS** shipping fee **PER BOOK.**

(Mail Order **MUST** come from inmate directly to receive discount)

Shyt List 1	_____	$15.00
Shyt List 2	_____	$15.00
Shyt List 3	_____	$15.00
Shyt List 4	_____	$15.00
Shyt List 5	_____	$15.00
Shyt List 6	_____	$15.00
Pitbulls In A Skirt	_____	$15.00
Pitbulls In A Skirt 2	_____	$15.00
Pitbulls In A Skirt 3	_____	$15.00
Pitbulls In A Skirt 4	_____	$15.00
Pitbulls In A Skirt 5	_____	$15.00
Victoria's Secret	_____	$15.00
Poison 1	_____	$15.00
Poison 2	_____	$15.00
Hell Razor Honeys	_____	$15.00
Hell Razor Honeys 2	_____	$15.00
A Hustler's Son	_____	$15.00
A Hustler's Son 2	_____	$15.00
Black and Ugly	_____	$15.00
Black and Ugly As Ever	_____	$15.00
Ms Wayne & The Queens of DC **(LGBT)**	_____	$15.00
Black And The Ugliest	_____	$15.00
Year Of The Crackmom	_____	$15.00
Deadheads	_____	$15.00
The Face That Launched A Thousand Bullets	_____	$15.00
The Unusual Suspects	_____	$15.00
Paid In Blood	_____	$15.00
Raunchy	_____	$15.00
Raunchy 2	_____	$15.00
Raunchy 3	_____	$15.00
Mad Maxxx (4th Book Raunchy Series)	_____	$15.00
Quita's Daycare Center	_____	$15.00
Quita's Daycare Center 2	_____	$15.00
Pretty Kings	_____	$15.00
Pretty Kings 2	_____	$15.00
Pretty Kings 3	_____	$15.00
Pretty Kings 4	_____	$15.00
Silence Of The Nine	_____	$15.00
Silence Of The Nine 2	_____	$15.00
Silence Of The Nine 3	_____	$15.00

Prison Throne	_____	$15.00
Drunk & Hot Girls	_____	$15.00
Hersband Material **(LGBT)**	_____	$15.00
The End: How To Write A	_____	$15.00
Bestselling Novel In 30 Days (Non-Fiction Guide)		
Upscale Kittens	_____	$15.00
Wake & Bake Boys	_____	$15.00
Young & Dumb	_____	$15.00
Young & Dumb 2: Vyce's Getback	_____	$15.00
Tranny 911 **(LGBT)**	_____	$15.00
Tranny 911: Dixie's Rise **(LGBT)**	_____	$15.00
First Comes Love, Then Comes Murder	_____	$15.00
Luxury Tax	_____	$15.00
The Lying King	_____	$15.00
Crazy Kind Of Love	_____	$15.00
Goon	_____	$15.00
And They Call Me God	_____	$15.00
The Ungrateful Bastards	_____	$15.00
Lipstick Dom **(LGBT)**	_____	$15.00
A School of Dolls **(LGBT)**	_____	$15.00
Hoetic Justice	_____	$15.00
KALI: Raunchy Relived	_____	$15.00
(5ᵗʰ Book in Raunchy Series)		
Skeezers	_____	$15.00
Skeezers 2	_____	$15.00
You Kissed Me, Now I Own You	_____	$15.00
Nefarious	_____	$15.00
Redbone 3: The Rise of The Fold	_____	$15.00
The Fold (4ᵗʰ Redbone Book)	_____	$15.00
Clown Niggas		$15.00
The One You Shouldn't Trust	_____	$15.00
The WHORE The Wind		
Blew My Way	_____	$15.00
She Brings The Worst Kind	_____	$15.00
The House That Crack Built	_____	$15.00
The House That Crack Built 2	_____	$15.00
The House That Crack Built 3	_____	$15.00
The House That Crack Built 4	_____	$15.00
Level Up **(LGBT)**	_____	$15.00
Villains: It's Savage Season	_____	$15.00
Gay For My Bae	_____	$15.00
War	_____	$15.00
War 2: All Hell Breaks Loose	_____	$15.00
War 3: The Land Of The Lou's	_____	$15.00
War 4: Skull Island	_____	$15.00
War 5: Karma	_____	$15.00
War 6: Envy	_____	$15.00
War 7: Pink Cotton	_____	$15.00
Madjesty vs. Jayden (Novella)	_____	$8.99
You Left Me No Choice	_____	$15.00
Truce – A War Saga (War 8)	_____	$15.00
Ask The Streets For Mercy	_____	$15.00
Truce 2 - (War 9)	_____	$15.00
An Ace and Walid Very, Very Bad Christmas (War 10)	_____	$15.00
Truce 3 – The Sins of The Fathers (War 11)	_____	$15.00
Truce 4: The Finale (War 12)	_____	$15.00
Treason	_____	$15.00

By T. STYLES

(**Redbone 1 & 2** are **NOT** Cartel Publications novels and if <u>**ordered**</u> the cost is **FULL** price of $15.00 **each. <u>No Exceptions</u>**.)

Please add **$5.00** for shipping and handling fees for up to **(2) BOOKS PER ORDER**. (INMATES INCLUDED) (See next page for details)

The Cartel Publications * P.O. BOX 486 OWINGS MILLS MD 21117

Name: _____

Address: _____

City/State: _____

Contact/Email: _____

Please allow 10-15 BUSINESS days Before shipping.

PLEASE NOTE DUE TO <u>COVID-19</u> SOME ORDERS MAY TAKE UP TO <u>3 WEEKS OR LONGER</u> BEFORE THEY SHIP

The Cartel Publications is <u>NOT</u> responsible for <u>Prison Orders</u> rejected!

<u>**NO RETURNS and NO REFUNDS**</u>
<u>**NO PERSONAL CHECKS ACCEPTED**</u>
<u>**STAMPS NO LONGER ACCEPTED**</u>

CPSIA information can be obtained
at www.ICGtesting.com
Printed in the USA
LVHW042142200921
698281LV00001B/4

9 781948 373364